D1025267

IMAGINE US HAPPY

Also by Jennifer Yu

Four Weeks, Five People

JENNIFER YU

IMAGINE US HAPPY

HARLEQUIN®TEEN

ISBN-13: 978-1-335-01536-5

Imagine Us Happy

www.HarlequinTEEN.com

Printed in U.S.A.

for M,

*without whom I could never have written a book
about love & family.*

IMAGINE US HAPPY

Everyone always wants to know how it ends. That's the best part of love stories, right? The part when the prince comes back to rescue the princess with a white horse and a sword that sparkles and a smile that sparkles even brighter. Or when the second suitor with the slicked-back hair who came out of nowhere turns out to be a total jerk, and our heroine's love triangle resolves itself in a beautiful, heart-rending reconciliation with Mr. Right in the pouring rain. Or, if it's not that kind of love story, it's the part where our main character is left waiting outside in the rain all alone, cursing her naiveté and wishing she'd realized sooner that "true love" is nothing but Disney's greatest, most profitable invention.

There are a thousand different love stories and a thousand different ways that each of them could end, and believe me, I know—there's nothing worse than reading three hundred pages or watching two hours of a whirlwind romance expecting rose petals and wedding streamers only to get heartbreak instead.

I guess that's why I'm starting at the end. I don't want anyone to be confused about the type of love story I'm about to tell, or where it's going, or what to expect. And I don't want to disappoint anyone in search of a happy ending. I'll say it from the start: this isn't that kind of story.

68. THE LAST TIME

The last time Kevin and I fight, it's the second week of April.
A week straight of seventy-plus–degree temperatures have finally coaxed the trees in my backyard into full bloom. I'm
watching the leaves of the old oak tree sway as Kevin shouts
at me for the last time.

"Goddamn it, Stella," he says. "You can't even look at me,
can you?"

He's wrong. It would be easy to look at him. It always has
been. It would be easy to turn away from the window, to
walk to where he stands across the room, to take his hands
in mine and look him square in the eye. But then I would
start crying, I know, and he would soften in the way he always does when he's burned down the anger inside him and
doesn't have the energy to shout anymore, and then I would
forget in the way *I* always do that it's only a matter of time
before something reignites it and we start all over again.

"Stella," Kevin says. His voice cracks, and the sound of that is almost—*almost*—enough to break me. Even after all this time, after everything we've been through, after Jeremy and Columbia and the party in March, after *all that*, Kevin is still the only person who says my name like that. Like the key to something beautiful and secret is tucked between the syllables.

"I think you were right," I respond quietly. "This isn't going to work."

"Come *on*, Stella, you know that I didn't mean that," Kevin says. And all of a sudden, he's pissed again. I can hear it in the quickening of his breath, in the way his words start tumbling out of his mouth all at once, sharp like knives. "You're really going to give up on this? On *us*? Over some stupid thing that I said? Stella, you know I only said that because you ditched me to hang out with half the football team and didn't even tell me about it!"

It's 4:05 in the afternoon. My mother will be home from the grocery store soon, and Kevin will have to leave.

It's only a matter of time.

"Talk to me, Stella, *please*, come on," Kevin says. And then, when I don't: "You know what? Fine. I'm leaving. I'm not going to stay here and beg for something you obviously don't give a shit about."

Kevin pushes his chair back so violently that it falls over and hits the floor as he stands.

"I fucking love you," he says loudly. "I'm sorry if that's not enough for you."

He grabs his backpack off my bed, knocking half of my books off my desk in the process. I suppose I should be thankful that no one has thrown anything yet, unlike when we fought a couple of weeks ago and shattered my window in the process. I hear him stomp across the room and pause in my doorway. He's looking at me, I know. Waiting.

"You're being a coward. You know that? You're just fucking scared."

I barely register the words. The wind outside has picked up again and I'm watching the branches of the oak tree arch gracefully in the wind, leaves fluttering into each other. By the time Kevin swears one last time, storms down the stairs and slams the front door shut behind him, it feels like I'm listening from a place very, very far away, where none of this really matters.

The last time Kevin and I fight, there's a profound sense of anticlimax about the whole deal. The emotional pyrotechnics will come later, I know, but in the moment I am surprisingly calm. I do not yell. I do not cry. I do not run back into his arms and let myself fall headfirst, foolishly back in love with a mirage.

The last time Kevin and I fight, it is the second week of April. It's seventy-five and perfect outside, and the afternoon sun makes every particle of dust drifting through my room look like a tiny speck of gold. I have known Kevin for eight months, have sworn up and down that I love him for five, have fought with and fought for and fought because of him so many times the mere thought of it exhausts me.

The last time that Kevin and I fight, I sit back and stare out the window and let him go. Because yes, I am scared, and yes, I am being a fucking coward. But there is nothing left here worth being brave for.

0. A MEMORY

When we first moved from Hartford to Wethersfield, my dad hung a tire swing from one of the branches of the old oak tree. To my six-year-old self, that swing was magic. A way of escaping gravity that the scientists, cooped up in their offices and boring laboratories, somehow missed. I would have sworn that I went faster on that swing than cars moved on the highway.

One afternoon, I fell off the swing and broke my arm. It hurt like hell, but what hurt more was getting back from the hospital and seeing that my dad had cut the tire swing down. I didn't care that I had to wear a splint for two months, or that all the kids at school started making fun of me for being clumsy, or that I had to learn to write left-handed to take my spelling tests. I forgot the excruciating pain of hitting the ground with my arm bent the wrong way and the sickening *crack* of bone giving way underneath my weight the moment I saw that the swing was gone. Who cared about the pain? I just wanted to feel that magic again.

Sometimes I think of Kevin and all I can remember is that last fight. Kevin, calling me a coward and storming out of my house. And me, refusing to talk to or even look at him in a moment when the desperation in his voice could wring water from the desert. I remember that fight, and I wonder how two people who loved each other could grow to be so deliberately, vindictively cruel.

But I guess that to understand what happened that last day, you have to understand who Kevin and I were before—before he became a boy screaming at the girl he swore he loved, and before I became the girl loving him right back even though I knew I couldn't. You have to understand everything that happened to us between August of 2016 and that day in April. You have to start at the beginning, to when that boy just wanted to read his copy of Modern Philosophy: An Anthology *and get into Columbia and the girl was just trying to survive junior year with minimal emotional fallout. Back to the first day of school, to our first class with Dr. Mulland, to the first time I met Kevin.*

1. RESOLUTIONS FOR JUNIOR YEAR

Find somewhere to hang out with Lin and Katie in this town that ISN'T Porky's Pizza, the roller rink or, for fuck's sake, THE MALL.

Get an 1800 on the SATs, or whatever it takes to get into a school on the opposite side of this country.

Break twenty minutes in the 5K by our last cross-country meet of the season.

Convince Mom and Dad that if they're going to scream at each other all the time, the least they can do is get me some nice speakers for Christmas.

Spend more time in therapy listening to Karen talk, and less time coming up with unlikely escape routes from her office.

Ditch Homecoming, on account of the fact that it is a glorified high school mating ritual.

Ditch prom, on account of the fact that it is a glorified high school mating ritual.

Convince Katie to ditch Ashley Kurtzmann's house parties, on account of the fact that they are ALL GLORIFIED HIGH SCHOOL MATING RITUALS.

Hate people less, despite their unreasonable obsession with glorified high school mating rituals.

2.

Lin, in typical Lin fashion, arrives at my house on the first day of school at 7:15 a.m. sharp.

I, in typical Stella fashion, spend fifteen minutes lying in bed after my alarm goes off trying to work up the motivation to get dressed instead of actually doing it, and don't make it out the front door until 7:22 a.m.

Lin is wearing a black T-shirt that says:

THINGS ADO:
1. Nothing

Her long, brown hair is pulled into a high ponytail, and I notice as I clamber into shotgun that she's put on eyeliner today, which is about as much makeup as Lin ever wears. That's how I know that Lin is taking the first day of school Very Seriously.

"Stella!" Lin says, and wraps me in a hug. "God, it feels like it's been forever. How *are* you?"

I can feel the grin spreading across my face before I even know why I'm smiling. Maybe it's the fact that Lin looks so happy to see me that she doesn't even say anything about how late I am. Maybe it's that she's forgotten to put the car in Park before reaching over to hug me, and we start rolling down the hill before she goes, "oh, shit," and brakes hard. Maybe it's that it really does feel like it's been forever—it's been a long morning, and an even longer summer—but now that I'm sitting in Lin's car, half-terrified that her shitty 1996 Ford Taurus is going to roll right into my front porch, it also feels like nothing's changed at all.

"I'm good," I say automatically, because I've learned that responding to "How are you?" with any answer other than "Good" is a great way to find yourself trapped in conversations you don't want to be having with people you don't want to be having them with. Then I remember that Lin is one of my best friends—not my parents, not my therapist, not Ashley Kurtzmann making her best bid for Miss Congeniality—and I try to be a little bit more honest.

"Well, as good as anyone about to suffer through another year at Bridgemont could possibly be, anyway, which is maybe not-so-good," I say. "And my parents are at each other's throats, of course, but what else is new? What about you? How's the college application struggle?"

Lin rolls her eyes as she pulls out of my neighborhood and starts driving toward Katie's house. "I have written two hundred and fifty drafts of my supplementary essays for Brown," she announces, "and every single one of them is terrible. Don't even get me started on the common application essay."

"Bleak," I say. If Lin doesn't think she can get into a good school, then I might as well just mail it in and take a full-time job at McDonald's now.

"You know what I realized, Stella?" Lin continues. "There is not a single thing I have ever done in my high school career that's original. I mean, here I am, starting senior year, and not a single nonprofit, patent or international peace prize to my name. Not a single lousy Olympic medal!"

"Not *one* Olympic medal?" I ask, faux-outraged.

Lin parks the car in Katie's driveway and makes a face at me. "That's not funny, Stella. Wait 'til you and Katie go through this when you're seniors next year. Speaking of—holy shit. What has she done with her *hair*?"

I turn around to get a better look, but the only thing I manage to get a glimpse of before Katie climbs into the car behind us is a flash of bright, bright purple.

"I FUCKING MISSED YOU GUYS SO MUCH!" Katie shouts.

"Your hair," Lin says, as we both crane our heads around our seats to stare at Katie. "It's—wow."

"Do you guys *love* it?" Katie asks. And then, before either of us can respond: "I think it really says—" she pauses, then adopts a bossy, confrontational tone and rolls her blue eyes upward "—'I know what I want and I don't give a shit what anyone else thinks.'"

"Oh, that's great," I say. "Seriously, Katie, everyone who's never had a conversation with you will be really convinced."

"Shut up, Stella," Katie says, laughing. "How was camp? How's *life*? I have so much to tell you guys."

The truth is, I am often completely bewildered as to how Katie and I are still friends. In the third grade, we were assigned to do a project on sequoia trees together, and I suppose the process of spending an entire afternoon drawing pictures of trees and pasting them onto a poster is the kind of lifelong bonding experience that's strong enough to withstand vastly divergent personalities and completely incompatible definitions of appropriate speaking volume. If it were anyone other than Katie, I would hate her—but the power of the sequoia, apparently, is mighty indeed.

"Let's not talk about camp," I say as Lin starts driving toward school. "I was having such a nice morning and I'd hate to ruin it. Even managed to get out of bed and everything."

"But was it amazing?" Katie says. "Did you discover yourself? Did you, you know, *meet anyone*?"

"Katie," I say, very seriously, because once Katie starts talking about boys, it's very important to rein her in before she goes off the wall. "I was at a camp for troubled teenagers. We were in therapy all day. Not exactly romantic circumstances."

"Don't call yourself a troubled teenager," Lin says. "You're not troubled. You're just—"

"Difficult? Emotionally disturbed? Had a complete meltdown in the middle of our American history final for no apparent reason and almost got kicked out of school?"

There's a beat of silence. "You," Lin finally says, "are going to have a killer common app essay."

3.

Every year, without fail, there's always that one class that you know you're going to remember for the rest of your life. Freshman year, there was Literature Around the World, which featured eight critically acclaimed novels replete with obscure metaphors for Communism and increasingly depressing monologues given by characters with increasingly unpronounceable names. Then, last year, there was my American history class, which I thought would be a yearlong testament to democracy, innovation and the joys of fried food, but instead ended up being a survey of all the people white men have ever victimized, which, as it turns out, is everyone.

Compared to freshman year English and sophomore year history, the first six classes on my schedule are remarkably uneventful. European History quickly devolves into a never-ending list of petty wars fought by men with large egos and even larger budgets. My decision to take normal CP biology is validated when Ms. Jensen announces that the school has purchased only enough fetal pigs for the AP class to dissect, leaving the rest of us, presumably, to spend yet another year learning that the mitochondria is the powerhouse of the cell. Calculus immediately reveals itself to be a joke when Mr. Tang throws his teaching degree to the wind and instead begins bribing the class by throwing candy at the people who raise their hands. In fact, going into last period, the only thing standing between me and a complete roster of forgettable classes is Philosophy, Room A208, Dr. Mulland.

Dr. Mulland is one of those middle-aged guys that seems completely ordinary. He's of average height and average weight, with brown hair that's graying at the temples and glasses that look about one size too big for his face. But everyone who has taken his class says that it's unforgettable, and the administration must agree, because they appointed him the Humanities department chair three years ago. Now it's almost impossible to fulfill the graduation requirements without taking either his freshman/sophomore history class or his junior/senior philosophy elective.

The first thing Dr. Mulland does when he walks into the classroom at 2:20 is pick up a piece of chalk and scribble, in long, sweeping strokes:

What.
is.
PHILOSOPHY?

He underlines *philosophy* twice, as if the caps weren't enough, and then turns to face the class expectantly.

"What is philosophy?" Dr. Mulland asks us. He glances around the classroom and must find something amusing about our blank expressions, because then he smiles, spins around and asks again, this time facing the chalkboard: "What…is…philosophy?"

The unmistakable silence of seventeen students who have just realized that they should have taken the underclassman history class is punctuated only by the sound of Becca Windham sneezing as chalk dust floats into her face.

Dr. Mulland spins around and narrows his eyes at the class. "Jesse," he says, pointing at a senior in the back row who snuck out of study hall fifty minutes ago and returned bearing the unmistakable scent of weed.

"Teach?" Jesse says.

"*What*," Dr. Mulland says, turning around to underline *Philosophy* three more times, "do you think of our little introductory question here?"

"What do I think?" Jesse repeats.

"There must be something, Mr. Turner."

"I guess it's just, like, the study of…things," Jesse says.

"Things," Dr. Mulland repeats. "Interesting." He picks up a piece of chalk and writes that down, next to the question. I stare blankly ahead at the chalkboard, which now reads:

Things.

Is this guy for real? I think. But he must be, because Dr. Mulland doesn't miss a beat as he turns to Jeremy Cox and asks: "Mr. Cox! What say you?"

Jeremy, a senior on the football team who surely has not been asked to memorize anything outside of a playbook in the past four years, blanches. "Er," he says. "I mean, it's just, you know—hey, can I go to the bathroom?"

"I am sure you can but you may not," Dr. Mulland replies. "Give us a guess, Jeremy."

There's a moment of silence during which I become convinced that Jeremy is going to start reciting fantasy football stats. But then he pulls himself together and says: "Trying to find the truth?"

"The *truth*," Dr. Mulland says, and writes that up on the board, too. "A noble pursuit indeed—don't you think, Becca?"

Becca sneezes.

"Bless you," I say reflexively.

"Ah, but that would be *religion*," Dr. Mulland says, spinning to face me. "Closely related—fundamentally inextricable, I'd say—but not quite this class, Stella. You may want to consider World Religion with Mr. Edwards."

"That's not what I…" I start, but Dr. Mulland just winks at me and looks around at the rest of the class. "Ashley, you're up."

"I mean, you have aesthetics, right?" Ashley Kurtzmann says. "But then also other stuff?"

Dr. Mulland writes:

Aesthetics.

Then:

Other stuff (?)

"Brady!" he says, without even turning around.

"It's the study of existence," Brady, class valedictorian and Harvard legacy three generations running, drawls.

"Excellent," Dr. Mulland says, copying that down. "Someone who read the syllabus. Kevin?"

"The pursuit," Kevin Miller says, "of wisdom."

Kevin taps his pencil against the desk once and looks thoughtful. Then he adds:

"At the end of the day, isn't that what we search for when we study philosophy? What it means to exist. What value there is in truth. Religion. Beauty. Existence. When we find those answers, or, perhaps, what we find *instead* of answers— it's all wisdom, isn't it?"

There's a moment of confused silence as the class processes the fact that someone has actually responded to Mulland's question, during which Brady looks pissed that someone has showed up his answer, Jeremy looks even more bewildered than he did before, and Becca looks impressed and…kind of turned on. Me? I'm just trying to figure out who the hell this Kevin kid is, and why he's so unfamiliar to me. Sure, he's a senior, but the school is barely 500 people. There's something about him that should trigger a memory—the brown hair, the shadowed blue eyes, the faintest hint of a smile on his face, as if he's appreciating the sound of his answer as he says it.

"Thank you, Mr. Miller," Dr. Mulland says. "And to the rest of the class for participating in my little exercise."

Then he throws the chalk down on his desk so loudly that half of the front row jumps.

"Philosophy," Dr. Mulland announces, "encompasses all that's been proposed today. It is, as Jesse proposed, the study of things—what defines an object, what makes it real, what constitutes 'being.' It is also, as Mr. Cox here suggested, the contemplation of truth—whether or not such a thing exists, and whether or not we have any hope should we dare and go seek it. Philosophy includes aesthetics: the realm of art and beauty. And, of course, philosophy includes existentialism, the particular focus of this class—a body of thought that seeks to understand the *nature of human life itself.*"

Another pause, during which I begin to understand why everyone at Bridgemont loves this class. I can't take notes fast enough to keep up with Dr. Mulland's monologue, so I settle for scribbling down particularly eloquent phrases—*Pursuit of wisdom. Contemplation of truth. Hope should we dare. Nature of human life*—and hoping that I'll understand when I reread my notes later.

"Like life, which at its richest is both transcendent and futile, both joyous and damning, the works we will be studying are profound, divergent and contradictory. Our journey begins Thursday."

Dr. Mulland dismisses us from class twenty minutes early. At our lockers, Lin and Katie ask me how the last period went and I describe Mulland's opening dramatics in painstaking detail, trying futilely to recreate the specific phrases he used.

"I loved that class," Lin sighs, looking nostalgic. She has four textbooks in her arms that she can't put away because Katie is currently using the mirror on the inside of Lin's locker to reapply her lipstick. "Made me think about Steinbeck's *East of Eden* in a whole new way, really."

"Any interesting guys of note?" Katie asks.

"No," I say. "But there was this one guy who gave a minispeech of his own. Something about philosophy as the pursuit of wisdom. Got really into it. Kind of seemed like he'd already taken the class."

"Was he cute?" Katie says.

"Uh," I say. I think of the guy from class and his messy

brown hair, the slight smirk on his face when he talked about philosophy. "In an artsy hipster kind of way, I guess."

"Huh," Katie says. She slides her lipstick back into her pencil case and slides out of Lin's way. "Well, that's better than nothing."

4.

I walk into the house after finishing my run on Tuesday afternoon to find my mom sitting at the dining room table clutching a cup of tea, an expectant look on her face.

"Hi, honey," she says, before the door has even finished swinging shut behind me. "How was school today? Did you have a good run? Care for some tea?"

Ever since the whole mental meltdown thing happened in the middle of the school year last semester, my mother has gotten really into *tea*, as if some particularly potent strain of chamomile is going to be able to soothe our family's nerves back into normalcy. Left to her own devices while I'm at school and my father is at work all day, she's somehow managed to amass six tea sets since Christmas, not to mention enough tea leaves to get the entire town of Wethersfield through a nuclear winter. I can no longer hear the sound of a kettle whistling without feeling my heart rate triple in anticipation of some serious family conversation that will be, presumably, terrible. The only bright side is that birthday shopping for my mother this year took two minutes flat.

I sit down at the table and pour myself a cup—*green tea*, I note, and that's a relief. There's a pattern to these things: green tea, or anything fruity, indicates that my mother is stressed, but far from peak neuroticism. Oolongs are a step above that: made in anticipation of conversations that range from awkward ("You know, the Kayes down the street mentioned that Brian is looking for a date to the next school dance…") to verbal waterboarding ("We're concerned about your grades, Stella. Are your whole…emotional *issues*…affecting your schoolwork?"). And black? Black teas are the real heavy-duty nerve soothers, which means it's probably best to just drop a Xanax into the cup as you sit down.

"School was fine," I say.

"Just fine?" she asks.

I don't know what it is that parents seem to have against *fine*. I'm a sixteen-year-old girl living in the heart of suburban Connecticut, whose primary goal for the foreseeable future is to graduate high school without doing anything scandalous enough to become the Wethersfield church crowd's weekly object of gossip. I'm not sure what part of that seems remotely conducive to a life that transcends the bounds of the adjective *fine*.

"Yes, just fine," I repeat. "As in, the idiots comprising fifty percent of my grade have somehow managed to make it out of yet another summer alive, but at least there were no punches thrown today."

My mom hums a little, sipping carefully. She looks—well, she looks *sad*, is the thing, which makes me feel kind of sad, too. I know that things with my dad haven't been great lately, and that she's probably been sitting at the table for a while, waiting for me to come home, and that I should probably be more—I don't know, *conversational*. But *conversational* has never been my strong suit, and even as I finish my cup and my mom pours me a new one, I'm mostly thinking about how quickly I could pull off an escape to my room.

"How are your classes?" she asks.

"Fine."

"Anything interesting on the schedule this year?"

"Eh," I say. "History'll be boatloads of flash cards as usual. No dissections in biology this year, thank God. The philosophy teacher that everyone loves seems cool, but let's face it—the class will probably be ruined by all the assholes who are just in it so they can graduate."

"You should give your classmates a chance, Stella," my mom says. She smiles a little ruefully, so that her eyes crinkle and the lines around her mouth come out. "When are cross-country tryouts?"

"Friday."

"You feel good about them?"

"Eh. I feel—"

"Let me guess—fine?"

I shrug. "Coach likes me, I think."

My mom squints at me. "And emotionally...?"

I shrug.

"You know, Karen mentioned that we might want to consider extending your sessions to three hours each week, or perhaps going twice a week as we enter the school year."

"*Mom*," I say.

32

"Transitions are tough, Stella, and junior year is stressful. This is the year that your grades really matter, and college—"

"Yeah, yeah, college applications next year. I know. I *promise* that I'm *fine*. Going to therapy for three hours a week is just going to make me go insane faster. Then I won't even make it to whatever colleges I get into next year! Also, I have to go start my history reading so I'll talk to you later bye!"

The sound of my mom's sigh follows me up the stairs.

Three hours of therapy a week, I think, after I've shut the door, shrugged my backpack onto the floor and fallen into the bed. *Jesus.*

5. A BRIEF EXPLANATION

Here is a fact:

Sometimes I just get...sad.

It feels something like this:

Like there's a black hole in the center of my stomach and it's pulling all of my vital organs into it and I'm slowly imploding into myself.

Or maybe like this:

Like there's no point in getting out of bed because that black hole inside me is going to suck everyone else's happiness into it, too.

Or, one time, like this:

Like the shouting in my head is so loud that I can't hear or think or read the questions on my American history final so I start screaming on the *outside* to try and drown out the noise on the *inside*, but the problem is that everyone can *hear* the noises you make on the outside, Stella, and now what have you done?

But it's all right. Because here is another fact:

I'm better now. I swear.

6.

On Wednesday, Katie, Lin and I make the most of what little remains of summer by eating lunch outside. We head to the back of the Lantiss Courtyard, where a line of trees separates the end of the campus from the road on the other side. From here, the only suggestion that there might be more in the world than Bridgemont Academy—more out there than the layers of red bricks towering above us and the tennis courts in the distance and the aggressively maintained grass that fills every possible square inch of space in between—is the sound of rushing cars on the road, filtering through the tree leaves. But even that noise is so constant that it eventually becomes white noise, barely noticeable, a sound that might as well be a part of the school itself.

The courtyard itself is never crowded. Only upperclassmen are allowed to use it for lunch, and most of the one hundred and twenty people in the two classes decide to go off-campus to eat lunch, anyway. Despite the room, Lin, Katie and I sit as far away from the entrance as possible because the only other upperclassmen who stay on-campus without fail are the athletes, who congregate in the center of the courtyard with their protein shakes and loud inside jokes and endless talk of balls and points and players and whatever the hell else. The end of the hour always devolves into yelling as they all abandon their lunches in a mad scramble to figure out which one player's turn it was this week to do the math homework for everyone else. If only Principal Holmquist knew that *this* was the "team spirit" his monthly pep rallies were fostering.

"Is it bad that I kind of hate them?" Lin says. She peers over the top of her laptop at the mass of jocks starting to file into the courtyard. Jeremy Cox is there, of course, and his cheerleader girlfriend slash inevitable homecoming queen, Jennie von Haller, then there's the quarterback Adrian and *his* girlfriend, then a quarter of the baseball team files in…

"Like, I've spent my entire life staying up all night writing papers and studying for tests and doing lab reports and double-checking math problem sets, and then dragging my ass out of bed at 4:00 a.m. in the morning to make it to swim meets, and then forcing myself to stay awake through biology so Jensen will write me a recommendation, and *then* staying after school for drama practice to develop my *creative side* so I can be, oh, I don't know, *well-rounded*," Lin continues. "And all Adrian's done is lucked into being six-three with well-developed biceps and he's going to have God knows how many colleges just *begging* him to go there. Where's the justice in that?"

"I'm not even a senior, Lin, and even I know that there's no justice in college admissions," I say.

"No justice," Lin agrees glumly. "Only sleep deprivation."

"That sucks," Katie says. She gives us three seconds of silent mourning for all of Lin's lost sleep before her pep returns. "But *anyway…*"

Katie places her fork down next to her half-eaten salad and looks up at Lin and me with the most innocent of innocent expressions.

"No," Lin says. She finishes chewing the bite of burger in her mouth and repeats the word even more emphatically: *"No."*

"You don't even know what I was going to say!" Katie says.

"You only make that face when you're about to ask us to do something you know we don't want to do," I say. "Like every time you tried to get me to ditch math class with you in freshman year. Or when you tried to convince Lin to host afterprom at her house last year just so we could crash it. Or when—"

"I get it," Katie says smugly. "I'm the *interesting* friend."

"Not," I say, "what I meant."

"Look," Katie says. "Lin, I know that you have to spend, like, eight million more hours filling out your college applications with every single award you've won since the fifth grade, and that you, Stella, are irrationally prejudiced against all things that any normal human being might consider to be *fun*. Buuuuuut Ashley Kurtzmann is having a back-to-school party this weekend and it's supposed to be—"

But we never find out what Ashley Kurtzmann's back-to-school party this weekend is supposed to be, because both Lin and I have groaned at the exact same time.

"The last time we went to one of Ashley's parties," Lin

says, "you ended up miserable because Casey Bishop decided to make out with Victoria Lee instead of you."

"Um, have you seen Casey Bishop?" Katie says.

"Um, you had a boyfriend?" Lin says.

"Oh, yeah," Katie says. She bites her lip. "Well, look how that turned out. *The point is*, I refuse to let you spend your entire senior year sitting in front of a computer screen writing sixteen different drafts of your common app essay when everyone knows Harvard is just going to take one look at your GPA and let you in, anyway."

"That's really not how college admissions works," Lin says, but it's no use.

"And Stella! After everything that happened last year, don't you think that you deserve to have a little fun?"

"Well—well, yes," I say, "but—"

"All you do now is listen to mopey acoustic music and go on long runs and listen to more mopey acoustic music and go on even *longer* runs and listen to *even more* mopey acoustic music *while* you're running. What happened to the Stella I used to know? The one who dressed up as Jekyll to my Hyde for Halloween? The one who egged Lucy Sherman's house with me after she made fun of my lunchbox?"

"That was in the *fifth grade*," I say, only to be cut off by Katie's increasingly hysterical implorations.

"I know this can be the hardest thing in the world to believe sometimes," she says, her sincerity now starting to reach levels of absurdity, "but you deserve to have some fun. You deserve to go to a party. You deserve *happiness*."

"Katie," I say. "Have you ever considered that Ashley's parties...aren't...really... fun?"

"How would you know?" Katie says. "You've literally gone to *one* in the last year! Come on, Stella, give it a shot."

"My parents—"

"Oh, give me a break, Stella. Your parents will be *delighted* that you've taken an interest in socializing, and you know it. You know what your mom told my mom at the book club meeting at my house last month? That she's starting to think they were *too* strict on you growing up and now you're afraid of talking to your peers."

I open my mouth to retort, and then close it again in disbelief. "They *talked about me*?"

Katie nods solemnly.

"At *book club*?"

I can hear Lin suppressing her laughter next to me.

"I'm moving out of the suburbs," I declare.

"So you'll come?" Katie says. The warning bell—signaling the start of fifth period in six minutes—rings, and I look sadly at my barely touched, barely edible excuse for a meal.

I sigh. "Fine. I will go to Ashley Kurtzmann's party," I start. And then, over the sound of Katie's squeal of delight: "*If*—if Lin also comes."

Katie turns to Lin.

"Fine," Lin sighs. "But you're going to have to find someone else to drive us, Katie. There's no way I'll get through one of those parties sober."

"Well, obviously," Katie says. "No one could get through one of Ashley's parties sober."

7.

Lin and I have study hall together in the library last period on Wednesdays and Fridays. This is great for my sanity, because Lin is exactly the kind of sympathetic-but-no-bullshit friend that I need after a long day of barely managing to slog through classes, but terrible for my productivity, because we inevitably end up talking the whole time.

The two of us take a table in the center of the study lounge—one of the good ones, with the plushy chairs instead of the plastic wheeled ones. I watch as Lin slides her laptop out of her backpack, closes her eyes and takes a deep breath. Some of her hair flutters in front of her face, then flutters upward when she sighs.

"Sorry," Lin says. "I know I haven't been very fun lately. Katie's probably on the verge of staging an intervention for my social life."

"Don't be ridiculous, Lin," I say. "If Katie was about to

start throwing interventions for that sort of thing, I'm sure I'd be first on the list."

"Their English program is just so good, you know? And the arts scene in Providence... And it's close to home but not *too* close to home, you know, so my parents can't make me come home every other weekend. Anyway, sorry to make you listen to all this rambling for like the eightieth time. I know you know how much I love Brown. I mean, *everyone* knows how much I love Brown. I should spend less time talking about how much I love Brown and more time working on my application, which is due in—"

I watch her do the math in her head.

"Six weeks. Oh, *God*."

"I thought people didn't have to submit their applications until the winter," I say.

"I'm applying early so I can find out early," Lin says. "This way I'll know by the middle of December if all of my dreams have been crushed or not."

"You're being dramatic," I say. I make a mental note to buy some chocolate at the end of November, just in case.

"This, from the girl who once said she had to drop out of Bridgemont because 'douchebag might be contagious.'"

"Hey."

Lin and I both look up at the guy standing next to our table, then look at each other in confusion, then look back. Standing before us is Yago Evans, Bridgemont's resident weed dealer, looking lankier, blonder and even more stoned than I remember him being last year. Next to him is the Kevin from my philosophy class yesterday, shifting uncomfortably. It clearly wasn't his idea to strike up a conversation.

"Me and Kevin are gonna take advantage of senior privileges and get out of here. We're going to Dr. D.'s. And you're the only other senior in this study hall, so…you wanna come?"

Lin looks too confused to reply. I'm fairly sure that neither of us has never ever talked to Yago before in our lives. In fact, I'm shocked that Yago even knows who Lin and I *are*. Thankfully, Lin manages to gather herself and say: "I think I'm going to stay here and hang with Stella. I was gonna give her a ride home after school, anyway, so it doesn't really make sense to leave. Thanks for the offer, though, really."

Yago shrugs. "No worries, dude. Maybe next time."

I watch until they're both out of the library before turning back to Lin. "That was…weird," I say.

Lin looks thoughtful. "You know, I had AP Lit with Yago last year and he was actually pretty smart. Which just makes it so much weirder that he—you know."

She mimes taking a hit from a bong, which is hilarious.

"Well, anyway," Lin says. "We should do some work."

"I guess," I say. Lin puts her headphones in and starts typing on her laptop, and I spend the rest of study hall flipping through our first philosophy reading of the semester and wondering what kind of parent would name their child *Yago*.

8.

After school on Thursday, Lin takes a fifteen-minute detour into Hartford proper on her way home so she can drop me off at LiveWell Connecticut Counseling in time for my 4:00 p.m. appointment.

LiveWell is housed in one of the tall, concrete buildings in downtown Hartford that all look pretty much the same. Karen's office is on the seventeenth floor, where you can see almost the entire city and lines of cars stuck in traffic on the highway. There's a desk in the back of the office with half a dozen framed pictures—Karen and her husband on her wedding day, some school photos of her kids. Behind the desk is a bulletin board where she pins a new, vaguely inspirational quote every couple of weeks. It currently reads:

What Are You Grateful For Today?

"So," Karen says, after I've poured myself a cup of water and sunk into her couch. "How are we feeling today?"

Karen asks me some variation of this question every week,

and for some reason she always uses the pronoun "we" instead of "you," as if her feelings and my feelings are fundamentally bound together by some weird therapist-patient emotional link.

"I'm all right," I say. Which is also pretty much a variation of the answer I give every week.

"Ten milligrams of the fluoxetine still working well for you?" Karen asks.

"Hasn't made me suicidal yet!" I say. I flash her a thumbs-up.

Karen does not find my joke amusing.

"I understand that you started school this week."

"I did indeed," I say, taking a long gulp of water. The worst thing about therapy is that I have this habit of lifting the cup to my mouth and drinking reflexively every couple of minutes, just to have something to do with my hands. I can never even tell that I'm doing it until I realize how urgently I have to pee thirty minutes into my eighty-minute session.

"Mmm-hmm," Karen says. "And how has that transition been?"

"Fine," I say. "Just trying to pass my classes. Stay out of the way of all the imbeciles at Bridgemont—which is, you know, everyone. Not have another meltdown. Normal junior year goals, you know."

"Mmm. How would you compare yourself emotionally now versus last spring?"

"I'm fine," I say.

Karen looks at me.

"Fine-*ish*," I amend.

Karen raises an eyebrow.

"Fine-*er*. More fine."

Karen taps the side of her pen against her notebook thoughtfully.

"What do you want me to say? I don't feel *good*, but I do feel better. Less..."

I waggle my finger around my ears. "Less crazy thoughts."

"No suicidal ideation?" Karen asks.

"No," I answer.

"No feelings of self-loathing?"

"Not like last year," I say.

I don't know how to explain it. It's like...it's like there's another me—this crazy, unpredictable, terrifying version of the real me—locked in an iron box deep inside my brain. And I *know* that it's really the same person, and that everything I felt last semester was as real to me then as how unreal it is to me now. But it just doesn't *feel* that way. It doesn't feel like I could ever be that off the rails again, even though I'm sure that's how I felt before everything started going to shit the first time around.

"Is there any way I could just be... I dunno, like, *cured*?" I ask. I know it's a stupid, naive question, but I can't keep the note of hopefulness from filtering in my voice.

"Mental health isn't something that comes down to being *cured*," Karen says. "What's more likely is that, last semester, many separate factors came together to put you in a bad place emotionally. Perhaps something in the nights before your history exam triggered you or pushed you over the edge. You're still experiencing symptoms of depression now, but you're more stable, so you're having difficulty relating to how you

46

felt then. But that *doesn't mean*," Karen adds, "that the same thing can't happen again."

"Great," I say. "So I'm a ticking time bomb, is what you're telling me."

"Of course not," Karen says. "However, this is why I'd like to focus on developing healthy coping mechanisms. So that in case the stress builds over the course of the school year or things aren't going according to plan or something does trigger you again, or in moments when you might feel the way you did last semester again—when you might feel less stable, less invincible, less *healthy*—you know what to do."

"But I spent my entire *summer* developing healthy coping mechanisms," I say. "Breathing, running, music—good. Eating, screaming, retreating into isolation—bad. What more is there to develop?"

"Emotional health is like a muscle," Karen says, and then launches into a long speech about how coping mechanisms need to be practiced. I find myself zoning out, thinking about latest class with Mulland, about Kiekegaard and the nature of despair, and about Kevin, who continues to make comments in class that suggest that he's already taken the class once or twice or five hundred times and has gotten a bit *too* familiar with nineteenth century philosophers and all their existential despair.

"…which reminds me, Stella, I wanted to ask you if you've discussed these things more openly with your parents?"

The long silence after Karen's question snaps me out of my reverie. "Um," I say.

She raises an eyebrow.

"Not…really."

"Mmm-hmm," Karen says. She pauses. Then, full speed ahead: "You know, Stella, I really think a family session—"

"Ugh, *again*?" I say, before Karen finishes the sentence. It sounds petulant, but Karen has been trying to get me to agree to a family session for the past six months. She seems to be under the impression that it will help my parents and myself understand each other better, which sounds well and great and all, except for the part where having to sit in this stuffy office for an hour and a half talking about my feelings with both of my parents and Karen mediating seems like a particularly cruel, twenty-first-century version of purgatory.

"From what you've told me, it does not seem as if you and your parents have an emotionally close relationship," Karen says.

"Well, yeah," I say. "We don't."

"Your parents are your most direct support network," Karen says. "Not to mention that your relationship with your own feelings is shaped by their relationship with you."

"My mom gets even more upset than I do when I tell her that I'm the slightest bit sad, even if it's over something trivial and ridiculous that I know will blow over in a few days. Plus, she's already so worried about me that if I told her something was wrong, she'd never leave my side ever again! And my dad—well, I don't know if I've ever even seen my dad have feelings. Do people that smart have emotions?"

"But those are issues that you should *discuss* together," Karen says. "Your mother's concern may be rooted in how little information she has to go on. And your father—"

"I'm just not interested, okay?" I say, throwing my hands up. "I know that it might be better in the long run, but I just—I really—it would just be so *uncomfortable* talking about these kinds of things with them. Like, what am I supposed to say? 'Oh, hey, Mom and Dad, sorry that I sometimes hate myself!' I can't even imagine it. Can we talk about something else, please?"

"All right," Karen says. "It's your decision." But the look on her face says that I haven't heard the last of this, not by a long shot.

9. WHY I RUN

Here's a funny story for you:

When I first tried out for the Bridgemont cross-country team, my parents were in the middle of one of their countless, endless fights. My dad had just gotten promoted the year before, which meant that he was working overtime almost every day of the week, which meant that my mom quit her job to spend more time at home. The thing is, though, that I don't think my mom actually wanted to quit her job. I think it was one of those things that she did because it seemed like the right thing to do at the time, and then by the time she realized that she actually really missed her job—well, it seemed like it was too late to go back.

The point is, by midway through September, my mom was perpetually miserable and resentful and angry; and every night when my dad got home they'd have these huge blowout arguments about how late he was working and whose responsibility it should have been to pick me up after school in which they said the exact same things, over and over again, night after night, just in angrier and angrier voices. So I thought to myself, well, Bridgemont sports teams have practices four times a week, for two hours every day, which comes out to eight hours a week that I don't have to be at home. Volleyball, soccer and tennis were all out, because an incident in middle school when a poorly aimed half-court shot landed squarely on my unsuspecting head left me with a crippling fear of all sports involving balls. Which is—well—almost every single sport. But running? All I needed to run was a pair of sneakers (old Nikes that I'd had for four years and used maybe three times) and a direction to run in (away from my parents) and I was set to go.

And that's how I ended up on the cross-country team.

The other funny thing is that I was terrible. I had the third-worst mile time of everyone who tried out, and I didn't even manage to finish the wind sprints before walking off the track, exhausted and dehydrated and depressed. But Bridgemont has a team for all the freshmen who spent their entire middle-school years watching YouTube videos of cats all day instead of training, and—voilà!—there I was, on the freshman cross-country team.

At first, I was pretty sure that I had made the biggest mistake of my life. When I signed up for the team, I had anticipated mindless—perhaps even relaxing!—jogs through the suburbs of Connecticut, a couple hours of peaceful trails a week outside of practice, a coach who yelled charming motivational phrases like "Pain is weakness leaving the body!" and "The battle is ninety percent mental!" and stuff like that. What I didn't realize was that no sane person would ever describe running for ninety minutes a day when you're already sore from the ninety minutes of running you did yesterday with an adjective remotely close to "relaxing." Or that I would have to spend hours doing wind sprints up *hills* to increase "power." Or that cross-country coaches are basically exempt from the rules of public decency in the name of their sport. I swear, at least one person went home crying every week from sheer terror, and this was the *freshman* team.

Which brings us to the last and biggest surprise of all: eventually, I actually…started to love it. Sure, it was exhausting, and I was sore for entire months at a time, and I had to spend fifty dollars on a new pair of shoes after the soles of my old ones literally fell off. But after the initial shock wore off, the exercise, the repetitiveness, feeling myself get stronger with each run—it became something I started to look forward to every day. Running became a time when nothing else mattered but the feel of my shoes hitting the ground, the sound of my breathing in my own ears, the miles and miles of tree-lined roads that flew by over the course of an afternoon. Katie might've always been prettier and more social and better at making friends and just plain *happier* than I was, and Lin—whom we befriended midway through October after bonding over a miserable English group project—might've been smarter and more creative and endlessly well-read, and I might have been drowning in more schoolwork than I'd ever had in my life, but none of that mattered when I was running. Because I had the roads. The roads, and the wind in my hair, and a personal best to set.

10.

Katie sends Lin and me eight text messages in a row before Ashley's party on Saturday, each more urgent than the last.

Katie Brook (10:51 a.m.): yoooo so im thinking we should meet up at like 8 to start getting ready. you guys wanna come to my house?

Katie Brook (12:30 p.m.): gonna take that as a yes. lin can you bring ur naked 2 palette? i have no idea where mine went.

Katie Brook (12:31 p.m.): oh yeah and please try and wear something cute...

Katie Brook (1:42 p.m.): yes? no? are you guys alive?? stella did xc tryouts kill you???

Katie Brook (1:43 p.m.): how did those go btw?

Katie Brook (2:57 p.m.): LIN IF U DITCH AT THE LAST MINUTE BECAUSE YOU FEEL THE NEED TO REWRITE YOUR COMMON APP ESSAY FOR THE THOUSANDTH TIME I SWEAR TO GOD.

Katie Brook (4:00 p.m.):...

Katie Brook (5:37 p.m.): why am i friends with you guys?

Stella Canavas (5:39 p.m.): JESUS. YES. WE ARE COMING TO THE PARTY. SEE YOU SOON UNLESS YOUR COMPLETE LACK OF CHILL GIVES YOU AN ANEURYSM BEFORE.

Stella Canavas (5:39 p.m.): p.s. made varsity.

Katie Brook (5:41 p.m.): :*

Katie Brook (5:42 p.m.): CONGRATS OMG.

Katie Brook (5:42 p.m.): we will celebrate tonight with shots aplenty.

By the time 7:30 p.m. rolls around, I'm actually feeling pretty solid about going to this party. It'll be good, I tell myself, to start junior year off on a fun note, to do something other than sitting at home and surfing the web and trying to ignore my mother's anxious questioning about whether or not I have any "plans" this weekend. The worst-case scenario is that the music at Ashley's party is insufferable or something, and if that happens, I can just walk the seven blocks between her house and mine. No big deal.

I put on the closest thing to "party" clothes that I can find in my closet—a tank top, a black skirt and a pair of leggings—and throw some makeup into my bag, figuring that it's better to let Katie make me look party-ready at her house than to make a mess of my face trying to do it myself. I grab my cell phone, head downstairs and—

—run promptly into my parents...both of whom I've forgotten to inform about the party.

"Oh—hi, honey," my mom says, looking up from the television. My dad just looks confused, which I suppose is a somewhat disheartening testament to my complete and utter lack of social life. I can practically read his thoughts: *Stella, out of her room on a Saturday night? What happened to my daughter?*

"Need anything?" my mom says.

"I was gonna go…um, *out*," I say. Then, in response to their blank expressions: "To this…thing."

I cringe, because that sounds *terrible*.

"Could you elaborate on that, please?" my father says. I try not to groan as he picks up the remote and switches off the television. I might be here for a while.

"Lin, Katie and I were going to get together and go over together to this other girl's house. Um, her name's Ashley? She's in Lin's year."

"Who else is going to be in attendance?" my dad asks.

"Um, well, Lin and Katie are coming, as I mentioned, and beyond that… I don't…really know? Some of the other upperclassmen, I guess. Ashley's house isn't *that* big, so it can't be too many people…"

I trail off.

"I see," my dad says. He pauses. "Is this the type of party that parents worry about letting their children go to?"

"Uhhh…no?" I say.

But he doesn't look convinced.

"Oh, let her go, Thomas," my mom interrupts. "I'm sure they won't get into too much trouble. Isn't that right, Stell?"

"Is there going to be drinking?" my dad presses, ignoring my mother.

"Umm…" I say. The honest answer is yes, of *course* there's

going to be drinking. It's a party for a bunch of bored suburban high schoolers; what *else* are we going to be doing? But by the time I consider lying, I know I've waited too long to speak and the answer is written all over my silence.

Should've thought about this beforehand, I think. *Should've asked Lin what she's telling her parents, should've worn normal clothes and changed at Katie's house...*

"Not tonight, Stella," my father says. Then, in his most lawyerly of voices: "We can discuss this at another time and set a policy for future events, but for tonight—"

"Oh, for goodness' sake," my mom says. She rolls her eyes so hard that for a moment it's easy to see a flash of myself reflected in her expression. "Stella, promise you won't drink."

"I promise," I say. "I don't even want to get drunk. I'm just going because Katie's really into, you know, *socializing,* and that kind of thing."

"There you have it," my mom says. "They're just going to socialize. Nothing wrong with that."

"Anne," my dad says. "It's not just about whether Stella and her friends choose to drink. It's about her safety, which is affected by the decisions of everyone else at the party. I don't want her going to some stranger's house where a—a *horde* of seventeen-year-olds boys are drunk and doing God-knows-what."

"Ashley isn't a stranger! We had math together in freshman year!" I say. I leave out the part where there were twelve other people in that math class and Ashley and I did not speak a single time all year. "And it won't just be boys! Girls will be drunk, too! Ugh, that came out so much worse than I wanted it to."

"Stella hasn't had a fun night out in *years*," my mom says.

"There's no need to exaggerate, Anne, I'm sure she's—"

"No, really—she's right," I say. "I haven't had a night out in years."

"After the rough time she had last semester, I think Stella's earned tonight," my mom continues. "And besides, she'll be with Lin and Katie, two very responsible young girls."

"Misfortune doesn't permit deliberate irresponsibility," my dad says. He readjusts his glasses, which means that he's about to go into full-on lawyer mode. That's the thing about my dad. In moments of emotional intensity, the only thing that changes about him is that his words get, like, an average of six syllables longer. Which was fine when he had to convince Principal Holmquist that I wasn't a danger to myself or others, but is less fine when my mom thinks he's keeping me from my one shot at having a normal, happy junior year. "And besides," he continues, "what are Lin and Katie going to be able to do if their excessively inebriated peers get out of control? They're a bunch of teenage girls, Anne."

"Are Ashley's parents going to be there?" my mom asks.

"Of course they are." I actually don't know whether Ashley's parents are going to be there, but I figure that now is about the time when I should take a hint from every television show about high school ever aired and just *lie*. Works on *Gossip Girl*, right?

"No," my dad says.

"Go ahead, Stella," my mom says.

"Anne!" my dad says.

"What?" my mom snaps. "Stella wants to have a night out, she's going with two responsible friends, the party will be supervised by adults. There's no reason for us to keep her here, where she'll just sit in her room and stew in her own thoughts all evening."

Part of me wants to step in and tell my mom that there's nothing wrong with my thoughts, but then I remember that she's on my side.

"Stella does not have to sit in her room and stew in her thoughts all evening," my dad says. "She could join us. Stella, we are watching the sixth Harry Potter film on ABC Family and Ron has just taken the love potion that Romilda tried to slip Harry—it's really quite amusing. You are more than welcome to join us if—"

"Thomas!" my mom says. "This will be *good for her*. Do you understand what I'm saying? It will be healthy. Normal. Fun. All concepts which you may be familiar with!"

"That's not an assessment you can make on your own, Anne," my dad says. I start to think that I could walk out of the house right now and they'd be so caught up in arguing that they wouldn't even notice.

"Really?" my mom says. "Since when have you been in tune with Stella's extracurricular activities? I don't see you picking her up from track practice every day, or dropping her off at the mall on the weekends to hang out with her friends, or even having conversations with her when she gets home from school. When was the last time you took an interest in your daughter's social life?"

"Okay, well, I'm gonna go now," I say brightly, as my dad launches into a long lecture about how it's hard for him because he's at work all day, but he knows that he and I have a great relationship—*Isn't that right, Stella?*—and my mom is misconstruing all of his statements, and he doesn't see why she needs to get so *emotional* in the middle of what should be a rational discussion. Neither of them looks up.

"Well, bye," I mutter, and I'm not sure whether I feel more relieved or disheartened when I finally slip out of the house unnoticed.

11.

"Oh, my God, Stella, I was so worried," Katie says, answering the door. She ushers me up the stairs to her room, where Lin is perched on Katie's bed, dressed head-to-toe in Katie's clothes, examining her eye makeup in Katie's handheld mirror. Her dark brown hair is in loose curls.

"Sorry I didn't text you," I say. "My parents went insane. Turns out, Dad wasn't huge on the idea of me running wild at some debauched, alcohol-fueled party full of horny high school boys."

"You told them you were going to a party?" Lin says. "Well, jeez, Stella, there's your first mistake."

"Hold still," Katie says. She pulls her long, purple hair in a high ponytail and grabs her makeup bag off her desk. "I'm just going to do your eyes."

"How are we getting to Ashley's?" Lin asks.

"A couple of seniors are giving us a ride," Katie responds, almost too quickly. "Um, Bobby L. and Markus...?"

My eyes fly open and I swat Katie's brush out of the way. "The football players? We're going to get into a car with two *football* players?"

Katie blushes. "Yeah," she says, sounding half defensive, half pleased with herself. "Bobby's in my bio class and said he wouldn't mind. He's cute, right?"

I groan. "No. No. *Nooo,* Katie. I thought you were done with jocks after the Christian incident?"

Katie rolls her eyes. "Just because Bobby gives us a ride to Ashley's party doesn't mean I'm going to end the night in some random closet with him. You people have no faith in me. You know, Mariana told Ashley the other day that she was 'concerned for me' after she saw that Bobby and I are lab partners this semester in bio? Just because I like flirting, and I'd rather talk about cute guys than, I dunno, the *recurrent motifs in Steinbeck's body of literary work*—"

"Hey!" Lin says. Everyone who's ever talked to Lin knows that Steinbeck is her favorite author. In fact, I think Lin is counting down the days until I have to read it for AmLit this semester, just because she'll finally have someone new to harangue endlessly about it.

"That doesn't mean I'm some stupid girl who doesn't know what she wants. Or, for that matter, what guys want. Plus," she adds, "just because someone is an athlete doesn't mean they're an asshole. So everyone just chill."

"I dunno," I say. "Christian—"

"Christian is an asshole who *happens* to also be on the baseball team," Katie says. "He is an asshole *and* an athlete. Two independent facts."

Katie steps away from me, takes the mirror out of Lin's hands and passes it to me. "Done."

"It looks—I look—*older*, I guess."

"Yes," Katie says. She sounds faintly amused. "That's the point."

Katie takes the mirror away, tosses it onto her bed and sits down in front of me. She looks me in the eye with huge, perfectly mascaraed eyes. "Look, Stella," she says. "Promise me that you'll be open-minded tonight. About, you know, people."

"I'm open-minded!" I say.

"Uh-huh," Katie says. "Which is exactly why you think Bobby is an asshole even though you've never spoken to him before. Just because he likes to play football after school, *which*, I might add, *we go and watch*!"

"True," Lin says. "No one hates the football players when they're on the field winning." I take a pen off Katie's desk and chuck it in her general direction.

"I just don't want you to have a bad time tonight because you've already written everyone who's going to be there off as stupid, you know?" Katie continues.

"I haven't written everyone who's going to be there off as stupid!" I say. "I've just written off the party as a *whole* as stupid. There's a difference."

Katie does not look amused, but her phone vibrates before she can reply. "They're here," she says, and she sounds pretty damn grim for someone who is about to attend a party.

12.

The first word I would use to describe Ashley's party is *loud*.

The second word I would use is:

LOUD.

The only sound that comes close to matching the aggressive dance-floor pop blaring through Ashley's speaker is the chorus of thirty drunk kids singing along in the living room while swaying back and forth, making out or both. In that last category falls Ashley herself, who is wrapped around her boyfriend, clearly oblivious to the picture frames that have been knocked off the table and onto the ground, the drink Markus just accidentally spilled on her carpet and the game of beer pong being played across the *top of her piano*.

"So," Lin says, turning to look at me. Katie has disappeared into the crowd with Bobby, but the two of us still haven't taken five steps inside the actual house. "You wanna leave?"

"We can't leave," I say. "We promised Katie we'd stay and try to have fun."

"What?" Lin shouts. Unfortunately, my attempt to repeat the sentiment gets drowned out by the onset of the chorus of Kesha and Pitbull's "Timber," and the sound waves that come out of my mouth are promptly quashed.

I shake my head instead, grab Lin's hand, and pull her into the kitchen, where fifteen or so seniors crowd around a table stacked with beer, vodka and bottles of soda. The music is quieter here, but the trade-off is that the room smells like every ounce of marijuana in central Connecticut has been smoked in this room. The seniors, I now see, are passing around a pipe.

"Might as well reap the benefits of this shitshow, right?" I say, grabbing two beers off the table and handing one to Lin. We walk over to the side of the room, where all of the chairs from the table have been relegated, and sit down.

"Cheers to that," Lin says, opening her beer. I follow suit.

The last and only other time I've gotten drunk was at a party that Katie threw—because, let's be honest, who else would invite me to a house party?—while her parents were out of town celebrating their twentieth anniversary. That ordeal turned out to be a massive disaster, because:

1) I got way too drunk after taking four shots in a row with Lin to celebrate her ridiculously high SAT score and ended the night throwing up in Katie's bathroom;

2) Lin got way too drunk and ended the night crying because of her ridiculously-high-but-not-perfect SAT score;

3) Katie got way too drunk and invited Christian, her asshole ex-boyfriend, to come to the party at quarter past midnight; and

4) Katie's parents ended up finding out about the en-

tire thing, anyway, because some imbecile got so drunk he BROKE THE CHANDELIER IN THE FOYER.

For obvious reasons, I've been wary of alcohol since.

But Ashley's party is surprisingly fun—at least, compared to last year's debacle. Yeah, it reeks of weed, and the song "Don't Stop Believin'" has been played four times by 10:30 p.m., but chilling in her kitchen getting buzzed off beer while talking with Lin is not actually that far from my ideal Saturday night. Eventually, the music has been blaring so insistently and for so long that it almost fades into the background, damage to my eardrums be damned.

It almost feels like I'm having a good time, right up until the point where I walk to the bathroom and am greeted by the unmistakable sound of someone retching on the other side. I knock. No response. Knock again. More puking noises. I wait two, three, five minutes. "Are you okay?" I call, when there's a temporary pause in the vomiting.

"I'm fine!" a male voice calls back weakly.

"Oh, great," I say. "Hey, do you mind if I just—"

But the rest of my words are drowned out as whoever is inside the bathroom dissolves into another round of puking.

"Kinda seems like a lost cause, if you ask me," a voice behind me drawls.

I spin around.

"Hi, Stella," Kevin Miller says. He has a beer in one hand and the other in his pocket. "How's your evening going?"

For a second, I'm not sure how to respond. Kevin is looking at me like the two of us are friends and it's totally normal for us to be making small talk at Ashley Kurtzmann's house at midnight on a Friday while the sound of the Backstreet

Boys' "I Want It That Way" drifts down the hallway. Then I remember that I'm at a party, and that this is what people *do* at *parties*, and that if Katie were here, she'd have pinched me in the back already to try and get me to say something half-normal, like: "It's going great, thanks—how's yours?" or "I'm *so* glad I came—have you seen Jennie's outfit?"

"I need to get this idiot out of the bathroom before I explode," I say instead.

Which I suppose is why I don't get invited to more parties.

"Well, as I was saying, he kind of seems like a lost cause," Kevin says, looking remarkably unperturbed by my disastrous attempt to impersonate half-normal.

There's some more retching noises that probably prove his point.

"But there's another bathroom upstairs, second door on the left. I had to find it earlier because—well…"

I'm already making my way toward the stairs.

"You're very welcome!" Kevin calls out from behind me. I can hear the smile in his voice.

When I get back downstairs from the bathroom, Kevin is sitting at the chairs where Lin and I had been before I left. I wonder if he's sitting there because he knew that that's where I was, or if it's just a coincidence. Probably just a coincidence, I decide. Or maybe he saw Lin sitting there and recognized her from a class that they took together at some point.

But Lin isn't there anymore, I realize. Because Lin has joined the ring of smokers crowded around the table.

"Is this a prank? Tell me this is a prank," I say, walking up to her. "Have you ever even smoked before?"

Lin shrugs. From the hazy, lopsided smile on her face, I'm guessing the weed is having an effect. "Nah," she says. "But you were gone for, like, twenty minutes, and I thought, hey, first time for everything, right? Plus, Katie is always telling me to relax." She takes the pipe from the girl next to her, breathes in deeply and offers it to me.

"And I feel," she says, "rela-a-a-a-a-a-a-axed."

Then she erupts into coughs.

"No, thanks," I say, while Lin takes a long drink from her beer to smother her coughing. She shrugs again, passes it to the next person. "I'm gonna go…back over there," I say. "Because no offense, but you all smell like crap."

Lin smiles demurely. "No offense taken, Stella."

"Right. Um, find me when you wanna head out? Are Katie and Bobby still here?"

Lin waves in the general direction of the living room, which is now playing "Iris" by the Goo Goo Dolls. I pray that the switch from brainless upbeat pop music to brainless *downbeat* pop music means that the party's nearing its end. "I'll find you," Lin says. Then she turns around and starts talking to the girl next to her, picking up a conversation that has apparently been going on for some time about whether Hemingway or Fitzgerald did more to capture the existential ennui of the Lost Generation.

I walk back to the Chairs of Social Irrelevance, where Kevin is now sitting.

"Hi," I say.

"Hi," he says. He does that thing again, where he smiles at me like we're old friends, and I immediately run out of things to say.

"Surprised you're here without Yago," I say. "Uh, not that you can't go anywhere without Yago and vice versa, just that I'm surprised that you're here and Yago isn't. It seems more of his scene, that's all I'm saying. Also, what kind of name is Yago?"

I clamp my mouth shut before I can ramble on any further.

"That's not his real name," Kevin says, looking bemused.

"Must be pretty bad if he chooses to go by Yago instead," I say.

Kevin laughs. "Must be," he agrees. He looks slightly mischievous, and I take a drink to avoid thinking about that look any longer than I need to.

"And also," Kevin continues, "it is more of his scene. But you know, I haven't been at Bridgemont for a year and thought, *What better way to jump back in than one of Ashley's parties?* Now, of course, I realize that that was totally idiotic, and that spending two hours of my night whacking myself in the head with a hammer would be a more efficient way of shedding unwanted brain cells."

So that's why he's so unfamiliar, I realize. He was gone all last year.

"What'd you do last year?" I ask.

Kevin takes a drink. "Oh, I was around," he says after a long pause. He waves his hand in the air.

"Um," I say.

"Don't worry about it," Kevin says. "What are *you* doing here? You don't look drunk and you won't get high and you're sitting here all alone, so—what's the draw?"

"My friend Katie dragged me here," I admit. "In the interest of saving my social life. But I'm pretty sure it was mostly so she had an excuse to make out with her biology lab partner for a few hours."

"Nothing sexier than dead frogs," Kevin says. He takes another drink. The corners of his eyes crinkle as he smiles.

"My thoughts exactly. Plus, if he's anything like his best friend Markus, he's a total jerk. Markus—he—he made the most inappropriate comment about Katie's boobs on the way over, as if he wasn't talking to two of her best friends? It was—gross."

"A high school boy obsessed with boobs," Kevin says. "That's something new."

"Just because something is predictable doesn't mean it can't also be disgusting," I say. "Every year during the open houses, Holmquist goes on and on and on about how much we value equality and how we don't tolerate sexist behavior and how we even offer a class on feminism and yada yada yada. But *clearly*—"

"No one takes Modern Feminism except people who are already feminists," Kevin says.

I glare at him. For his tone of voice—which is annoyingly similar to mine when I know that I'm right about something—and for interrupting me right as I was about to get into a really good down-with-the-system rant. "*Just because* you've never been catcalled or—or had people think you can't do something because you're a girl, or—"

"Hey," Kevin says. He puts a hand on my arm to calm me down, and for some reason my desire to slap it away is met head-on by an equal desire to grab it and pull him close to me. I pull back, alarmed by the strength of my own reaction. *It's the alcohol*, I tell myself, even though I've only had two beers.

"Just because I stated a fact doesn't mean I think it's *right*," Kevin says, his hand falling back to his side. If he's noticed my micro-panic-attack, he doesn't say anything. "I think it would be great if everyone understood feminism. But let's be realistic for a minute here. How many dudes were in your class?"

"Four," I say.

"Out of?"

"Twenty-five," I admit.

"And how many of them were gay?" he asks.

I pause. "I plead the fifth."

Kevin laughs, and I can't help but drink in the sound of it, his movements, the way he smiles. When was the last time I laughed like that?

"That's what I thought," Kevin says. "But hey, there's hope yet. There's, like, ten guys in our class and we're reading Beauvoir. Hard not to be a feminist after reading Beauvoir. Genius, that woman."

"Kevin," I say very seriously. "Don't take this the wrong way. But…why are you in this philosophy class? You clearly—like, you understood Kierkegaard and you've already read Beauvoir. What's the point?"

"Here's the thing about philosophy," Kevin says. "You know in math, say, you're learning calculus, right? You're learning how to do derivatives so you can calculate the maximum volume of some storage thing that fills at a rate of blah, blah, whatever. Eventually, you figure it out. You know how to do a derivative, and that's it. You move on to the next thing—integrals, maybe—and then you learn that thing, too, and then the next thing, and so on and so forth until you've finished the school year or gone insane. Whatever.

"Or, like, biology. Mitosis is the process through which cells replicate. There are twelve organ systems in the body. Blah, blah, blah. You read those chapters in the textbook, they tell you the information that you're supposed to know, then you take a test on it, you forget all about it and you move on to memorizing the next set of facts.

"But philosophy... Philosophy isn't like that," Kevin says. He's starting to sound like Lin explaining her feelings about the closing scene of *Of Mice and Men* or Katie talking about MAC's newest eye shadow palette. He is so, so into this, I realize, and something about the feverishness with which he talks makes it hard for me not to get into it, too; makes it hard to remember that ten feet away there's a pipe being passed around, and twenty feet away Katy Perry is blasting through the speakers, and fifty feet away the couple upstairs is probably naked and passed out by now.

"You're never *done* with an idea in philosophy," Kevin says. "You never close a text or a chapter or even a *sentence* for good. Instead, you read Camus, and you read Sartre, and you read Kierkegaard, and you try to find your way through that glorious, glorious mess, and eventually maybe you come through the other side with your own conclusions about the human condition, about meaning, about where we find the will to live.

"Or maybe—maybe, you know, you don't. Maybe you get through *Being and Nothingness* and you're like, damn, this Sartre guy is full of *shit*. Well, that's fine, too. Maybe you're just not in a part of your life when Sartre's faithless skepticism rings true to you. Maybe you'll die thinking that *Being and Nothingness* is the worst excuse for a philosophical magnum opus ever written.

"But the magic of it is—even if that happens, even if that's how you feel this time around, you never know when it'll make sense. You never know when you're going to pick up that book again and look up at the world around you and the life you've lived and realize that it all clicks into place, it all makes sense, and you understand *yourself* better for it."

Kevin finishes talking. Finishes his beer. I blink a few times as the smokers, the music, Ashley Kurtzmann's house—as everything surrounding us fades back into my consciousness. The party is ending, I realize. The music's been turned off; everyone's grabbing their coats or trying to find their purses or lamenting their newly cracked phone screens. Lin and Katie will be here soon: Katie, drunk and giggly from her night with Bobby; Lin, somehow even *smarter* when she's high, because the world is unfair like that.

"You give that speech to everyone you meet at parties?" I ask.

"Just to the smart ones," Kevin responds, not a beat missed, that half smile on his face, and then it's silent again and I'm at a loss. Me. Stella Canavas. I literally don't know what to say.

It's not that there's nothing I *could* say, because that—as my parents often remind me—might signify impending apocalypse. I *could* tell Kevin that it was a beautiful speech, almost as great as one of Mulland's, maybe even better because I actually understood it. I *could* tell Kevin that there's something charming about the way he talks, about his words, about his obvious, unabashed love of something other than scoring free beer, or who won Bridgemont's last football game, or,

God forbid, boobs. I could even tell him that there's a part of me that wants nothing more than to sit here and listen to him talk like this for the rest of the night, stringing together sentences that I want desperately to hear and to understand and to believe in. But the truth is that I can't tell him any of those things, not really, not now, and so instead I pick up my purse and say: "I have to go find Katie before she leaves—I'll see you on Monday?"

"Sure," Kevin says. "I'll see you, Stella—Mulland's class. When our *intellectual journey continues.*"

He contorts his face into a gravely serious expression and drops his voice so that he sounds like Mulland at the beginning of class, and I make a noise that is suspiciously close to but definitely not a giggle.

"Uh-huh," I say, instead of what I *could* tell him, which is that I'm looking forward to it—to seeing him again, to talking about Sartre and Camus and the *human condition*, of all things. These are things that I will tell Kevin later, when his laugh has become familiar and comforting; when that speech has become engrained in my mind so deeply that I could recite it to you backward and forward; when I've come to love the way he loves philosophy as much as he loves the subject itself. But right now we're just two strangers who happened to be sitting at the same place at the same time at a party neither of us really wanted to be at. And it's not the time for that, not yet.

48.

It's midway through February, and there's a snowstorm howling outside my bedroom window. Six inches of snow overnight, said the meteorologist. Wind speeds topping forty miles per hour. Trees toppling over like Lego towers.

But all I can hear is the shouting.

This hasn't happened in a while. Then again, my dad hasn't been home in a while, either.

The digital clock on my nightstand reads 2:04 a.m. in red, spidery letters. They called the snow day six hours ago.

What do you want from me, Anne? You want me to go to work, bill sixty hours a week so I can provide for this household, track all of Stella's academics, run all the errands, fix the car, save the world while I'm at it?

Next to the clock is a big stuffed animal bear that I got as a gift from my grandparents for my third birthday. His name is written on a button stitched to his chest in my grandma's cursive: *Grizzly.*

I want you to BE PRESENT in this household. INVOLVED. As a FATHER. As a HUSBAND.

A stupid name for a bear, I know, but what more can you expect from a three-year-old?

You haven't exactly made this a welcoming house to be involved in.

The shelf above my writing desk has five framed photographs on it. The first: me and my parents at the San Francisco Zoo when I was four. The second: me and my grandparents and cousins at my oldest aunt's wedding when I was six. A classic Canavas family photo in which no one, *no one*, is looking at the camera. The third: me walking down the aisle, an explosion of pink-white tulle, as a flower girl at that same wedding.

So you just—you just leave?

The fourth: me, Katie and our moms at the beach the summer after fifth grade. The fifth: me, Katie and Lin smiling together, all braces and pimples and unnecessary hairspray, at the fall dance in freshman year of high school. I should just rip the Band-Aid off and take that picture down, because things between Lin and me are never going to be like they were in that photograph ever again, no matter how many hours I spend staring at it. But the three of us look so happy, and I know Lin has the same photograph hanging in her room, and every time Katie comes over she says that Lin hasn't taken hers down yet, either. So the photograph stays.

I haven't left. I'm here, aren't I?

You haven't been here in weeks, Thomas!

I was here five days ago.

You were here five days ago to pack a new bag!

The sixth photograph is new. It's a photo that Katie took

of me and Kevin while we were trying to build a snowman in my backyard over winter break. It's a horribly unflattering picture actually—we're both wrapped in so many layers that we look like giant cotton puffs, and neither of us knows that Katie's taking a picture. We're in the middle of an argument about whether or not our snowman's middle is too big for its bottom, but our faces are exaggerated, almost comically set, as if the outcome of our argument will determine the fate of the known universe. Kevin, mid-eye-roll, hands thrown up in the air in fake surrender; me, mouth half-open in some long-forgotten retort.

Earlier this year, after one of my many fights with Kevin, I was sitting at my desk writing and deleting text message after text message, trying to come up with something to say that would fix things between the two of us this time around. Desperate and nearly delirious from crying, I texted Kevin a copy of the photograph that Katie took and said:

Look how crazy we look right here. How comical in our anger. This is what this fight will look like in hindsight, too, you know. We're going to laugh about this one, too.

And, miracle of all miracles, it worked. Kevin came over and we spent the afternoon reliving that day, that argument, that moment; laughing together at our expressions; trying (and failing) to re-create them. Periods of calm never last very long between Kevin and me—that one certainly didn't—but in that moment, I felt like I had figured it all out. *This photograph*, I thought, *is going to make everything okay.*

I was wrong, of course, and it wasn't long until the next argument escalated, until I was storming out of his house and he was shouting after me that we were done, for real this time, *I fucking mean it*. But by the time the temporary euphoria of making up wore off and I realized how stupidly naive it was to think that a photograph could ever be anything more than just a photograph, I had already framed it and put it on my desk. And because hope is the cruelest of prisons, I haven't been able to bring myself to take that one down, either.

—*how to do this, Anne. I don't know how to feel at home here anymore.*

You MAKE IT feel like a home, Thomas. You COME HOME AFTER WORK and you SPEND TIME WITH YOUR WIFE AND DAUGHTER. That's how.

It's nearly three in the morning now. I wish the walls in my house were thicker. I wish I could text Lin about this. I wish Kevin were here. Mostly, I wish I could go downstairs with a camera and take a picture of my parents that would make them laugh together, if only for one night.

13.

By the time the tension between my parents reaches its apex in the spring, I will have spent many sleepless nights replaying their argument before Ashley's party, thinking that *that* fight was *the* fight that did them in for good.

I don't realize the significance of that argument at the time, of course. Even as the weeks in September unfurl into the beginning of October and my parents go from fighting once a week to twice a week to permanently snippy, I don't *really* think anything of it. There are just so many other things on my mind. My teachers, for starters, seem to be under the impression that with junior year comes an unlimited capacity to do homework. My life becomes a series of worksheets, readings and essays. I start looking forward to weekends because they provide forty-eight uninterrupted hours during which I can catch up on everything I didn't have time to do during the week. I do so many calculus problems that I begin doodling *the integral sign* absentmindedly in my other classes.

My biology lab partner dislodges Katie from her longstanding position at the top of my "Most Frequently Texted" list. I begin to resent the whole of Europe for fighting so many goddamn wars in the nineteenth century, all of which I am somehow supposed to memorize.

"Why couldn't they have just signed some kind of permanent peace treaty?" I complain to Lin one afternoon while we're holed up in her room doing homework.

Lin snorts. "A permanent peace treaty. That's cute. Wait 'til you see how that worked out in the *twentieth* century."

Then there's cross-country. It's not that I come to dislike the eight hours a week I spend in practice, because I don't. The beginning of fall—when the temperature is cooling down and the air around you feels *crisp*, feels somehow *new*—has always been my favorite time to run. And running is still the only effective escape that I have from the stress that sometimes feels like it's taking over my life. Karen says that quitting cross-country is the *last* thing that I should do, and for once, my therapist and I are on the same page. It's just that by the time I get home after every practice, it's already half past five, and the mountain of things I still have to do feels absolutely insurmountable.

To top it all off, there's Lin. Lin is anxious about Brown. Lin is more anxious about Brown than ever. Lin is so anxious about Brown, in fact, that I start to experience *secondhand* anxiety about Brown. Sometimes I find myself going down this train of thought while daydreaming in English class: *If I get a C on this paper, is it going to tank my GPA? Will Brown think I'm a major slacker if I only take one AP class senior year? Are my*

SAT scores so bad that even pulling all A's next semester won't save me? Wait a second, I haven't even taken the SATs yet.

Lin is so stressed that even Kevin and Yago have started sitting with us during our shared last period study halls to try and make her feel better, which usually goes something like this:

Kevin: You know, one almost feels bad for Nietzsche. So brilliant, yet so unhappy.

Lin: [Stares at laptop screen.]

Yago: You know what Nietzsche needed? Weed. He needed weed.

Kevin: That's one suggestion.

Lin: [Stares at laptop screen. Her eye twitches.]

Me: Was Nietzsche a, um, recreational user of many drugs?

Yago: Dunno. But if he was, he definitely wasn't smoking weed.

Lin: [Stares at laptop screen.]

[An uncomfortable silence descends.]

Yago: Lin, have you considered smoking some weed? I really think it might help.

Not exactly a scene out of a rom-com.

The worst part of it all is that I can't help but feel somewhat disappointed as the weeks stretch on and Kevin and I remain nothing more than friendly-but-distant acquaintances. No matter how many times I tell myself that the chemistry I thought we had was all in my head, and that I barely even know the guy, and that he's horribly pretentious, anyway (who reads Beauvoir for *fun*?), I can't ignore the fact that when he speaks up in Mulland's class or slides into the seat next to me in study hall, I feel…well, stupidly giddy. And I can't help but spend nearly all of my calculus classes in the month after Ashley's party conjuring up scenarios in my head, all of which seem to end in Kevin professing his feelings for me in deep, philosophical terms that I can barely understand. I spend half of my time feeling swept away by a torrent of irrational desire, and the other half of my time feeling mortified that there's nothing I can do to stop it.

The problem is that the fifty percent of my brain that thinks it might be a good idea to make an innocuous first move—you know, something "casual" and "cool" like asking Kevin if he wants to hang out after school sometime, or striking up a conversation during study hall that doesn't revolve around Yago's various drug recommendations—is combated by the other fifty percent of my brain that is terrified of rejection. I replay the following scenario in my head and physically cringe from the mortification so many times that Lin asks me if my anxiety is starting to manifest in a physical tic.

Me: Hey, Kevin. So, uh, no pressure, but, like, do you maybe want to hang out this Friday?

Kevin: Oh, hey, Stella. Is Ashley having another party or something?

Me: Oh. Um, no, she's not. I meant, you know, just the two of us, together. But not like, just the two of us, alone, together. Like, just the two of us, hanging out together, in a place where there's more than just the two of us. You know, like a movie theater. Or, um, a zoo? Or...a public library!

Kevin: You...want to go to the library on Friday?

Me: [Melts into the ground, becomes one with the Earth, am reincarnated as an inanimate object that does not bear the burden of socialization.]

"You have to help me," I say to Katie at lunch one afternoon. "I feel like I'm going crazy."

"You'll get your alone time, Stella," Katie says. "Sooner or later the unresolved tension will become so unbearable that the two of you will have no choice but to shove each other into the janitor's closet and rip each other's clothes off. And my bet," she adds, smirking, "is on sooner."

"Are you speaking from personal experience?" Lin asks, looking up from her laptop. There's a sticky note on it that reminds us that the Early Decision application deadline for Brown is twelve days away.

"Was that supposed to be reassuring?" I ask.

Katie just smiles and tosses her hair—still magnificently purple—behind her shoulder.

"Maybe you should just try to forget about it for a while," Lin says. "You clearly have a lot on your plate right now, and do you really think that getting with this random mysterious philosophy dude who may or may not have spent his last year on a serial killing spree across the country should be at the top of your priorities list?"

"Hmm," I say. "I don't think Kevin's the serial killer type. He's too honest. Maybe arson, you know, or—ooh, graffiti. Are there any underpasses in Hartford with Sartre quotes spray-painted on them?"

"Let's all focus on the facts here," Katie says. "Which is that Stella thinks this guy is cute, and he clearly thinks that she's cute, and—"

"Objection," I say. "There is zero—and I mean *zero*—evidence supporting that second conclusion."

"You hung out at Ashley's party last month," Katie says. "And he sits with you guys during your study hall."

"He sits with us from study hall because he's concerned that Lin is going to go catatonic from the stress of her Brown application," I say.

"A reasonable concern," Lin admits.

"And we hung out at Ashley's party last month because you abandoned Lin and me to make out with Bobby all night and then Lin abandoned me to get high!"

"And who did you turn to in your hour of greatest need?" Katie says. She pretends to swoon.

"The only person available," I say. "Who *happened to be* Kevin."

"Bobby's friend Markus was available," Katie says.

"Bobby's friend Markus? Oh, the one who really likes your boobs? Yeah, I'm sure he's a riveting conversationalist."

"Ooooh. Is Kevin a…*riveting conversationalist?*" Katie's voice gets low and salacious.

"Okay," I say, determined to put an end to this conversation. It's been half an hour and I've barely even touched my lunch (although, given the look of today's "eggplant Bolognese," that might be a good thing). "Am I into Kevin? Sure. He's cute and not a total imbecile, which, given the state of our fellow classmates at Bridgemont Academy—"

I gesture around the courtyard. A group of wannabe punks sits to our left, with enough hair dye between the four of them to cover the entire spectrum of visible light. Past them are Brady and his circle of Harvard aspirants, who would probably rather go 0-for-8 on the Ivies than hang out with someone not on the AP track. And in the center of the courtyard, the entire football team is crowded around one completed math worksheet, all jostling for optimal copying position.

"—is unfortunately pretty much where my standards are. But I'm not you, Katie. I'm not the kind of girl who can just waltz into some guy's brain and, I don't know, make him want to make out with me."

"So you *do* want Kevin to make out with you!" Katie says.

"Is that really what you got out of what I just said?"

"All right, Stella," Katie says. There's an air of finality in her voice that means there's no point in protesting. "Here's the plan. You're going to invite him to hang out with us at Homecoming."

"I'm not going to Homecoming," I retort immediately. "It's a glorified high school mating ritu—"

"Not the homecoming *dance*," Katie says, rolling her eyes. "I gave up on trying to get you guys to go to that years ago. No, I'm talking about the homecoming pep rally. Sit in the bleachers. Watch the dance team. Rah-rah-Bridgemont, rah-rah-Tigers. That sort of thing. We all have to go, anyway. You might as well tell him to hang out with us while we're there. And it's a low-key ask. It's just like—"

Katie does an impression of me and Kevin talking to each other that makes me want to transfer schools immediately:

"'Yo, I'm *so over* these pep rallies.'

"'Yeah, I know, right?'

"'Well, Lin, Katie and I are gonna be in bleacher four if you want to suffer through it together.'

"Then, *bam*. You're in the bleachers, getting it on."

"Have you ever considered reading some cutesy chick-lit novels?" I ask. "Because I really think you're their target audience."

"Have *you* ever considered reading some cutesy chick-lit novels?" Katie retorts. "Because I really think your life is in desperate need of some romance."

"Have *either* of you ever considered reading *East of Eden*?" Lin says. "Because it's the greatest American novel of all time—I don't know if you guys have heard."

"Okay, fine," I say. "Maybe I will ask Kevin and Yago to sit with us during the homecoming rally."

"You're *going* to ask Kevin and Yago to sit with us during the homecoming rally," Katie says.

"How can you possibly know that?" I ask.

Katie's smile turns wicked. "Because if you don't ask him, I will. And I'm sure you can imagine exactly what I'd say."

14.

"LAAADIES AND GENTLEMEN, BOOOOYS AND GIIIRLS! IT'S THE DAY WE'VE BEEN WAITING FOR. THE DAY WE'VE BEEN COUNTING DOWN TO SINCE THE FIRST DAY OF SCHOOL. A DAY THAT ONLY COMES ONCE EEEEVERY YEAR. IIIIIIIT'S HOOOOMECOMIIIIING!"

If there's one thing I've learned at Bridgemont Academy, it's that pep rallies are serious, serious business. This is not some poorly planned day party where students just mill around the gymnasium cheering halfheartedly until everyone can go home and start pregaming for the football game later in the evening. No, the Bridgemont Academy Homecoming Pep Rally is planned down to the minute. With every cheer, boom from the speakers and dance set to the latest pop hit, the amount of pent-up, repressed teenage energy in the audience doubles, triples, quadruples, until even the alternative, emo kids in the very back of the gym can't pass off their enjoyment as "ironic." And yes, even I—avowed hater of unruly crowds and social nobody with zero school spirit—find myself standing and cheering as the band marches around the gymnasium, cymbals clashing, drums pounding.

"It's funny," Kevin says over the cheering. "I never would've taken you for a pep rally kind of girl."

"Don't let the sarcastic exterior fool you, Kevin. Stella can be *very enthusiastic* when she wants to be. Isn't that right, Stel?" Katie waves her noisemaker in the air and winks at me while I consider pushing her off the bleachers.

Fortunately, everyone's attention is diverted back to the floor as the cheerleaders run out in uniforms so tight that it's a miracle they can move at all, much less do a round-off back handspring while someone backstage cranks the volume up to earsplitting levels.

Jennie von Haller grabs a microphone and shouts: "I'LL TELL YOU WHAT I WANT, WHAT I REALLY REALLY WANT!"

She holds the mic out to the crowd, and the crowd responds: "I'LL TELL YOU WHAT I WANT, WHAT I REALLY REALLY WANT!"

I shoot Kevin a helpless look. Kevin makes a face and rolls his eyes in mock exasperation.

Jennie, now even louder: "I'LL TELL YOU WHAT I WANT, WHAT I REALLY REALLY WANT!"

The crowd, stomping so hard all of the bleachers are shaking: "I'LL TELL YOU WHAT I WANT, WHAT I REALLY REALLY WANT!"

The sound of an airhorn blares through the speakers. Out run the girls' and guys' dance teams, who join the cheerleaders on the floor in a routine that is ten percent acrobatics and ninety percent gyrating. Needless to say, it's a real crowd-pleaser.

"HAS NO ONE NOTICED THAT THIS IS HORRIBLY EMBARRASSING?" I shout over the crowd.

"EVERYONE'S TOO BUSY HAVING FUN!" Katie shouts back.

"I THINK I'M GOING TO GO DEAF!" I say.

"WHAT?" Lin says.

"I THINK I'M GOING TO GO DEAF!" I repeat, shouting as loudly as I can.

Lin shrugs and mouths the words *Too loud, can't hear*, before turning back to the action. I turn to look at Kevin, who has an expression somewhere between a grin and a grimace on his face.

"DOROO WANNA GUESS AN EAR?" Kevin says.

He catches the blank expression on my face, opens his mouth as if to repeat himself and then seemingly changes his mind. Instead, he points once at me, then at himself, and finally at the gym doors.

The meaning is obvious, but I'm so distracted by the extreme nervousness that has just detonated in every fiber of my being that I don't actually manage to give Kevin a response. Instead, I gape at him.

Kevin mistakes my shock for confusion and tries again. He points at the exit and mimes walking with two of his fingers.

"All right, then," I manage to say, nodding weakly. And I barely have time to turn around and signal to Lin and Katie that I'm leaving—ignoring Katie's shit-eating grin and Lin's wink—before Kevin is on his way down the bleacher steps and I'm scrambling to keep up with him.

The second the metal gym doors clang shut, trapping most of the noise behind us, I breathe a sigh of relief.

"That was…" Kevin starts.

"Loud," I say.

"Yes. That. It was definitely very loud."

He makes a face and starts walking, stopping when we reach a set of lockers a few halls down from the auditorium. Then he sinks down to the ground, sitting with his legs extended in front of him, his back slouched against the lockers, his hands folded in his lap. There's a smile on his face that should be irritating—he is making fun of me, after all—but I can't bring myself to feel anything remotely resembling anger. Kevin looks so at ease. Like there's nothing at all unusual about the two of us sitting next to each other right now, in this empty hallway, completely alone.

That thought, of course, is enough to send my pulse skyrocketing again.

"Well, anyway," Kevin says after silence has settled around us. He leans a little closer and the air between us starts to feel like a flimsy, physical barrier; one that I could reach out and rip right through. "You wanna get out of here?"

He lifts his blue eyes to mine and grins so innocently that it takes me a second to understand what he's just said.

"Get out of here," I repeat. "As in, like…"

"As in, like, leave," Kevin says. "Exit the building. Flee the premises. Abscond, if you will."

"Oh," I say. "Right."

Of course, I think. *Of* course *he wants to get out of here. What did you think the two of you were going to do, Stella? Pace around the halls for three hours?*

Kevin must take my speechlessness as hesitation, because he adds, "I mean, the good part of the pep rally is pretty much over. Unless you really want to know who makes it onto the Homecoming Court, I guess."

"Right," I repeat weakly.

"Plus…" Kevin says. He lowers his voice so that it's almost a whisper and leans into my ear. "It'll be *an adventure…*"

The last time I was this close to a guy was when I ended up making out with Titus Liu in the middle of Katie's living room at her ill-fated house party last spring. And let me tell you: the quarter-cup of vodka that robbed me of my better judgment that night has *nothing* on the hormones currently staging a coup in my brain.

"That sounds like it might be fun," I say, swallowing hard. "And also like it might be totally against the rules. But…that's fine. That's cool. *I'm* cool. I'm totally cool. What are rules, anyway? Ha. Ha, ha."

Kevin laughs. The nicest thing, I think, is that even when I've said something completely idiotic, Kevin still doesn't laugh like he's laughing at me. He laughs like he's inviting me in on my own joke.

"It's Homecoming," Kevin says. "No one is going to notice."

"Lin," I manage to say. And then, ever the picture of eloquence: "Katie." And then: "Yago?"

"You know, I feel like they're the type of friends who would tell you to go," Kevin says.

"My parents will kill me if they find out."

"They won't find out," Kevin says.

"You sound like you've done this before," I say, narrowing my eyes.

"Bridgemont has a lot of pep rallies," Kevin responds. He doesn't sound the least bit guilty. In fact, he's smirking.

"Aren't you worried that *your parents* will find out?"

Kevin rolls his eyes. "My mom doesn't care if I go to Homecoming, Stella. It's *Homecoming.*"

"Oh," I say.

"They've got bigger fish to fry," Kevin says grimly.

"Oh," I say again. I wait for him to elaborate but he just shrugs. "You in?" he says.

I take a deep breath and consider my options.

Option A: I tell Kevin that it's really important to me to be there for Jennie von Haller's big moment of being crowned homecoming queen even though we've never shared a single conversation and she probably doesn't know who I am. I endure abuse from Katie for the rest of the year—no, the rest of *my life*—for passing up what may well be my only opportunity to have a cutesy chick-lit moment. Lin refrains from commenting out of politeness but makes that face that she makes every time Katie and I blow off her desperate attempts to get us to read *East of Eden.*

Option B: I leave with Kevin. We go who-knows-where and do who-knows-what. If I'm lucky, no one at Bridgemont notices that two delinquent teenagers have gone AWOL and calls my parents. If I'm somewhat lucky but also kind of unlucky, my parents do find out but wait to murder me until after I tell Katie that I've finally done something exciting with my life, so that at least my best friend can attend my funeral with pride. If I'm not lucky at all, I get home this afternoon to find my mom mainlining black tea and my dad pacing back and forth and, well, that's the end. But in that scenario, I get out of taking my calculus test next Friday, so really, it's a win/win/win situation.

"All right," I say. "Let's do it."

15.

Kevin drives a gray sedan so beat up that it gives Lin's Ford a run for its money. First of all, there's a dent the size of a basketball above the right back wheel. The hood is freckled with so many paint chips that, from a distance, the car resembles a gray-and-white mosaic, sparkling underneath the afternoon sun. I have to slam the passenger door three times before it latches shut, rattling in protest the entire time.

Needless to say, I start to have serious reservations about Kevin's driving ability.

"Don't worry," he says, before I've even said a word. "I didn't do all that. The car's a hand-me-down from my cousin Brett. And Brett—as you can see—is a real shit driver."

Kevin slides the key into the ignition and the engine hums awake, deceptively strong underneath the scratched-up exterior.

"Was my fear that obvious?" I ask.

"The look of terror on your face was a bit of a dead give-away, yeah," Kevin says, smirking. He reaches for the parking brake like he's going to take the car out of Park, then drums his fingers on it a few times and seems to change his mind.

"So," Kevin says, turning to face me. He places his elbow on the center console between our two seats, and leans in.

And in.

And even farther in.

And then, in a tone of voice so transparently flirtatious that it takes me a solid ten seconds to process the actual words: "Where to, Miss Canavas?"

Here's the thing: normally, I consider myself a fairly eloquent person. I mean, I'm no Dr. Mulland, and Katie could talk circles around me any day of the week, but I don't often find myself at a loss for words. If anything, my problem is that I always seem to have *too many* words.

The point is, I should have something to say right now. I should be able to parry Kevin's low, suggestive "Where to, Miss Canavas?" with something equally disarming, something that would leave *him* wordless and fighting down a blush. But it's not just his words that my brain is suddenly struggling to process—it's also everything about his physical presence: the way his clothes smell like fresh, still-warm laundry; the way the blue of his eyes is darker on the outside of his irises than near the pupils; the way I can almost, almost, *almost* feel his hand, so close to my arm, resting between our two seats. It's like all of my senses have gone into overdrive at the same time, leaving me—well, senseless.

"I didn't really have anything in mind," I manage to say. My voice sounds all wrong in the small, silent car: strangely amplified, too casual, slightly shaky. "Know of any good get-away spots?"

"Are you trying to get away?" Kevin responds softly. The fact that we are sitting in the school parking lot and that any-one—one of my friends, one of his friends, Mr. Tang, Doug from biology class, Principal Holmquist, anyone!—could walk by and see us right now is completely and utterly obliterated from my mental radar as Kevin slides his hand over and runs his thumb down mine.

There is a tiny, tiny corner of my brain that is still online that takes the ensuing silence as an opportunity to shout: *That was not that much contact, Stella! Say something clever. Pretend you're in a dramatic rom-com and this is the scene they're going to put in the trailer while a string quartet plays in the background.*

"Aren't you?" I say.

Okay, my brain says. *I think you may have overshot a bit.*

Kevin makes a sound that's half scoff, half laugh, and breaks our eye contact for the first time in what feels like hours. "Touché," he says. He shakes his head almost ruefully, then turns back to the wheel and shifts the car into Reverse. The rest of the world comes flooding back, and I feel…well, I don't know how I feel. Confused? Deflated? Sad? All of the energy that was just crackling between us dissipated all at once, and now the car feels empty.

"Well, I do have somewhere in mind, as a matter of fact," Kevin says. He takes the car into first, then second, then third gear, the engine revving slightly louder with every change in gear. "It's not very glamorous, but it's…nice. Quiet and secluded and nice."

My brain selects "secluded" from the list of adjectives that Kevin has just provided and latches on to it.

"Lucky for you, I much prefer quiet and secluded and nice to glamorous."

"You know, I would've guessed as much," Kevin responds. His lips curl into a wry smile. "Although I also would've guessed that you'd be the last person to hightail away from Bridgemont during school hours with someone like me. And look at us now."

"Someone like you?"

"Oh, you know. Strange. Mysterious. Best friends with a drug dealer."

Kevin pauses, looking very grave, and then adds: "And incorrigibly handsome, of course."

"Well, I'll certainly give you 'strange,'" I say. Kevin laughs—*really* laughs, his eyes crinkling, the tension flooding out of his body.

"But hey," I say. "Sorry to defy those expectations of yours."

"Don't be sorry. It's always…"

Kevin trails off. The sound of cars rushing by around us on the highway fills the car. "Well, it's always nice to be surprised by someone," he says.

"Yeah, it is," I say softly.

Kevin smiles and whistles a few notes of a song I don't recognize under his breath. The sun is directly overhead, a constant reminder that we really should be in school right now. I reach for my phone to see how many times Katie and Lin have texted me—because they've definitely texted me by now—but change my mind the second my hand hits the case.

Right now, right here, this car feels like its own little universe. A universe with exactly two people: a boy who never thought the girl would be the type of person to ditch school with him on a random Friday, and a girl who never thought the boy would be the type to whistle peacefully to himself while driving. And the truth is, I don't want to bring anyone else—not even Lin, not even Katie—into the world I'm sitting in right now.

"Can I ask you a question, Kevin?"

"Voltaire once said that it is better to judge a man by his questions than by his answers," Kevin responds.

"Okay, well, I'm going to take that as a yes," I say.

"Go for it."

I take a deep breath and plunge in. "Where were you *actually* last year? I tried to ask you at Ashley's party, but you were…evasive."

Kevin's been expecting the question. "You really want to talk about this?" he says.

"We don't *have* to. I'm just curious, that's all."

Kevin takes a sharp right and pulls into a tiny parking lot that's almost invisible from the road. Describing it as a "lot" is actually generous: there are four spots nestled in a patch of trees, all of which are currently empty.

"Welcome to Prospect Park," Kevin says. Then, before I can press the question: "Like I said, not very glamorous. It's one of those locally funded neighborhood parks the state of Connecticut maintains with all that property tax we're paying. Well—all that property tax our parents are paying, anyway. But, of course, the state of Connecticut forgot to take into account one small detail—no one goes to parks anymore."

Kevin locks the car behind him as we step out. It's one of those early fall days when the air is crisp and the temperature is that perfect cool-but-not-cold medium and it's easy to forget that four and a half months of snow and misery are about to descend upon all of New England. It's apple-picking weather. Sweater weather. Running weather.

"Do you come here a lot?" I ask, following Kevin up a tree-lined hill that leads into the park. We take a right when we get to the top and then take a path that winds through a field of tall, dandelion-ridden grass. The city noises fade as we walk, and I think that if I had a car I'd come here after school every day—to run, or perhaps just to get away from it all.

"I get out here a couple of times a month when the weather's nice," Kevin says. "You know, to read or write or just think. I used to come here a lot more with Yago, but he's so busy now with college applications and all that shit that we can never find the time. I guess I should be working on college apps, too, but there's not nearly as much of a rush for me because I'm not applying anywhere early."

"Not sure how I feel about being a Yago stand-in," I tease.

Kevin stops so suddenly in front of me that I walk into him. He turns around, and the look on his face is so intense that I reflexively take two steps back. It's not that he looks angry, or sad, or frustrated—there's not really *any* identifiable emotion on his face. He just looks…intense.

"That's not what I meant," he says.

"I know," I say.

"Yago is my best friend," he says.

"I know," I repeat.

"But I'm not only hanging out with you because he's busy this semester. You're not a stand-in for any other person."

"Kevin, I know. I was just making a joke. I know I'm not a stand-in for Yago. My name is 'Stella,' for God's sake. Not nearly weird enough. You'd go with, I dunno, Brixa-Marie from Mr. Parker's homeroom. God, I'm so glad my parents didn't name me Brixa-Marie."

"All we have," Kevin says, ignoring my rambling, "are our words. You know? Everything comes down to the words that we say to each other. And the meaning we try to convey with those words. And the hope that when we convert the meanings that live in our heads to the words that come out of our mouths, the two are close enough so that the person we're talking to can walk across the gap and arrive at the right conclusion about what we're trying to say to them."

Kevin steps toward me and places his hands on my shoulders. He bites his lip. His voice is soft. "I know you aren't offended and it may not seem like a very big deal—just standard miscommunication, just said the wrong thing when actually I meant something else, whatever. But I am not the type of person who is careless with my words, Stella. And I don't want you to think that I am."

"Okay," I say.

"Okay," Kevin repeats. He hesitates, then turns forward again and resumes walking. "We're almost there, just give it a minute."

The truth is, I've never even thought about the perils of being "careless with words," much less associated them with specific people, much less associated them with Kevin just because he made an offhand comment about not being able to hang out with Yago at this park after school. And the fact that Kevin just got so dramatic and serious about something that I literally wouldn't have given a second thought to otherwise is definitely weird. But also, I can't help but think, kind of hot. As I fall into step next him, my brain replays his *"I am not the kind of person who is careless with my words, Stella,"* over and over again, soaking in the gravity of his voice, the feeling of his hands, how easy it would have been to kiss him just to shut him up. Then I pull myself out of that daydream, mortified.

"All right," Kevin says. "This is it."

We're standing in front of a concrete pergola in the middle of a garden. Or, more accurately, what probably was once a garden but is now a field of overgrown grass with random flowers spread throughout, waving lazily in the wind. The pergola also looks like it's been abandoned for many, many years: the stone is worn down and uneven, and the blocks scattered across the ground as makeshift chairs are speckled with dirt.

But what's really striking about the pergola is the graffiti. Almost every inch of the stone columns is covered in quotes, drawings and random musings scribbled in spray paint, marker and even plain black Sharpie. I imagine roving bands of high schoolers continuing to visit the park long after the groundkeepers and gardeners abandoned it, sneaking out of their house after dark to leave their mark on this strange, crumbling landmark. How many illicit cigarettes have been smoked here by "rebels" all desperately trying to impress their friends? How many nervous first kisses has this garden played host for? How many angsty teenagers have made their way here to write their latest revolutionary thought in hopes that someone else might read it one day and find it profoundly meaningful?

"Wow," I say.

Kevin sits down on one of cleaner concrete blocks and looks around. "Yeah," he says. He points at the arch at the center of the back wall, above which three words are etched into the concrete:

Garden of Remembrance

I say the words out loud as I read them, feel them drift away in the breeze.

"It's an ironic name for a garden that's been abandoned," Kevin murmurs.

"Not just ironic," I say. I think of someone planning this beautiful garden, someone planting the flowers and laying down the rocks for the pergola, all in the name of remembrance. Only for this, too, to be forgotten. "It's sad."

"You're right," Kevin says. "It is sad. But I think there's something about this place that transcends the irony and the sadness of it all. I've probably spent hours just reading through all the graffiti, thinking about who all these people were, and why they wrote what they wrote, and when they wrote it. And yeah, some of it is just obnoxious couples scribbling their initials everywhere, and at least another ten percent are lyrics from bad emo songs, but someone wrote that stuff here for a reason. They wrote it because it meant something to them at the time. Something important. And whenever I'm here, I just think about all of those people, all of that emotional energy, all of the heartbreak and euphoria and angst that they've put onto the walls because they didn't know what the hell else to do with it…it makes the place feel alive, you know what I mean?"

"I do," I say. I keep my voice soft, because we can hear the wind rustling through the leaves of the trees and because to speak too loudly in a place like this feels wrong—sacrilegious, almost.

"This guy wrote, 'So what if we're all just machines?'" I say, reading the words on the column in front of me. "That's deep, right? I kind of like that."

"It's interesting because it could go one of two ways, you know?" Kevin says. "He could be saying, 'So *what if* we're all machines?' As in, could it really be possible that everything about our lives—everything that's intricate and sublime about the human experience—is just the product of a bunch of biochemical impulses? Or he could be saying, 'So *what* if we're all machines?' As in, even if we are indeed all slaves to a bunch of biochemical impulses, does that somehow invalidate all that is intricate and sublime of the human experience?"

"Damn," I say. "That *is* deep. Perhaps I should give the delinquent youth of this town more credit."

"Or maybe you shouldn't," Kevin says. "The one right under 'So what if we're all machines?' just says, 'TC sucks dick.'"

Kevin and I spend the rest of the afternoon in the garden, moving from column to column, reading our way through the endless lines of graffiti. By the time it's 4:00 p.m. and we get back to his car, my head is a blur of lyrics and Kerouac quotes and made-up aphorisms. I haven't checked my phone in three hours. Kevin peers over my shoulder from the driver's seat as I pull it out of my bag and turn on the screen, fingers crossed that I don't have fifty-six frantic voice mails from my parents. Which brings me to the good news, and to the very, very, very bad news.

So here's the good news: I do not, in fact, have fifty-six missed calls from my parents, which means that no one has noticed my spontaneous absence from Homecoming.

The bad news is that I have nine missed text messages from Katie and Lin, all of which appear, clear as day, on my screen the moment I turn it on, all of which Kevin reads at the exact same time as I do.

Katie Brook (12:01 p.m.): where did you GO omfg

Katie Brook (12:02 p.m.): are you and kevin making out in the janitor's closet right now??? or the library??? rec room??? student union??? FOURTH FLOOR GIRLS' BATHROOM???

Katie Brook (12:02): i mean, get it, girl. he is ☺ ☺ ☺ ☺ ☺

Katie Brook (12:02): ☺ ☺ ☺ ☺ ☺ ☺ ☺ ☺ ☺ ☺ ☺ ☺ ☺

Lin Chen (12:15 p.m.): hey do you still need a ride home this afternoon?

Katie Brook (12:30 p.m.): she can't answer you. she's too, ahem, ~busy~ with Kevin.

Katie Brook (12:31 p.m): ☺

Lin Chen (12:35 p.m.):...wait but seriously do you still need a ride home this afternoon?

"Oh, God," I say. "Oh, *God*."

Kevin turns the key in the ignition and starts pulling out

of the parking lot as if he hasn't just witnessed my best friend describing him with thirteen straight winking emojis, but the barely suppressed smirk on his face is a pretty clear indication that he knows exactly what he just saw.

"If you're trying to pretend you didn't just see those texts, you're doing a horrible job," I say. I prop my elbows up on top of the glove compartment so I can shove my face into my hands and never emerge.

"You should put your seat belt on," Kevin says, very seriously. "Put safety first and all that."

"I'm going to punch you in the face."

"Hmm. Don't think punching the driver in the face qualifies as putting safety first."

I can hear Kevin shifting gears every couple of seconds, and we're going considerably faster now, so we must be getting back on the highway. "I live at 14 Belmont Drive," I tell him. "Right off the shopping plaza with the Shaw's and the Staples and that shitty Chinese restaurant no one can pronounce the name of. Please drop me off and leave me there to die."

That actually gets a laugh out of him. "Stel. You know it's not actually a big deal, right? There's nothing wrong with finding me attractive. The one thing about people our age that baffles me the most is how ridiculously gun-shy people get about being attracted to other people. Like, we're sixteen. It's fine."

Kevin's statement is delivered with just enough easy confidence that I feel like I am completely and utterly out of my depth. This activates my default response to situations in which I feel like I've lost control: spirited defiance. Or, as Karen prefers to call it, "lying."

"Don't call me Stel," I say. "That's not my name. And also, I'm not attracted to you."

He's silent for a moment, like he's not sure if I'm joking or not. Then, in a tone of voice that's completely calm—pleasant, even, as if I've just informed him that the weather is seventy degrees and breezy: "All right, then."

"Seriously. I mean, Katie is. Obviously—you saw the text messages. And she's totally hot. But I think she's really into her lab partner right now. So...you might have some competition there."

"Katie is quite attractive," Kevin says. "But I'm actually not interested in her."

"It's fine if you are, you know," I say. "I'll even—I dunno—I'll give you her number, if you want. But yeah, you might get punched in the face by Bobby on the football team, and then you can't say I didn't warn you."

I don't know what's come over me. It's like I'm so mortified by the possibility that Kevin is going to think I'm some silly, pathetic girl who spends all her time pining hopelessly after him and his stupid blue eyes that I'll literally say anything to make him think otherwise. Including, apparently, that he should date Katie.

"I appreciate the offer and the warning," Kevin says. "But I don't think that'll be necessary. The number *or* the punching. Because Katie's not my type."

I lift my head. We're two blocks away from my house, where I will crawl under my covers and try as hard as possible to be absorbed by my bed. Beds don't get themselves into situations like this. Beds never even have to leave their rooms.

"Katie's everyone's type," I say.

"Okay," Kevin says easily. "What's your type?"

"My type?" I say, blindsided by the question. "Uh."

Kevin raises an eyebrow. I say the first thing that comes to mind before the silence can stretch on any longer. "I guess my type is…smart guys. You know, like…our math team. You know they won the state championships last year? That's pretty hot."

I am officially ready for this conversation to be over.

"Okay, then," Kevin says. He pulls up to the curb outside of my house and parks the car, looking as relaxed as he sounds. Which is irritating, to be quite honest. I just told him that I don't find him attractive, for Christ's sake. The least he could do is act a little bit disappointed.

"Okay, then!" I repeat, compensating for horror that is threatening to swallow me whole from the inside with way too much enthusiasm. I am experiencing so many emotions at once that I feel vaguely like I'm drowning in them. There's relief that he's not making fun of me mixed with outrage that he's so being aggressively casual mixed with the barely suppressed giddiness I feel whenever I'm in close quarters with him mixed with a wild urge to kiss him *right now* because Jesus Christ am I attracted to him.

GET IT TOGETHER, my brain yells.

"Well," Kevin says, "I had a lot of fun with you today, Stella." He looks at me and smiles—just *smiles*—and it hits me that furiously protesting my attraction to Kevin has actually made me ten times *more* attracted to Kevin, because the universe is cruel and unfair. This isn't enjoyable at all, I think. Isn't attraction supposed to be enjoyable?

"I had a lot of fun today, too," I say. "I just want to make sure that we're on the same page about how I feel about you. These things can get awkward when people don't communicate properly, you know, and that's the last thing I want to happen…between…us."

The last three words get lost on their way to my mouth, because Kevin has done that thing again, where he turns and leans all the way in and then he's there, *right there*. "I think…" Kevin starts. He draws out each word softly and slowly, like he's thinking very, very carefully about them.

I am not the type of person who is careless with my words, I remember him saying. That conversation feels like it was weeks ago.

"I think you've made it very clear how you feel about me, Stella," Kevin says. I can't tell if I'm imagining the faint smile on his face.

"Just wanted to make sure," I say weakly.

"Have a good weekend, all right?" Kevin says. I take this as my cue to open the door and step out of the car.

"Thanks, Kevin," I say, trying so hard to keep my voice casual that the words come out totally flat. Then, of course, I overcompensate, and my "You, too!" sounds positively manic.

Kevin winks at me before he drives away, which leaves me standing in my driveway 1) slightly dazed, and 2) in need of a cold shower.

"That was fine," I tell myself, walking up to the garage. "That. Was. Fine. That was totally fine. Oh, who am I kidding? That was a disaster."

I replay this afternoon time and time again over the course of the weekend, going over every word and every loaded pause until I start to feel like I'm going crazy. But what I forget to mention—what doesn't occur to me until weeks later, long after I've exhausted every possible implication of the sentence "I had a lot of fun with you today" ad nauseum—is that Kevin never did answer my question about what he was doing last year.

16.

"So let me get this straight," Lin says. "You just...lied?"

"It's not my fault," I say. "It was like a self-defense mechanism kicked in and the next thing I knew, I was vehemently insisting that I could only be attracted to a mathlete."

"A mathlete?" Katie says blankly. "Like Brady Thompson mathlete?"

The three of us are having brunch at this diner near Lin's house, an emergency Saturday morning meeting I called the minute I got home last night. Joe's Kitchen & Coffee is probably one of the most beloved places in Wethersfield, so much so that you can never get a table without waiting at least thirty minutes. But the guy who runs the diner, Mark, always manages to squeeze us in because Lin has been tutoring his daughter in English for the last three years. It's a testament to how god-awfully boring Wethersfield is that one of the perennial topics of conversation is how a restaurant called Joe's Kitchen

& Coffee came to be run by a guy named Mark. This is what constitutes cosmic irony in this town.

"Brady is cute," I say weakly. "He's got that, you know, bookish-geeky vibe going for him. Lots of girls are into that."

"Look," Katie says, turning to me. "Stella."

Katie chews thoughtfully on a piece of her omelet before proceeding.

"I feel like you should think of this Kevin situation as an opportunity," she says.

"I *am* thinking of it as an opportunity," I say. "It's an opportunity to drop out of school and relocate to a sparsely populated desert in the Pacific Southwest."

"*No*," Katie says. "An opportunity to laugh off something a little bit embarrassing that happened and realize that when you don't take your screw-ups so seriously, no one else does, either. And an opportunity to be honest with Kevin, for once, instead of playing everything off like a joke. An opportunity to be vulnerable."

"I don't like this advice," I say. "Can I resubmit my request and get a new piece of wisdom instead?"

"No," Katie says flatly. "That's my advice and that's what you get. And we all know I'm right."

"I don't want to be *vulnerable*," I whine. "Being vulnerable opens yourself to being—oh, I don't know—*vuln*-ed."

"My friendship," Katie announces, "is wasted on you."

"Thank God you still have Lin," I say.

Lin clears her throat, picks up her glass of water, and then puts it down again.

"I have Lin for ten more months," Katie says, "before she runs off to Brown and abandons us for members of the artsy, literary crowd who all have cogent opinions about literature in the American Jazz Age."

Lin clears her throat again.

"Yes, Lin?" I say. "Is there something you'd like to share with us?"

"I have news," Lin says.

"We figured from all the *ahem*-ing," Katie says. "What's the news?"

"The news," Lin announces, "is that I finally figured out what I actually want to write my common application essay about. Like, for real this time."

"Thought you were writing on the genius of *East of Eden*," I say.

"I was writing on the genius of *East of Eden*," Lin says. "But every single draft ended up being over twelve hundred words. And the limit is six hundred and fifty. And they all sounded like academic papers. College essays are supposed to be about *you*, not about a long-dead author, and especially not about a long-dead author who didn't even go to the university you're applying to. They're supposed to be *personal*. So…"

She pauses dramatically.

"So?" Katie says.

"So I am writing about a deeply important relationship that has shaped me into the woman that I am today."

Lin has obviously rehearsed this declaration in front of a mirror a few times.

"You're sure you're not still writing about John Steinbeck?" I say.

"*I am writing*," Lin continues, "about my relationship with two people who have always supported me, even if they insist on getting in six million unnecessary sarcastic comments while doing so. I'm writing about you guys."

Katie's mouth drops into a comically perfect O.

"Wow," Lin says. "Glad you guys are so touched at being the topic of the *most important essay I have ever written*."

It's Katie who regains her senses first. "Oh-my-God-Lin-of-course-we're-touched!" she says, as if it's all one word. "Aren't we, Stella?"

"So touched," I say. "But, Lin—are you sure this is a good idea? Katie and I aren't very interesting. In fact, we're so uninteresting that it seems like we should be the last people you'd write about in such an important essay. I mean, I just dragged you guys out of bed at 10:00 a.m. on a Saturday morning because I'm having boy problems. Please don't tell Brown that I once called an emergency Saturday morning brunch for boy problems. In fact, don't tell Brown anything about me. Write about—write about your parents! Didn't they immigrate to America with, like, five dollars in their pockets? That's much more inspirational than Katie and I could ever be."

"Yes," Lin says. "The story of my parents' immigration is, in fact, much more inspirational than anything I could write about you or Katie, who are both sixteen years old and have never faced anything remotely resembling political persecution. But when I suggested that to my college counselor, she said, and I quote, 'It's a nice idea, but runs the risk of coming off as generic or overdone.' Which I'm pretty sure is just a polite way that guidance counselors tell Asian kids that every other Asian kid is also going to write a sappy essay about their parents, Lin, are you sure you want to do that, too? Plus, I don't want to write an essay about my parents. I want to write an essay about me. And I think my relationship with you guys says a lot more about me than my relationship with my parents. I mean, I didn't *choose* to be my parents' kid. But I choose to be friends with you."

Lin smiles, as if the matter is now closed. "So yeah. I'll send you guys a copy when I'm done."

Katie raises her glass of water and says, "To Stella finding vulnerability and to Lin getting into Brown with her bomb-ass essay that only she could possibly write."

And then, simply: "To us."

Lin picks up her glass and clinks it with Katie's. They both turn expectantly to me.

"It's just—we're being so *corny*," I say.

Katie rolls her eyes, picks up my glass, and does it herself.

"To us," she repeats. And while I don't drink to that, I do smile when she does.

44. MARCH

In hindsight, I think, staring at the distorted reflection in the spoon on the table in front of me, this entire thing was a horrible idea.

"*Stella*," Kevin says forcefully. He reaches across the table, picks up my spoon and drops it onto his plate, where it clinks and clangs before finally falling silent. My omelet—the Joe's Kitchen special—is cold, and Kevin hasn't even touched his toast.

"Kevin," I say quietly. "We've been talking about this for an hour. I don't want to discuss this anymore."

"Well *I do*," he says. Kevin's got this look on his face that I can barely stand to look at. Anger makes Kevin look like an entirely different person—someone ten years older, someone who I've encountered only in the form of a television villain or an over-the-top movie antagonist, someone the real Kevin would never want to be around. Someone I don't even want to be around.

"It takes two willing participants to have a conversation, Kevin. And I am no longer a willing participant."

"You haven't answered my question," he presses.

"Oh, but that's the thing, Kevin," I say. "I *have* answered your question. I have answered it a thousand times. There is *nothing* going on between the two of us. We are doing a *project* together, that's all. He has a *girlfriend*, for fuck's sake! The real problem isn't that I haven't answered your question. The real problem is that you *don't believe me*."

I can feel my voice rising. This is not the correct response, I know. If I get angry and frustrated, it's only going to fuel Kevin's anger and frustration, which will make me even *more* angry and frustrated, until the two of us are just a self-sustaining cycle of anger and frustration that neither of us knows how to get out of. There's just this part of me that wishes, hopes, *prays* that this time will be different. That this time, if I just plead enough, if I just show him how ridiculous he's being, if I just manage to say in the right words that I love him, I really do, so much so that it fucking *terrifies* me, then it will be different.

"How could I believe you, Stella?" Kevin says, his voice up another couple of decibels. I always used to think that my dad's default response to conflict—to shut down his emotions and go absolutely calm—was the worst possible way of handling arguments. Of course, now that Kevin is yelling at me in a crowded diner on a Sunday morning that was supposed to be a date, I'm reconsidering that assessment.

"How could I believe you?" Kevin repeats. "You—"

"Oh, I dunno," I say, cutting him off. "How could you

believe me? Maybe…trust me? You know, like people who are dating are supposed to trust each other?"

"You spend *all of your time with him*, Stella!" Kevin says. "After school. After cross-country. During the weekends. Between class—"

"First of all, that's not even true. I spend at least six hours a week arguing with you about how much time I spend with him, which may very well be more time than I spend with him. Secondly, we're *doing a project together*. We are literally *forced* by the Bridgemont curriculum to spend time together. So take it up with Holmquist, not me!"

"That's funny," Kevin says, "because I did the same project two years ago, and I don't remember being forced to spend every single free afternoon at my partner's house. In fact, we only met, like, once every other week!"

People are starting to look at us. People *we know* are starting to look at us. Becca Windham and her boyfriend, Casey. Jesse Rogers's parents. Four other adults I recognize from my mom's book club. I can feel them stealing glances at Kevin and me every few minutes, probably thinking about how they knew *all along* that a *pair like the two of them* would just *never work out*.

But there's one person in the diner who doesn't seem to be paying any attention to the two of us at all. She's sitting in a corner booth buried in a history textbook that's four inches thick, headphones jammed into her ears, scribbling furiously in a notebook. I've seen this expression on her face countless times—that relentless concentration, the sense that she's blocked out everything other than the words and dates she's currently committing to memory. And the fact that she's shut me and Kevin out is even more devastating than having our very public blowout witnessed by Mrs. Rogers and the post–Sunday school crowd.

Lin.

I shut my eyes. Count to five. *I am not going to cry*, I tell myself. *I am not going to cry. I am not going to cry.*

"Look," I say. Precise, measured. Controlled. There will be no tears, not today, certainly not here. "Could we just stop? Let's just go to your house. We're causing a scene."

"Oh, who gives a shit, Stella?" Kevin says at full volume. Everyone at the diner (*except Lin, except Lin, except Lin*, my brain says) turns around to look at us.

"Kevin," I say.

"Don't say my name like that," he snaps. "I'm not your fucking kid."

I have nothing left to say.

Kevin sighs. His voice softens. "I'm really struggling with this, Stel," he says. "I'm *trying*. But I'm really struggling with this."

"I know," I say, softly.

"Do you believe me?" Kevin says.

The desperation in his voice is like a punch straight to the gut.

"Of course I believe you!" I say. "But I don't know how to help you, Kevin. I can't—I can't just half-ass this project. My parents are already on my ass about my grades and there's no excuse for getting a C in *health class*, for fuck's sake."

"You're not going to get a C in health class."

"I know it doesn't seem like this from your perspective, but there's really—I mean, we don't even spend that much time working on it. It's just Saturday afternoons and sometimes after school during the week and that's it."

"That's it?" Kevin says incredulously. "Stella, you realize that we haven't seen each other in a week, right?"

"But that's not because of this project! It's because of all the other homework that I have, and you know I'm taking the SAT in a month, and my parents are—"

"Yeah, I get that you're busy," Kevin snaps, his voice rising again. "Not like I'm also taking six classes and writing a forty-page research paper for senior seminar or anything. But I still make time to see you, Stella, because that's a *priority* of mine. Your number-one priority with what precious little free time you do have is *obviously not me*."

I push my chair back and stand up. The chair legs screech loudly against the floor—not that it matters, because everyone is already staring at us—and Kevin looks taken aback. "What are you—"

"Look," I say, fumbling with my purse. I'm trying to get a twenty out of my wallet, but my hands keep shaking. "I can't—I can't have this conversation anymore. I'm sorry, Kevin, I'm just—I'm about to lose it, okay? I'm sorry. Here—this should cover my food. You can text me later if you want to come over. But I can't argue about this anymore."

"Nice. Running away, that's cool."

I don't even bother to respond.

When I'm a few steps away from the door, I look over my shoulder and take in the scene I'm leaving behind—or, as Kevin puts it, running away from. Becca and Casey, pity written all over their faces. Mrs. Georges, disdainful as she takes a sip of her coffee. Mr. Rogers, who averts his gaze the second my eyes meet his. And then Lin, who's finally lifted her head out of her history textbook.

It's the first time our eyes have met in months.

For a second, I think—I *hope*—that she's about to stand up, shove all of her schoolwork into her bag, rush up to me and walk me home. This is *Lin* we're talking about, for Christ's sake. She's always the first person ready with a pep talk, a box of tissues and a reassuring hug. This is the same Lin who stayed with Katie for a week straight after her breakup with Christian so she could "make sure she didn't do anything stupid, like regret dumping that jackass." Lin will come up to me and wrap me in a hug and know exactly the right words to say to make me feel better, because she always does, and she always has.

But she doesn't.

Instead, she looks back down at her textbook. The concern on her face dissolves back into deliberate, determined focus. She picks up her pencil again and starts writing.

45.

It takes me forty minutes to bike home and it starts raining half an hour in, which pretty much confirms my suspicion that I am sitting pretty at number one on the universe's shit list. By the time I get home—miserable, tired, angry at Kevin, angry at myself, angry at the universe and soaking wet—the last thing I want to do is talk to my mom. But there she is: sitting at the dining room table, a pot of tea in front of her, staring expectantly at the front door.

"Please," I say. "Just let me go upstairs. Take a hot shower. And hibernate in peace until Monday."

Unsurprisingly, my plea goes unacknowledged.

"I got a call from Jesse Rogers's mom about half an hour ago," she says. "She had some very troubling news."

"Did you seriously just ignore everything that I said?"

"Stella," my mom says gently. "Please sit down."

"I'm going to drip all over the floor and ruin the carpet if you don't let me go upstairs," I say.

"Stella, you are so much more important to me than the carpet," my mom says, already weepy. This is the last thing I want to deal with right now, but what choice do I have? I get a towel from the laundry room, throw it over the chair and sit down.

"Sometimes when you're young," my mom starts, and I have to hold back a groan. No good conversation has ever started with a parent telling her child, "Sometimes when you're young…"

"Sometimes when you're young, and you're—and you think that you're in love, it can make you feel like you're invincible. I know this, honey, because I was young once, too."

"Mom," I say. "Please—"

"And I remember what it was like to be your age, Stella, and in my first serious relationship," my mom continues. "It was my freshman year of high school, and his name was William—Willie—Jenkins. He had this beautiful head of curly blond hair, and all the girls in the grade wanted to—"

I can't listen to this anymore, not one more word about what all the girls in the grade wanted to do to William "Willie" Jenkins and his beautiful hair. "Okay, Mom, I get what you're trying to do here, but there's really no need. Trust me, I'm not feeling invincible right now."

"Mrs. Rogers sounded very concerned about you," my mom says.

"That's really great of her," I say. "Really. Tell her thank you from me. And also tell her that her son Jesse has missed three philosophy classes in a row now because he keeps getting too high during his study hall and can't find his way back from the parking lot to the classroom, so she *might* want to consider redirecting her concern."

"She said that Kevin sounded very possessive and that you both lost your tempers, and it was quite the spectacle."

"Glad Kevin and I could fuel conversation for the next book club meeting," I say. "Wouldn't want the only item for you guys to gossip about to be Andrea Goldstein's nose job."

"She also said," my mom finishes, "that it didn't seem like you and Kevin have a very healthy relationship. That it didn't seem like you two were very good for each other."

My mom pours herself a new cup of tea. And me? I listen to the rain fall outside for a few seconds, the steady *patter* of the drops hitting the deck. And then—

"Where's Dad?" I say.

"What?"

"*Dad*," I repeat. "My father. Your husband. Partner at Porter and Canavas LLC. Haven't seen him around lately—work must be pretty busy. Tell me something, Mom—do you think that you and Dad have a very healthy relationship?"

"Stella," my mom says, looking shocked. Her hand shakes a little, and the tiniest bit of tea splashes over the edge of the teacup and onto the dining room table.

"You guys ever *lose your tempers*? Cause a *spectacle*? Probably not at the most popular diner in town on a weekend afternoon, I guess—boy, would that be immature—but, oh, I don't know, maybe in the middle of the night while your sixteen-year-old daughter is trying to sleep upstairs?"

I shouldn't be saying this—I shouldn't be saying any of this—but I'm so angry—*livid*—and all I can think is *how dare she say that about Kevin*. How dare she say *anything* about

Kevin when she and my father have been—when they've—three times a week, for the past few months, before one day it all suddenly stopped because…because—

"Kevin is the only thing," I say, and my voice is surprisingly steady—disturbingly steady, actually, because it feels like I'm shaking on the inside. "The *only thing* that's been keeping me sane this semester. Do whatever you want with your relationship. But leave mine alone."

I've barely shut the door of my room before I start crying, and then it's like the floodgates open and I'm *really* crying, hiccupping with the tears and trying to keep the snot from dripping into my mouth. What I want, I think, is to go back to the beginning, when Lin and I were still friends, when my dad still lived at home and I didn't say horrible, horrible things to my mom in fits of anger, when Kevin and I looked at each other like the two of us were living in a game that no one else knew the rules to. Back to the fall, when the leaves were just starting to change colors and the humidity had just begun to leech out of the summer air; when you could have told me that things with Kevin would crash and burn and I still would have dove in, headfirst, hand-in-hand and eyes squeezed tightly shut.

Because that was fall, and that was the beginning, and that's how it always feels at the start, you know? Like no amount of eventual hell or high water could make the high of the moment any less sweet.

17.

After I get home from brunch with Lin and Katie on Saturday, I spend the rest of the weekend trying to figure out how to be honest enough with Kevin so that I can find out if he's into me or not without being so honest that it's awkward for us to be friends if the answer is no. This involves no less than ten internal pep talks, four three-way calls with Lin and Katie and an entire monologue that I write out for myself.

Now, I know what you're thinking. *Isn't this a bit excessive? All you have to do is go up to Kevin and say that you may or may not have been completely full of shit when you fiercely denied being attracted to him, and ask him if he feels the same way. He took you to a park, for fuck's sake! Who ditches school and goes to a park with someone they don't like? Making an entire speech out of this is only going to prolong the embarrassment.*

Which is true. But Lin—who is probably at home trying to finish her common app essay and slamming her head into the wall every time my number shows up on her phone—tells me halfway through call number three that even Cicero back in 100 BC knew that the best way to organize your thoughts was to write them down. Now, it's true, I've never really felt the need to be organized, but look where that got me on Friday afternoon: babbling incoherently about mathletes. So I decide to give Lin and Cicero a shot. Here's what I come up with:

Me: Hey, Kevin.

Kevin: [Makes that face that he makes every time we talk that's fifty percent smile and fifty percent extremely serious glare that is a) completely indecipherable, and b) ridiculously hot.]

Me: Look, I know that Friday was weird. I mean, don't get me wrong—I had a really good time, and I hope you did, too. But there was that whole part during the car ride home when I was just babbling and I, um, may have insulted you by saying that I'm...not at all attracted to you.

Kevin: Yes, I do recall something about mathletes.

Me: Right. Yeah. I'm glad you remember. So what I wanted to say was, that statement that I made, you know, about me not being attracted to you and you not being my type and me not wanting you to get the wrong impression about us—it was actually...not entirely true.

Kevin: Oh?

Me: Yeah. Like, if I had to rate those statements on a scale of truthfulness, I would give them maybe a five.

Kevin: Out of ten?

Me: Out of a hundred. I would give them a five percent.

[A pause as Kevin struggles to process this revelation.]

Me: It's not that I wanted to lie to you. Because I didn't. I mean, I never want to lie to anyone except maybe my parents sometimes and Lin when she asks how far I've gotten in *East of Eden*. It's just… I don't know, you had seen those text messages that Katie had sent, and even though you kept saying that it wasn't a big deal to you, it was a big deal to me. Katie says I have issues with vulnerability. My therapist also says that. Actually, now that I'm thinking about it, most people I know have said that to me at one point or another.

The point is, I didn't want you to think that I was—that I am—attracted to you because I didn't want you to laugh at me, or to make fun of me, or to think I'm some silly girl who loses her wits just because she has a crush. And I guess I may have self-sabotaged there because I totally lost my wits just because I had a crush.

Kevin: Wow. That was so eloquent and self-aware and honest. Did you practice that?

Me: No. I did write it out, though. Because Cicero.

Needless to say, I will not be pursuing a career as a screen-writer after graduation.

I'm full of nervous energy by the time Lin picks me up on Monday morning. While I wouldn't go so far as to describe it as a *good* feeling, I will say that it's surprisingly not unpleasant. There's definitely a part of me that's scared shitless that I'm going to come face-to-face with Kevin, immediately forget every-thing I learned this weekend and end up recanting my attrac-tion to mathletes only to profess my "real" attraction to, I don't know, the Weeaboos of Bridgemont Academy (a real club, mind you). But there's also a part of me that's nervous in a fluttery, excited way; part of me that thinks there might be something really amazing on the other side of this ordeal that makes it all worth it; part of me that really just wants to see Kevin again.

I don't know if I've ever really felt like this before. I've had crushes, of course, and I've even gone to a couple of dances with guys who I liked well enough. But this nervous energy is on another level. I spend the entire car ride bouncing my foot up and down and fidgeting my thumbs and I don't even *notice* until Lin, halfway through the ride, says: "Good *Lord*, Stella, could you stop that? It's making it impossible to drive!"

The other thing Lin points out is that I've been smiling the whole time. And I guess that's really the best way to de-scribe it: it's the kind of mind-numbing, terrifying, illogical nervousness that leaves you smiling.

There's just one tiny hitch that reveals itself after I get to school on Monday, ready to come clean and show Cupid who's boss. And that's that Kevin has started avoiding me.

18.

At first I don't realize that something's up. Kevin and I don't have lockers or homeroom in the same wing because we're in different grades, so it makes sense that we don't really see each other in the morning. When I walk by him between third and fourth period and he practically sprints down the hall, I figure that he's in a rush and just didn't see me. Then he's not at lunch—but that could be for a number of reasons, right? Meeting with a teacher. Working on a project for class. Buried himself in a philosophical treatise and forgot to re-surface. But then it's right before last period and I'm walk-ing to art class and Kevin is directly down the hall, walking in my direction, and there's this moment when we make eye contact. Then, of course, I break into a smile—because I'm happy to see him, stupidly happy to see him, *surprised*, even, by how happy to see him I am—and he promptly turns left into the hallway that leads to the *cafeteria*. So unless Bridge-mont has created a special last-period lunch for seniors that I just never found out about, I think it's safe to say that Kevin is avoiding me.

It takes longer than a day for the reality of this to settle in. On Tuesday, I'm mostly just confused. He didn't seem angry or bothered the last time when we were in the car together, and how much could possibly have changed over the course of half a week? A part of me actually thinks that I'm going to be able to catch him after Dr. Mulland's class and ask him what the hell his problem is, but then he's out the door the second the bell rings, before I've even managed to finish putting my books in my backpack.

"Why don't you just text him?" Lin asks at lunch on Wednesday. The food is miserable today, and it's so cold and windy that it's no longer enjoyable to sit in the courtyard. Some of the athletes are still outside, but then again, they probably have a winter coat's worth of insulation permanently wrapped around their bodies in the form of muscle, so there's that.

"I can't text him," I say. "I don't have his number."

Katie stares at me in disbelief. "After *all this*," she says. "After all of that flirting and ditching school together and—and you *still don't have each other's numbers*?"

Katie slumps in her seat. It seems that my romantic incompetence has really done her in this time around. Even the purple of her hair seems to fade a little bit in despair.

"You don't have to tell me that I'm pathetic, Katie. I already know."

Lin puts her copy of *The Moon Is Down* on the table and looks at me sympathetically. Then she says: "You know, the word *pathetic* derives from the Greek *pathos*, which means 'suffering' or, more broadly, 'emotion.' I guess most experiences involved suffering in those days. Anyway, my point is that if you break it down to the roots, the word *pathetic* just means 'full of feeling.' 'Evocative,' oftentimes in a sad or melodramatic way. 'Emotionally rich.' It's not a bad thing."

"Thanks, Lin."

"That wasn't helpful, was it?"

"No, it was totally helpful. I mean, not with Kevin, really, but if I work it into the English paper I have due tomorrow, Mrs. Trout might be impressed enough to give me an A."

Kevin hightails it out of philosophy so quickly on Thursday that I've barely even had time to gather my notebook and pencil before I'm watching the back of his head disappear out the door. On Friday, I arrive at the library for study hall to find Yago sitting in a corner desk and Kevin nowhere to be found.

Enough is enough, I think, and I do the only thing I can think of. I march up to Yago, pull out the seat next to his and stare expectantly at him until he looks at me.

Yago is doing homework for AP Physics, which is an oddly incongruous picture. I can't even imagine Yago doing homework for a regular class, much less trying to learn—it takes me a minute to read his paper upside down—how to calculate the magnetic field of an infinitely long wire with a current of 9.5 amperes running through it. Lin mentioned that he was in AP Lit with her, but writing ten-page papers about how a bright green light in the distance is actually a symbol for the American dream while high is one thing, and doing equations that involve more letters than numbers while high is a whole other thing entirely.

"Hey, Stella," Yago says uncertainly.

"Hey," I say. "How's—"

I wave at his paper, because why make awkward small talk with words when you could instead make awkward small talk with vague hand motions?

"It's fine," he says. He flips his paper over like he doesn't want me to see it, which is weird. I'm not even taking AP Physics this year.

"Listen, do you know what's up with Kevin?" I ask.

"I don't know what you mean," he says, and swallows so hard that his Adam's apple dips.

"You are a terrible liar, Yago," I say.

"I think he's been stressed about homework," Yago tries.

"Yago," I say, exasperated. "We've had a dozen study halls together and I've never seen Kevin so much as pick up a pen for a class other than Mulland's. Will you tell me what's really going on?"

Yago buries his head in his hands and mumbles something that sounds like, "Knew I never should've gotten involved in this crap."

"Hmm?" I say.

He lifts his head out of his hands. "I said, 'I knew I never should have gotten involved in this crap.'"

"So what's going on?" I say. "Is it his parents? Are they upset with him ditching the homecoming rally?"

"Huh?" Yago says. "No, that's—Kevin's mom isn't like that. She doesn't care about that stuff."

"So what is it, then? I thought there was a chance that he liked me, but then he just—"

"He does like you," Yago says, as if it's obvious.

"But then, if it's not his parents, then why—"

"Look, Stella," Yago says. "He likes you. God help me for telling you this, but I think he actually likes you a lot. Kevin just has some—some extenuating circumstances going on right now, I guess," Yago says.

"Extenuating circumstances," I repeat flatly.

"Yeah, those," Yago says.

"Extenuating circumstances," I say again.

"He probably just needs some time to come around."

"How much time is 'some time'?" I ask. "I'm not just going to wait around for Kevin to pull his head out of his ass because some 'extenuating circumstances' prevent him from talking to me."

"And that's totally fair," Yago says. "I've told him that he's being an idiot."

"You told him that he's being an idiot?"

"Yes," Yago says, sounding more and more exasperated. "Because he *is* being an idiot. But he won't listen to me. He's consulting Nietzsche instead."

I try to come to terms with the fact that this is my life now: pining over a guy who consults Nietzsche for relationship advice.

"I really need to do this homework now, Stella," Yago says. "I have band practice after school today."

I look at Yago—the pleading expression on his face, the constellation of acne across his cheeks—and sigh. "All right. Thanks, though. For…you know. Talking to me about this."

"Sure," Yago says. He smiles.

Yago is a nice guy. It's too bad about his asshole friend.

"And could you just—" I start.

"I won't tell Kevin we talked," Yago promises.

His head is already back in his worksheet.

19.

In the coming months, I'll often think back to the two weeks between the afternoon Kevin and I spend at Prospect Park and the night things finally come together. I'll think of how ironic it is, the way I was just starting to forget about him and put those endless daydreams of miraculous get-togethers and movie-scene proclamations of love out of my head when, all of a sudden, there he is in front of me again, standing outside underneath the night sky with a knowing smile and a half-finished PBR in his hand, wearing a black T-shirt and a pair of ripped jeans.

But I'm getting ahead of myself. Because the chain of events that gets Kevin and me together that night goes back, way back, so much so that it almost does seem like some mischievous cosmic force must have been tugging at strings all along. Where this story really starts is with Ashley Kurtzmann's party in September. It starts with Brian Patterson, captain of the Bridgemont football team, getting way too drunk and deciding it would be fucking *hilarious* to replace all of the water in Ashley's parents' fish tank with beer from the keg. Needless to say, Mr. and Mrs. Kurtzmann aren't too thrilled when they come home and find a) their fish tank full of beer, and b) all of their fish dead. They ground Ashley for the rest of the calendar year, which is devastating for Ashley, because now she can't leave her house after 6:00 p.m., and also devastating for the rest of Bridgemont, because now the annual Halloween party is off and everyone has to find somewhere else to blow off all their repressed sexual frustration. That is, until Katie—the softhearted, purple-haired angel that she is—begs and pleads until her parents finally cave and agree to let her have the party at her house. Lin has finally submitted her Brown application, which means that she has no excuse for not going, which means that *I* have no excuse for not going. And that's how I end up at Katie's house on the night of Friday, October 28, wearing head-to-toe black and a ski mask.

"What are you, a robber?" Katie says, wrinkling her nose as she opens the door to let me in.

"I was going for ninja," I say, voice muffled by the mask. "But close enough."

Katie is in a gold-and-black number with flashy geometric cutouts, piles of costume necklaces and a Cleopatra wig. Behind her, the party has already started. Bobby and his friends are standing around with beers, someone has plugged their phone into the speakers and is blasting the latest pop hit, a few girls mill around in heels that I could never walk in. I note the costumes as I walk to the kitchen to get myself a drink: Becca, in a black leotard and Catwoman mask; Victoria Lee, a pirate in a bustier and very little else; Chrissy, a cowgirl in plaid and denim. And then men: Jesse, a shirtless firefighter; Casey, a shirtless Aladdin; Bobby L., a shirtless Indiana Jones. And, of course, Jeremy and Jennie, looking like they belong on a Hollywood movie set instead of a high school house party, as Marilyn Monroe and James Dean.

"What'd you tell your parents?" Katie asks.

"Oh, I just said I was sleeping over for the night," I say.

"What?" Katie says. She frowns, and pulls the ski mask down so that it's around my neck instead of covering my mouth. "Points for effort, but I can barely hear anything you're saying. Try again."

"I told them I'm sleeping over," I repeat. "They're in the middle of fighting over who should be responsible for driving me to cross-country meets on Saturday, so I don't think they'll even notice I'm gone."

Katie makes a sympathetic face, but before she can comment, Lin comes up behind us and throws one arm over each of our shoulders. "Looks like your dream of having your house taken over by a bunch of intoxicated buffoons might finally come true," she says to Katie.

I hand her a beer. "And here's to *your dream*," I say, cracking one open for myself, "of submitting the perfect college application essay. How's it feel to be done?"

"Feels good," Lin says. She pauses, takes a sip of beer. "Actually, it's pretty freaking stressful. Nothing to do now but wait, you know what I mean?"

"Lin, if Brown doesn't let you in, I will personally spearhead a boycott and convince everyone else at Bridgemont not to apply there out of protest. That's how ridiculous it would be."

"What would I do without you?" Lin says drily.

Lin is wearing a billowing forest-green dress with lacy sleeves and puffy shoulders. Her hair is in some kind of complex French-braid combination that looks like it must have taken hours. I'm pretty sure she's dressed as a character from a Jane Austen novel, but I haven't read any of them other than *Pride and Prejudice* from our freshman year summer reading list, and I'm afraid that if I ask which one, she'll launch into an impassioned ten-minute speech about Victorian society, marriage and feminism. I say this because two years ago on Halloween, Lin dressed as a character from a Shakespeare play, and when I asked which one, she launched into an impassioned ten-minute speech about Elizabethan society, marriage and feminism. Since then I've learned not to ask.

I can't believe I'm saying this, but Katie's party is actually pretty fun. People rotate in and out of the house all night, but I spend most of the first two hours hanging out with Katie, Bobby, Jeremy, Adrian, Jennie and Victoria. Although a more accurate assessment is that *I* hang out with Katie, and *Katie* hangs out with Bobby, Jeremy, Adrian, Jennie and Victoria, none of whom have the heart to reject the host's ugly duckling best friend. I don't say very much, because the conversation revolves around the latest hit television show (which I don't watch) and the big play that won us last week's football game (which I didn't go to) and whether or not Ashley and her boyfriend, Taylor, are really done for good this time (which I don't care about in the slightest). But it's interesting, watching Katie blend seamlessly into the conversation, so comfortable that it almost seems like she's always been a part of that social scene. The conversation takes a sharp turn sometime around eleven, when everyone—myself included—is three or four drinks in and really starting to feel it.

"*This guy*," Bobby says, slapping Jeremy in the chest, "is a *beast*. You guys know that? He's the one making our quarterback over here look good."

"It's 'cause I have a great team around me," Jeremy says. But you can tell he's pleased with himself.

"But I gotta tell you, his *real talent*," Bobby continues, "lies off the field. Lay? Lays? Fuck that word."

Bobby picks up a can of beer and hands it to Jeremy.

"Oh, God," Jennie says. "Do we have to do this every party?"

There's a crowd forming around us now, which is disorienting. I mean, I'm usually the one standing in the corner of the room as the crowd forms, staring judgmentally at all of the football devotees who have nothing better to do than throw themselves at guys like Bobby and Jeremy just because they look good without a shirt on and can throw and catch a ball. Now I'm standing in the middle of it all, so close that I can almost feel the excessive testosterone radiating from their bodies.

Bobby pulls out his phone. "Personal best is 4.7 seconds," he says.

"You know I'm gonna crush that shit," Jeremy says, grinning. He pulls out his keys and lifts the beer can to his mouth horizontally. You can tell that he really feels at home here, half-naked in front of the crowd, which is so ridiculous that it's almost admirable.

"One…two…three," Bobby says, and on three, Jeremy

sticks a key into the beer can and chugs it in one, smooth motion. The people around us actually *cheer* while this happens.

Jeremy turns to me and Katie, grinning, like the entire exercise was for our benefit.

"Wow," Katie says. "I mean—wow."

I nod vigorously. "You are ready for college, J. Did I just call you J?"

Jennie, standing next to me, laughs. "Let's not get ahead of ourselves here—have you seen his calc grade?"

"Aw, babe," Jeremy says. "Don't throw me under the bus like that." But he's got this goofy, boyish smile on his face, and he slides his arm around her shoulders as he talks. It is remarkably cute. And remarkably revolting.

"I'm gonna catch you later," I tell Katie. She and Bobby have split off into their own conversation, and Katie keeps playing with her necklaces and giving him that look from underneath her eyelashes, which means that it's only a matter of time until they're making out. I figure I should do what any good friend would do in this situation, which is to get the fuck out of there.

"Cool," Katie says. She says the word without taking her eyes off Bobby, and in a tone of voice that sounds way more like "take me now" than "cool."

"Text me if you need anything," I say. "Like another beer. Or a condom."

Then I fight my way through the crowd before Katie can hit me.

I run into Lin in the hallway back to the kitchen. "Stella!" she practically shouts. "Where have you been?"

"I've been with Katie and Jeremy and that whole crowd,"

I say. And then, upon seeing the look on her face: "It's a long story. Jeremy shotgunned a beer and then Jennie acknowledged my existence via conversation. It was bizarre. Where have *you* been?"

"No time for that now," Lin says. "Listen. Kevin is upstairs."

The first thing that happens is that my stomach drops, so immediate and forceful that I have to take a couple of deep breaths before I can talk again.

The second thing that happens is that I get really freaking annoyed. I've spent the better part of three weeks trying to get over this guy, refusing to look at him during philosophy class, generally ignoring his existence, pushing him out of my brain every time his stupid blue eyes show up in a daydream. And all it takes is one mention of his name and now here I am, caught up in that feeling that's at once sickening and giddy and terrifying and desperate. There's something profoundly unfair about that.

"What?" I say.

"Kevin is upstairs."

"No, I heard you. But…what?"

"They're on the balcony. Him and Yago, I mean. I don't know, Stella," Lin says. "Katie did send the Facebook invitation out to the entire senior class. But still, I wasn't expecting him to actually show up. Like, whose house does he think this is? You're Katie's *best friend*. He should leave. I should—I should go tell him that he needs to leave."

Lin narrows her eyes and sets her jaw. It's the same face she had the entire two weeks leading up to her SAT date.

"No," I say, grabbing her arm before she can go upstairs

and a) cause a huge scene, b) maim Kevin, or c) both of the above. I drag her into the kitchen. "I can handle this."

"Can you?" Lin says.

All the beer's gone, but there is a bowl of punch sitting on the counter. It's green, slushy and surrounded by bottles of liquor.

I ladle myself a cup.

"Trust me. I can handle this."

"Stella," Lin says. "Stella, listen. I know you think—Jesus, are you trying to drink all of that at once? Oh my God, *Stella*!"

Lin pulls my arm down and looks in the now-half-finished cup. "I don't really see how aggressive inebriation is going to help you here."

"Liquid courage," I say. And then I finish the rest of the cup.

"How much have you had?" Lin says.

I think back: the first beer, right when I arrived two hours ago. Another, halfway through the conversation with Jeremy and Bobby. And one right before Jeremy shotgunned the beer.

"Just, like, a couple," I say to Lin.

"A couple," she repeats.

"One or two," I say.

I turn around to make my way up the stairs.

"Wait, Stella, listen," Lin says. She runs so that she's standing in front of me and grabs my hands like she's about to give me the most important pep talk of my life.

"Listen," Lin says. "I'm not going to stop you from going and talking to Kevin. But just...think about what you want to get out of the conversation, all right? And stick to that. Don't let yourself get too caught up in the moment once you get up there. Figure out what you want to say to him—whether it's why he stopped talking to you or if he was offended when you said you weren't into him or whatever else—and then... then just make sure you get that and get out. Okay?"

"You know you're perfect, right?" I say.

"Not nearly," Lin says, smiling. "But I'm glad I have at least one person fooled."

There's this moment. It's when I'm standing behind the French doors that lead to the balcony, looking at Kevin and Yago's backs as they lean on the railing over Katie's front yard. Yago has a lit joint between two of his fingers that he raises to his mouth every minute or so. Kevin is restless, shifting his body weight from one leg to the other and drumming his fingers on the railing. There's an open can of beer sitting on the railing next to him. I wonder if they're deep in conversation, if they're standing in companionable silence, if either one of them has thought of me, even in passing, in the past few weeks. And I think to myself: *Maybe I should just go back. Maybe this is going to be horribly awkward. Maybe I'll step outside and Kevin will get so freaked out that he'll jump and end up breaking his leg and Yago will be too high to do anything and then the police will show up and Katie's parents will kill her and it'll be all my fault.*

But then it's like something takes over my body—maybe it's the alcohol, or maybe it's plain desperation—and I'm thinking, *Just do it, Stella, goddamn it*, and the next thing I know I've pushed the doors open and I'm standing outside, staring at two very taken-aback expressions.

It's silent for a solid ten seconds as Yago and Kevin take in my presence. Yago's expression goes from confused to surprised and then back to confused again. Kevin is unreadable.

"Oh, hey, Stella," Yago finally says.

"Hey," I say.

And then it's silent again.

It's right around now when I realize that I haven't actually planned anything to say. No deliberately casual questions about how their nights are going. No offhand comments about the state of the party downstairs. I don't even have an excuse ready for why I came up here in the first place.

Yago extinguishes his joint on the railing and slips it into his pocket. "Well, I'll talk to you later, Kev," he says. He nods briskly in Kevin's general direction.

"Yago," Kevin says, through gritted teeth. His eyes are locked onto mine and he keeps squinting, like there's a message written on my face that he can't quite read.

"Good seeing you, Stella," Yago adds, walking by me. I hear the French doors swing shut.

And then it's just Kevin and me.

"I heard you were here," I say. I take a few tentative steps forward, because the distance from the doors (where I've been frozen) to the railing (where Kevin is standing) feels awkwardly distant for two people who are trying to have a conversation. Of course, those steps put me three feet away from Kevin, which now feels both awkwardly distant *and* awkwardly close.

"Here I am," Kevin says. He unfolds one of his arms so that it's lying along the top of the railing and shoves his other hand into a pocket. "Nice costume," he says. "The ski mask is a nice touch. Bank robber, right?"

"Actually, it's supposed to be—oh, never mind. Yeah, I'm a bank robber. But what are you supposed to be? You look—you look like—well, you look totally normal."

"I don't really dress up for Halloween," Kevin says.

"Oh," I say.

I wait for Kevin to say something else.

He doesn't.

During the ensuing silence, Kevin takes his right arm off the railing and slides it into his pocket, and takes his left hand out of his pocket and slides it along the railing. I hold my breath and take one, two, three more steps forward. There are two feet between us now, close enough for me to see the wrinkles stretched across his black T-shirt, the stitching on the seams of his jeans.

I try to think back to what Lin was telling me before I ran upstairs: *figure out what you want to say to him and then get out.*

The problem is that now that I'm actually standing here, I have no idea what exactly it is that I want to say. Maybe at some point, I knew. Maybe before those beers. Maybe before that cup of punch. Maybe before being close to Kevin for the first time in weeks, maybe before I remembered what it's like to want so badly to throw yourself at someone, to throw yourself *into* someone. But now my thoughts are slow and sluggish and they keep getting interrupted by these random observations and all I can think is:

We are on Katie's balcony.

Kevin is looking at me like I am some kind of riddle, like I am something unexpected.

It is cool outside. There is a trail of goose bumps running down the skin of my arm.

Kevin is standing in front of me, less than two feet away, in a black T-shirt and ripped blue jeans.

He is running a hand through his hair.

There is something about this time of year that makes everything feel so temporary. Like the world around us is about to disappear.

His hair is dark, dark brown. Shines under the moonlight.

"I am attracted to you," I blurt.

Kevin raises his eyebrows. "Are you drunk, Stella?" he says.

"Damn straight I'm drunk," I say. I take two more steps forward to cement the point.

Kevin looks down, laughs softly. "I really like that about you, you know. You're—you're...*unabashed*." The word unfolds slowly, coming out of his mouth syllable by syllable before it rolls to a stop somewhere in the two feet of space between us.

"You can't just say that," I say. "You can't just ignore me for two straight weeks and then—now that we're on Katie's balcony together and I'm drunk and you're...whatever you are—you can't just start saying things like that to me now. It's not cool."

"Okay," Kevin says. He cups his face in his hands, then looks up at me and nods. "Okay, you're right. You're absolutely right. Look, I'm sorry. I'm sorry about that afternoon at the park and I'm sorry I made you uncomfortable on the ride home and I'm sorry I never said anything afterward. I should have said something."

He takes a deep breath.

I am so close to him.

"Why?" I say, simply. I don't really want to talk anymore,

not here, not now, not when he's so close and there's so much else I would rather be doing. But I want to know why.

Kevin sighs. He tilts his head back and massages his temples. This is clearly not the conversation he wants to be having right now. But he is trying. And there's something about that, something about that deliberate seriousness, the way he moves with such gravity, the way he *thinks* about everything. The way he tries to say the right things, the truthful things, even when it's almost midnight and he's been accosted on a balcony by someone he probably didn't even want to see tonight.

I am not the type of person who is careless with my words.

"Stella, I just… I got too caught up in everything, you know? I came back to Bridgemont after being away for so long and all of a sudden there you were—this smart, amazing girl who wasn't afraid to cut the crap and see things for what they really are, even if what things really are is total shit. And I thought, God, I can't let myself fuck this one up."

"You *didn't*," I say. "You didn't fuck it up. Look, Kevin, the stuff I said in the car—I don't know why I said all that. I just panicked. I didn't want you to think that I was some stupid girl who could be convinced to ditch school with a random guy she barely even knows just because her friend thinks he's worth thirteen winking emojis. So I just…lied."

"Stella," Kevin says, and for some reason he's *smiling*, for God's sake, and now there's a part of *me* that wants to jump off the balcony.

"*What is funny?*" I say. I try to keep my voice on the calmer side, but the thing about being drunk is that you really no longer have that kind of control over your vocal chords.

"I'm sorry," Kevin says, still sounding like he's holding

back a laugh. "No, really, I am, don't look at me like that. Stel—c'mere," he says. He reaches out, takes my hand and pulls me over to the railing so we're standing face-to-face in front of it. By the time I've fully processed the fact that he actually reached out and *held my hand*, he's already let go. It's the strangest feeling: giddiness and desire and disappointment colliding all at once.

But he is so, so close.

"Stel, I know what you said in the car was total bullshit. No one works so hard to deny that they're into someone unless they're...really into that someone."

"All right, then," I grumble. "If I was that obvious, then I retract my apology. And stop calling me Stel."

"It wasn't about that," Kevin says.

"So what was it about? All I know is that the next Monday I came in with a whole freaking speech prepared, and every time I got within ten feet of you, you hightailed it out of there like I was out to kill you or something. Seriously, the last time a guy has run from me like that, it was back in the third grade when cooties were a scientific and very terrifying reality."

"I just started thinking, you know, *What if things go wrong?* Stella, you were so freaked out. Which made me freak out, and then I thought, *Things are already going wrong. If things are already going wrong, how bad is it going to be if I actually get with this girl?* And then I realized that this entire *thing*, this entire idea that you and me should be together, that *I* should be with *you*—I realized that it was all a horrible idea!"

"How," I say, "*how* is it a horrible idea?"

"I just..." Kevin starts. He trails off. Bites his lip. Picks up the can of beer sitting on the railing and takes a drink. And I honestly, honestly have no idea what's happening inside my head right now. I feel wild, uncontrollable. I want to rip the beer can out of his hands and throw it over the railing and kiss him. I want to take his hand and jump off the balcony together, because something about that seems like the appropriate thing to do right now, seems romantic and beautiful and free.

I should not have chugged that cup of punch.

"You just what?" I say, instead of doing any of the above.

"I don't think that I..." Kevin says slowly. He pauses before he continues. Then: "I don't think I would be very good for you."

"Give me a break," I say.

"No, I'm serious, Stella!" he says. "You should be with someone who'll take you to the movies after school instead of convincing you to ditch halfway through Homecoming. Someone who doesn't spend half of his time talking about depressing continental philosophy."

"Give me a *break*," I repeat.

"It's not even really about ditching school or thinking about Camus all the time. It's more just about—I don't know, I'm the type of person who ditches school and thinks about Camus all the time, you know? That's not the type of person you want to be involved with! And if you knew what my last year was like, why I wasn't at school, then you'd understand—"

"GIVE ME A BREAK," I shout.

Kevin shuts up. Looks taken aback.

"Are you being serious right now, Kevin? You sound like you think you're some kind of modern-day Heathcliff, moaning and groaning and whining your way through Victorian England feeling sorry for yourself in all your romantic, tragic isolation. You think you're the only person who's ever existed in the history of forever who's needed to take a year off school?"

"It's not just that I had to take a year of school, it's that—" He cuts off.

"*What*?" I snap.

"I didn't miss school because I was doing something cool, Stella. I wasn't spending the year in Europe or volunteering full-time or bumming around New York working on a philosophy book. I missed school because I literally couldn't go to school. Like, I would think about going to school, and I would just freeze. I couldn't get out of bed. It was pathetic," he says bitterly.

Extenuating circumstances, I think. *Holy shit.*

"I'm not the guy you think I am, Stella. I'm—"

"Depressed," I say, flatly.

Kevin must take my tone of voice as a bad sign, because he cringes. "Yeah," he says. "Look, I don't expect you to understand, because—"

"Because why?" I demand. "Is there something about me that says, 'I don't have empathy'? Or perhaps, 'I am a judgmental asshole who looks down on people for having feelings'?"

"*No*," Kevin says. "You just shouldn't have to deal with—"

"I was at camp this summer," I say.

Kevin cuts off.

"Okay," he says.

"It was called Camp Ugunduzi. You should Google it.

Really nice, down in the middle of nowhere in upstate New York. Lots of hiking. Lots of…meditation."

Kevin looks like he thinks that I've lost my mind. "That sounds fun, Stella, but what does—"

"'Camp Ugunduzi is an experimental four-week therapeutic wilderness program for teenagers aged fifteen to seventeen who may be experiencing a variety of mental health issues,'" I recite. God, my mom read that brochure to me so many times.

"'Ugunduzi operates upon the principle that teenagers struggling with emotional illness deserve a summer camp that is as recreational as it is therapeutic,'" I continue. "Yeah, it was fun, I guess. Other campers were a bunch of tools, but I liked the part where we played mental health charades and I got stuck acting out 'cognitive dissonance.'"

A pause. Kevin runs his free hand down the front of his shirt, smooths out the wrinkles. For the first time in the conversation, he looks away from me. Katie's voice plays back in my head, a line in a conversation that I'd forgotten about until now: *That's your problem. You're all so goddamn afraid to be vulnerable.*

"If you had been here last year," I say wryly, "you would know that I didn't exactly have the best year, either."

I reach out and take his hand, watch as his eyes fly back up to meet mine in surprise. And I feel like I know exactly what he's thinking. And exactly what he's feeling. That mix of desperation and apprehension. That hope.

"So what you're telling me," Kevin says, "is that you get it."

"Oh, I don't know if I get it," I say wryly. "But I think you should probably give me the chance to try."

Kevin places his can of beer back down on the railing. "Okay," he says. Deliberate as ever.

"Okay?" I say.

"Okay," he repeats.

"Thank God," I say. I feel my lips curling into a grin. "You really have no idea how ridiculous you were starting to sound there, all *you wouldn't understand me* and *I'm so attractive but so emotionally unavailable* and *only assholes are obsessed with Camus.* Jury's still out on that last one, by the way, maybe I should wait until we get around to him in Mulland's class before deciding whether or not you're—"

"Shh," Kevin says. And he kisses me.

20.

"JESUS CHRIST!" Katie shouts. She flops onto her bed and throws one arm over her forehead in mock distress. "Stop. This is too much for me. I can't listen to this anymore."

I've just finished telling Katie and Lin what happened on the balcony last night, and Katie, needless to say, is beside herself.

"For someone who spent half of the night glued to Bobby at the lips, you're awfully worked up about a kiss," Lin says. She's sitting at the foot of Katie's bed, still in her pajamas despite the fact that it's almost noon.

"Shush," Katie says. "This isn't about me. This is about Stella! So then what happened?"

"Thought you couldn't listen anymore?" Lin says.

"I recover fast," Katie says.

She turns to me expectantly.

"Oh. Well, that's...pretty much it. I was halfway through an extremely witty imitation of Kevin's whole Heathcliff act—I literally used Heathcliff as an example, Lin, you should be so proud of me—and he just cut me off and kissed me."

"Then what?" Katie asks.

"That's it! *Fin*, the end, story's over."

Katie rolls her eyes like she can't believe she even has to explain this. "Yes, but *how was it*?"

"How was what?" I say.

"*How was the kiss?*" Katie practically shouts.

Lin snickers.

"*Oh*," I say. "It was good! At least, I think it was good. It's not like I have a lot of experience to compare it to."

"That's funny, because I clearly remember you and Titus getting it on in this very house last year," Lin says. She frowns. "A little too clearly, actually."

"That didn't count," I say. "Nothing from that night counts. Can we just make that, like, a general life rule? If you're so drunk that the room is spinning, nothing you do counts."

"And didn't you go out with Patrick a few times in freshman year?" Lin adds.

"Yeah, but that was freshman year. That should be another general life rule. Nothing from freshman year counts, because we were freshmen, and therefore dumbasses."

"Stop avoiding the question!" Katie says.

"I'm not!"

Katie gives me A Look.

"Okay, fine," I say. I take myself back to last night, try and remember how it felt the moment Kevin stepped in and kissed me. His hands, one in my hair and one at my waist, pulling me closer. The breeze in the air. That spark.

"It was very…overwhelming," I start. "Like, I know that

it was just a kiss, and people kiss other people all the time and have totally forgotten about it by the next day. But I had been thinking about this for so long, you know, and I've been talking to you guys about Kevin for months now, and there have been so many times when this could have happened but didn't, or when I wanted it to happen but couldn't make myself do anything, or when *he* obviously wanted it to happen but I told him I would rather get with Brady Thompson. And then, last night, it just felt like it was all happening at once, like there was so much waiting and angst and excitement all leading up to that one moment, right there, and then it was so…natural. It was so easy. And it was so easy to get lost in."

Silence from Lin and Katie. Lin is biting her lip. Katie has this expression on her face that almost looks sad, which is both confusing and slightly concerning.

"Did that sound stupid?" I say. "See, this is why I didn't want to get into it. Because I knew I would start talking and sound ridiculous and now I'm completely embarrassed and—"

"No!" Katie says. "That wasn't embarrassing at all! I just didn't know what to say because—well, because I don't know if I've ever actually felt that way before. When I'm with Bobby, I'm happy, obviously, and I think he's a cool guy, and I'm very attracted to him, but it's nowhere near that level of—what's the word…"

"Intensity," Lin says.

"Yeah! I'm into him, but there's very little *panic* and *angst* and *craziness*," Katie says, waving her hands in the air to punctuate the words. "When we make out, I mostly just feel… fun. I feel fun, and I feel flirty."

"Fun and flirty," I repeat. "What's that like?"

Katie throws her pillow at me. "Don't act like you can't be fun and flirty, Stella! Otherwise, we'll have to call up Titus and ask him to serve as a reference for—"

The rest of her sentence is cut off because I've thrown the pillow back at her face.

"It's not even really about me," I say, over the sound of Lin and Katie laughing. "It's Kevin. It's Kevin and his whole…"

I squint my eyes and tilt my head to the side, trying to imitate that look that Kevin gets sometimes. Like the meaning of life will become clear if he just ruminates hard enough on whatever happens to be in front of him at the time.

"The point is," I say, when my impression gets nothing more but raised eyebrows from Katie and a puzzled look from Lin, "the two of us could be playing Scrabble and it would probably feel momentous and emotionally loaded. Because it's Kevin, and that's the type of person that he is."

"Uh-huh," Katie says. She pauses. "And do you…like that?"

"I don't know," I say. "Makes things interesting, I guess."

The one thing I haven't shared with Katie and Lin is the whole Kevin-being-depressed thing, because I still don't know what to make of it, and it doesn't really seem like my secret to share. If there's a time to say something about that, it's probably now, while the conversation is still serious and we're already on the topic of Kevin and his emotional constitution. But then I hesitate—because do I really want to bring this up?—and Katie starts talking about how she and Bobby might go on a double date with Victoria and her boyfriend next weekend, and then Lin mentions that she and some senior on the debate team really hit it off last night, and then Katie spends the next hour grilling Lin about this guy. The next thing I know, it's midafternoon and we only have an hour and a half to clean the entire house before Katie's parents get home from their two-day trip.

So I put the rest of my thoughts and feelings about Kevin's thoughts and feelings on the back burner, figuring we'll have a chance to talk about all that another time. It's been an eventful enough Halloween, anyway.

So there's one thing that I have to say.

I know that what comes next must all seem very silly, and un-necessarily dramatic, and perhaps even predictable. I know that the red flags were there from the very first night, up there on Katie's bal-cony, if only I had been able to really look at Kevin instead of being blinded by every look he threw my way. And I know that love stories between people so recklessly desperate to write a love story with each other very rarely end the way they do in the movies.

But I only know all that now—only in hindsight. At the time, I'm...well, infatuated. I'm caught up in the rush of stumbling into someone like Kevin when I had planned to spend the rest of my time in Bridgemont avoiding everyone and hoping college would be bet-ter. I spend all of my time lost in his words, or his eyes, or his touch, and every time I'm pulled back into reality, I want less and less to do with it.

Which I guess brings us to the one thing that I can't say. Which is that no one tried to warn me.

27.

I've missed my last three therapy sessions, and, unsurprisingly, Karen is not happy.

"Help me understand this, Stella," she says, on the blustery Thursday afternoon I finally drag myself into LiveWell after she leaves voice mails on my home phone, my cell phone and my father's work phone. "You just…haven't 'felt like coming in' for the past month?"

Karen's gotten a haircut since I last saw her, and replaced one of the pictures of her kids on her desk with a new one. The quote on the bulletin board behind her desk now reads:

Always Remember That You Deserve Happiness.

"It's not that I haven't felt like coming in," I say. "It's just that I've been…happy. Really happy. And do I really have to come to therapy if I feel happy?"

Karen takes a deep breath. Then she puts her pen down on the table very gingerly and folds her hands.

And that's when I know that I'm screwed.

"Stella, of course I'm grateful and relieved to hear that you've been feeling happier lately. But therapy isn't just about coping with sadness. It's also about understanding yourself more. Building healthy relationships with other people. Learning how to manage your emotional responses so that when you're *not* as happy, you're empowered to make good decisions."

"Uh-huh," I say.

Karen makes a face. A couple seconds of silence tick by. I can tell that Karen is trying to get me to say more, but I stay pointedly and resolutely silent. I've been in therapy long enough to recognize the ol' draw-them-out-with-silence tactic, and I'm not falling for it.

After half a minute, Karen gives in and changes the topic. "How are things with your parents?" she says cheerfully.

"Oh. I mean, they've been fighting with each other so much that half the time I don't think they realize that I do, in fact, still reside in the Canavas household. So I guess things are worse, but also kind of better—no one's yelled at me about my chemistry grade in, like, two months."

"What do they fight about?"

I roll my eyes. "What *don't* they fight about? Money. Groceries. Who's supposed to drive me to cross-country practice. My dad has started going to these poker nights with a bunch of his friends from work, so they also fight about that. And then they fight about whose fault it is that they fight so often."

"Have you had time to give some more thought to the idea of having a family session with you and your parents?" Karen says. "Because I really think that—"

I groan before I can stop myself. "I really think that… No," I say.

Karen pauses. "And why's that?" she asks.

"Because," I say. I try to think of a reason that isn't *Because I don't want to.*

"Your mom expressed interest in having one in our discussion a few weeks ago," Karen says.

"Of course she did," I say. "And my dad will think it's a colossal waste of time, and they'll never come to an agreement about it. It'll just get tacked on to the list of things for them to scream at each other about after dinner."

Karen purses her lips and then switches to another tactic. "Is it hard to be caught in the middle?" she says. "I imagine it must be very draining."

"Not really," I respond.

Which is definitely not the answer that she's looking for.

"I mean, it's not great," I add. "Sometimes it bothers me, especially when it's late at night and I'm trying to sleep, or when things get so heated that I can hear that my mom is trying not to cry."

I pause and try not to picture it too clearly. Because I'm not heartless, you know? There's something about it that's incredibly sad—who wants to lie in bed listening to their mom cry?—and if I think about it too much, I start to feel overwhelmed and emotionally shaky.

"But it hasn't been too bad. I haven't been in the house as much, anyway."

"Oh?" Karen says. "And why's that?"

"Oh, you know," I say. "I've been doing drugs every day

after school in the parking lot. Amazing, how easy it is to kill time when you're high as balls."

I learned long ago that sarcasm doesn't fly very well in therapy, but it hasn't stopped me from trying.

"Uh-huh," Karen says.

"Yep," I say.

Karen tries the silence thing again. When that doesn't work, she sighs and says, "Stella, let's try to be serious."

"Well, I have cross-country practice. And sometimes I stay after school to go to office hours for calc help, because I have to get my grade up to a B+ before the semester ends or my dad will make me quit the team. And I've been spending a lot of time at Kevin's."

"Kevin?" Karen says.

"Oh," I say. "I guess—wow, yeah, I guess you haven't heard about him."

Even though I understand it logically, there's still something about that fact that seems incredibly weird to me. It's been less than a month since Halloween, but it already feels like Kevin has become this defining, central part of my life. We're with each other so much now that it's hard to imagine what I did with all of my time before the two of us started dating.

"I've started dating this guy," I say. "His name is Kevin. He goes to Bridgemont."

"Ah," Karen says.

"He's really cool," I say. "I mean, not in the way that Katie is cool, because most of the people at Bridgemont who are cool in the way that Katie is cool are terrible human beings. But Kevin is cool in like a real, nonsuperficial way—do you know what I mean?"

Karen nods slowly. "Ah," she says again.

"He's a senior, and we actually only know each other because we're in this philosophy class together. Kevin is really, *really* into philosophy. It's strange, and it used to throw me off whenever we were just hanging out and having a normal conversation and he randomly started talking about the nature of existence or the meaning of humanity or whatever. But now that I'm used to it, I think it's actually really admirable. I mean, so many people at Bridgemont only seem to care about passing their classes or carefully tracking the social hierarchy or when they can next get drunk. And it only takes half a conversation with them to tell that they are totally, totally fake. But Kevin—he would never *try* to fake someone out, you know? He just is who he is, even if who he is doesn't make sense to most of the people we go to school with."

Now that I've finally started talking, I'm expecting Karen to be a little bit more enthusiastic about the conversation. After all, this is what she's been trying to get me to do for the entire thirty-five minutes that I've been sitting in her office. But instead, she just furrows her brow a little bit and says, yet again: "Ah."

"That's it?" I say. "I've finally dragged myself out of the pit of misery that is my existence, and all you have to say is 'Ah'?"

"At the beginning of this session, you mentioned that you haven't been coming to therapy because you've been happy," Karen says, completely overriding my question. "Is this why?"

"Um, it's definitely part of it," I say. "I'm also happy because, you know, Katie is really happy with Bobby—that's her new...um...well, I don't really know what they are, but whatever it is, they're happy. And Lin is so much less stressed now that she's submitted her Brown application. So I'm happy that they're happy. But I guess if I had to say what it *mostly* was…it'd be Kevin."

Karen looks very focused. And sounds very silent.

"I don't know," I say, feeling the need to explain myself even though I'm not sure why. "It's just… It's nice to be able to be *real* with someone, you know? I'm never afraid to tell Kevin what I'm really thinking. Or to tell him how I really feel. And I don't know if that's ever really happened to me before. Of course, I tell Katie and Lin about everything remotely notable that happens to me, which is not very much. But I'm always slightly worried that Katie's going to decide that I'm way too much of a freak to be friends with her, or that Lin's going to realize that I'm really not smart enough to understand half the things she says. With Kevin, I just tell him things. And he agrees, or he disagrees, or maybe he drags Camus into the conversation. But I always feel—what's the word I'm trying to find here?—I always feel safe."

Karen nods. "I see," she says.

The two of us sit there for a bit.

"Well," Karen says, "we actually only have a couple more minutes. I want to say that I'm glad you felt comfortable sharing that with me. And I'm so happy that you've been feeling happier lately, Stella. The fact that you've found someone that you feel safe with—well, that's really something valuable."

She takes a deep breath.

"But I also want to caution you. Relationships can be a wonderful thing, Stella, and they can really enrich a person's emotional life. That's partially because they create such a wide range of powerful feelings. But that's why it's especially important in a relationship to be in a good place emotionally when you're on your own, and to really know yourself and trust yourself and trust your *feelings*. Does that make sense?"

"Uh-huh," I say.

"I've seen this pattern of behavior quite frequently with young men and women this age, where they think that the solution to all of their problems lies in this other person. And it's—well, it's worrisome to me, Stella, I'll be honest with you. You want to love someone because they complement you and make you a better person, not because you need them or because they're distracting you from other issues in your life or because they fulfill a need that's going otherwise unfulfilled."

"I don't think Kevin is the solution to all of my problems," I say. I understand that Karen is my therapist, and it's literally her job to bring up stuff like this. But does her job have to be so goddamn annoying? "I don't think Kevin is the solution to *any* of my problems—well, except maybe my embarrassing lack of experience with guys. Kevin is just what makes it worth it to get out of bed in the morning to deal with all those other problems."

This, unsurprisingly, does not go over very well with Karen.

"I want you to think about what you just said, Stella," she says, "and think about why it might be worrying."

I roll my eyes. "I thought we were almost out of time."

"We are," Karen says. "But think about it. For next time."

"Okay, Karen," I say.

But I don't. In fact, I don't even make it to my appointment the following week. Because Kevin and I decide to take an impromptu after-school trip to the movies, and, well, who needs to go to therapy when everything in their life is going fine? I'm happy, and Kevin's happy, and Karen probably has better things to do than spend time with someone who doesn't have anything to talk about, anyway.

30.

It's the beginning of December: one week after the first snow leaves all of the sidewalks and roads lightly coated in white, like they've been dusted in powdered sugar, and it's two weeks before the first nor'easter rips its way through New England and causes mass power outages throughout Connecticut. If someone were to ask me to name my best friends, the two people I trust more than anyone else in the world, I wouldn't miss a beat. "Katie and Lin" would leave my mouth the second I fully processed the question, because Katie and Lin *are* my best friends, just like they've always been.

My answer would be so automatic that I wouldn't have time to think about how I haven't been spending very much time with my self-professed best friends. I wouldn't really think about the fact that Kevin has been driving me to school for the last three weeks, because it only seems natural for the senior you're dating who has his own car to pick you up in the morning. I wouldn't really think about how I've been spending more and more of my lunches in the library catching up on work that I didn't do the previous night, because when you first start dating someone, of *course* you spend entire afternoons cuddled up on the couch watching movies instead of doing your homework. I wouldn't realize that I've been going days at a time without seeing Lin and Katie, because something about those early weeks with Kevin pulls me into a separate universe, one where my best friends, my classes at school and my relationship with my parents all seem like distant aspects of a life separate from the one I've suddenly been transported into.

It all happens so quickly, is the thing. I'm so giddy and enchanted by this universe Kevin is pulling me into that I don't even realize I'm leaving something behind.

But the real world, as always, asserts itself sooner or later. Kevin comes down with a cold toward the end of November, forcing me to text Lin and ask her for a ride to school for the first time in nearly a month.

"Hey, stranger," Katie says, when I climb into the car that morning. Her hair is so long now, down to the small of her back, and the purple sheen is starting to fade. "What's new with you?"

"Nothing," I say. It's a reflexive answer. Usually—well usually, there *isn't* anything new with me, and the answer is so ingrained that it's left my mouth before I realize how ridiculous it must sound to two people who I've been blowing off for nearly a month.

"Well, that's obviously not true," Lin says. "Considering we haven't seen you in eons."

From the backseat, I can't see Lin's face, so I can't tell if I'm imagining the strange tone in her voice right now.

"I see Katie every day in history class!" I say.

Katie rolls her eyes. "Yeah, me and the eighteen other people in our history class. Sitting through lectures on the prolonged dick-measuring contest that was Cold War–era global politics doesn't exactly count as quality time."

It's a good point.

"I mean, I really haven't been up to very much," I say. "I've just been hanging out with Kevin a lot and trying not to fail my classes."

Katie nods. "I texted you to see if you wanted to come out with Bobby and me last week," she says. She doesn't need to say the rest of the sentence: ...*but you never responded*.

"Oh, yeah," I say. "I guess I just...forgot."

No one says anything.

"I feel like you guys wouldn't want to go out with me and Kevin, anyway," I offer. "We're not very...social."

"Clearly not," Lin says.

The weirdness in her voice is harder to ignore that time.

"Have you heard from Brown?" I ask.

"No, I haven't," Lin says. "Which is stressful, because I'm *dying to know*, but also kind of a good thing, because I'm *terrified to find out*. I think I'm just pretending I never applied and it's not happening and I should think about everything and anything other than whether or not I'm going to be moving to Providence in less than a year. Nothing soothes the nerves quite like fierce denial."

Those sentences are so completely Lin-like, so normal and familiar, that a flood of relief washes over me. It's a strange experience: being consumed by relief when I didn't even realize I had a reason to be nervous.

"Well, in that case," I reply, "I won't ask you when you're supposed to find out."

Katie snorts. "December 10," she says. "I know this because Lin talks a good game about staying calm and pretending she never applied and all, but then lunch hits and it's back to *Did putting chess club on my résumé turn me into a walking stereotype? And, Oh, God, I should have written my common application essay about my parents instead of you two bozos.*"

Katie's imitation of Lin's panicking-about-college voice is spot-on.

"What did I do," Lin says, smiling despite herself as she pulls onto the Bridgemont campus, "to deserve such supportive friends?"

"Hey, I support you," I say. "I know you would never say the word *bozo.* You would use something much more sophisticated. Like *imbecile.* Or *cretin.* Or *ignoramus,* that one is nice and Latinate."

Lin snorts. The three of us clamber out of the car and swing our backpacks over our shoulders, so familiar it's almost synchronized.

"Whatever happens, on December 10," I say, "we'll go to Joe's that weekend. To celebrate. And if not to celebrate, to commiserate."

"That'd be really nice," Lin says, looking touched.

"I'm always down for an omelet from Joe's," Katie says.

"I have to run to homeroom," Lin says, as we walk through the parking lot and into the building. "But I'll see you two at lunch?"

"Definitely," Katie says.

Katie and Lin turn to look at me.

"Uh," I say. And wince. "I have to finish this paper at lunch today," I explain. "It's due seventh period, and I totally should have just finished it last night, but I just—well, that's not important. But tomorrow—I promise."

Lin nods, expression inscrutable, and then disappears around a corner. "Well, I'll see you in history," Katie says.

"Yeah, I'll see you."

There's something really, really unsettling about this situation. It's not that we're talking about anything particularly awkward, and Katie, as far as I can tell, is exactly the same cheerful person she's always been. What's making me feel weird, I realize, is that I'm even thinking about the possibility that things between us might be uncomfortable. When you've been friends with someone for as long as Katie and I have been, that stops being a thing you worry about. And the fact that I feel weird enough to think that there might be something weird between us—well, it's jarring.

Katie spins to walk away—the tips of her hair flying off her shoulders—and then seems to change her mind and turns right back.

"One more thing," she says.

"What's up?" I say.

"I'm really happy that you're happy with Kevin, Stella," Katie says. She bites her lip.

It looks like there's something else that she wants to say, so I don't respond. But then the seconds tick by—one, two, three, four, five—and she's still silent, and it's pretty clear that even if there *is* something else that she wants to say, she's not going to say it.

So I say: "Thanks."

Katie nods.

And then she heads to her locker.

It's the beginning of December, and if you were to ask me who my best friends in the world are, I'd say Katie and Lin before you even finished asking the question. But I don't know that either of them would answer with the same lack of hesitation anymore. And I guess what I'm trying to say with all of this is that I don't know if I could really blame them for that.

I'm not trying to defend myself here. Believe me, I think I was as stupid for not listening to Karen and Katie and everyone else in the world just as much as you do. And I don't know if I'll ever really get over the regret of throwing away Lin's friendship over a guy. Everyone was right. I fell too hard, too fast, too blindly.

Of course, I didn't think about these things when Kevin and I first started seeing each other. I didn't think about how my best friends were my best friends for a reason, so maybe I should listen to them, or how Karen was a licensed therapist, so maybe she had a good point, or how maybe all along I was just romanticizing the idea of finding someone as fucked up as I was. At the beginning, I was just caught up in the feeling of finally being with someone. Someone who made me feel smart, and understood, and safe.

And you know what? Even all this time later, even knowing everything that I know now, I still get that.

Because it was nice to feel that way. It really was.

21.

The second time Kevin kisses me, we're sitting in his car, parked on the side of the road in front of my house. I've just gotten out of cross-country practice, and Kevin—who often stays after school on Tuesdays to have long, postclass conversations with Dr. Mulland—has offered to drive me home. We haven't talked at all about the conversation we had at Katie's on Friday. We also haven't talked about what happened after the conversation we had at Katie's on Friday, after he cut me off midsentence, after he leaned in, in, in—

Stop this, I tell myself, and try to focus on the actual words that Kevin is saying instead of the way that his lips move when he talks. The only time when that's possible is when I'm not looking at Kevin (and his lips, and the way his hands are resting on the wheel, and the line of his arms up to his shoulders, and the color of his eyes) at all, so instead I turn my gaze out the windshield—at the dark brown leaves carpeting the ground, the washed-out gray of the sky.

"What I really like about Dr. Mulland is that he's not just interested in my thoughts about philosophy," Kevin is saying. "He asks me a lot about life in general. My family. My plans for the future. I'm going to ask him to write one of my recommendations for Columbia."

Kevin pauses, and I take the moment as an opportunity to steal a furtive glance at him. Unfortunately, my furtive glance proves to be not particularly furtive, because Kevin is looking right at me. We make forceful, fleeting eye contact for three seconds, which, of course, immediately floods me with mortification. I jerk my gaze back straight ahead, where it lands on the thorny, bare branches of what used to be Mrs. Holloway's rose garden.

"You okay?" Kevin says. "You seem nervous."

I force myself to turn my head and look at him. "I'm not nervous," I say.

Kevin nods. "Okay, then. You're not nervous."

"I don't really *get* nervous," I say. "I'm not really a nervous person. I think it has to do with the fact that I've pretty much resigned myself to the fact that no matter what I do, my life will be futile and awkward and embarrassing, and once you've accepted that as an inevitability, well, there's not much reason to be nervous anymore."

Oh God. I'm doing that thing again, that thing that I do when I get nervous. Babbling. I'm babbling.

"How very existentialist of you. Sartre would be proud."

Kevin is smirking. Which makes me nervous. Which makes me defensive. Which makes me babble more.

"Yeah, I can't say that I really *get* Sartre, Kevin. First of all, I can't fucking pronounce his name. Second of all, *Being and*

Nothingness was a doozy. And third of all, while I haven't actually read *Nausea* yet, even you have to admit that it's not a very promising title."

"You should read it," Kevin says. "It's a quick read, and I think you'd like it."

Kevin leans into the space between our two seats, looking bemused.

"A quick read relative to what? To *Being and Nothingness*? Because that's not saying very much."

Kevin adjusts his body so that we're at eye level, then reaches out with one hand and cups my chin.

My breath catches.

"Are you nervous?" Kevin says. A hint of a smile on his face.

"No," I say.

A few inches closer.

"What about now?"

"No," I repeat.

"That's reassuring," Kevin says. And then, before I can respond, he kisses me.

It's different this time. The first time Kevin and I kissed, on Katie's balcony, there was this urgency, this desperation, like if we didn't do it right there, right then, we might miss our moment completely and it would never happen. It was intense, and overwhelming, and disorienting in the best possible way.

The second kiss is definitely still intense, and being so close to Kevin—close enough to smell him, to feel his body next to mine, to be able to run my fingers through his hair—still leaves me dizzy and flustered, feeling off balance even though I'm sitting down. But it's also easier this time, like we're getting to know each other instead of praying that it isn't too late to try. This time, Kevin kisses me like we have all the time in the world.

"Let's go on a date," he murmurs, seconds or minutes or perhaps hours later.

"When?" I say. He trails his lips down the side of my neck, which sends involuntary shivers through my body.

"Tomorrow," he says.

"Tomorrow?" I say. I push him away, somewhere between giddy and incredulous at the suggestion. "Tomorrow's Wednesday. We have school, Kevin."

"After school," he says. Then he goes back to kissing me, which interrupts the flow of thoughts in my brain for another solid ten minutes.

"What about homework?" I manage eventually.

"We can do it afterward. C'mon, Stel," he says, pouting, and I wish I were a strong enough woman to resist how goddamn adorable it is. "There's an art museum in Hartford that I've been dying to go to. I'll drive."

"You want to go on a date to an art museum. Tomorrow. Of course you do."

"There's a collection of black-and-white photographs on exhibit," Kevin says, as if what he's proposing right now isn't utterly absurd. "I think you'd like it, Stella. It's supposed to be very...noir. You know, like—"

But Kevin never gets around to explaining the intricacies of noir, because I've just glanced at my phone and realized that we've been parked outside my house for *over an hour.*

"Jesus," I screech. I turn around and grab my backpack

from the backseat. "Can you pop the trunk? I need to get my track bag."

Kevin blinks. "I wasn't aware you had such strong feelings about photography. They also have a collection of ceramics on display, although I must admit that ceramics have never really—"

"It's not the *photographs*," I say. "It's the fact that it's 6:13 and my dad's going to be home soon."

"Oh," Kevin says, looking slightly taken aback. "Sorry. Sometimes I forget about stuff like that."

"Stuff like what? Like having parents?"

"Stuff like having parents who *care*," Kevin says. "My parents—well, my mom, since they got divorced ages ago… Let's just say that she is an ardent subscriber to the laissez-faire method of parenting. She's a painter, you know, all about independence and the beauty of solitude and all that."

Suddenly, I am incredibly thankful to be taking my boring, tedious European history class, because that class is the only reason I know what *laissez-faire* means when Kevin says it.

"Well, that's lucky, right? What teenager doesn't want hands-off parents?"

"I mean, sure," Kevin says. "It's great for those nights when I want to go out and smoke a joint with Yago, I guess. Not so great for those days when one of my tires goes flat halfway back from school or, God forbid, I need help with a homework assignment. But hey, enough joints with Yago and you forget that any of those things are important. So maybe I am lucky."

Kevin smiles and rolls his eyes the second the words have left his mouth to try and cover himself, but what he doesn't realize is that I've done the very same thing so many times that I see right through it. No, there's real bitterness there, real hurt, real vulnerability.

"Whatever," Kevin says. "First-world problems, right? Surely nothing compared to the suffering our poor, cynical Nietszche endured. I can only imagine what he'd say if given the chance to hear me griping over my mother..."

He's trying to distract me with theatrics now, a half smile curled across his face, but like I said—I know the moves too well to let them slide. I reach out, touch his arm and forge past the rush of embarrassment when he cuts off and looks up at me sharply. I feel a jolt as his blue eyes meet mine.

"Hey," I say. "It's okay, you know? Like...if you're bitter or angry about your mom. You don't have to pretend that it's not a big deal and you couldn't care less, if it is, and you could, and you really do."

The expression on Kevin's face is inscrutable.

"We also don't have to talk about this if you don't want to," I add hastily. "I know it's kind of...personal."

One second of silence stretches into two seconds of silence stretches into three seconds of silence stretches into me contemplating if Kevin is about to lose his shit and throw me out of his car.

"Thanks," he finally says. Half word, half exhale. His eyes flicker to and away from mine, as if he can't decide whether or not to look at me.

I offer up a wry smile, try to hold his gaze. "No problem."

Another beat of silence. He's still not looking at me. And then—

"Okay, well, text me about tomorrow. I really think that you'll like the exhibit. The *New York Times* called it—"

I unlatch the front door and kick it open, step out of the car and then turn around to look at Kevin, this ridiculous, unbelievable boy who is now smirking at my exasperation like he's won some kind of chess game.

"Yes," I say. "Yes, I'll go to the art museum with you tomorrow, even though it means I have to come up with an excuse to be home late for the second day in a row. I'll meet you in the parking lot after I get out of practice and you can explain everything you know about noir photography to me on the ride over. All right?"

"Sounds good," Kevin says. He smiles—like, *really* smiles—at me, and that is almost, almost enough to get me to climb back into the car and start kissing him all over again, angry fathers be damned.

22.

When Kevin asks me to go to the Hartford Museum of Art with him to look at a photography exhibit, I figure it'll be a fun, if slightly pretentious, way to spend an afternoon with a boy that I really like. I do not, however, anticipate that the photographs on display will resonate with Kevin as much as they do. I do not anticipate that Kevin will spend the rest of the week giving long, impassioned speeches about their raw, unflinching honesty, their cold assessment of life in 1950s America and their *pathos*, oh, their pathos. And I *definitely* do not anticipate that our cute date to the art museum will so inspire Kevin that he wants nothing more than to spend the next few weeks visiting literally every single art museum within two hours of Wethersfield.

So that's how I end up at the Institute of Contemporary Art in Boston, spending my Saturday afternoon staring at a wall-size rectangular canvas that has been painted gray.

No, I'm serious. The paint is lumpier in some places than others, but it's…literally just the color gray.

"This is very…*interesting*," Kevin says. He squints a little and runs a hand through his hair. The tone of his voice makes me want to punch him in the face, and then drag him into a closet and make out with him.

"It's very textural," he adds.

"Shut up, Kevin," I say.

"Textural," he repeats thoughtfully. "Tactile. Synesthetic, one might even say."

"Might one say that? Might one *really*?"

"Perhaps," Kevin says. "If one were looking at this work expecting it to be a primarily visual experience—under the assumption, of course, that the power of painting as an art form is routed through the sensory experience of *seeing*—then yes, one might be surprised to find oneself reacting to the textural interplay of this piece of artwork in a physical way."

He pauses. I imagine him adjusting a pair of imaginary glasses on the bridge of his nose. "And it's really the physical that defines one's reaction to this piece, don't you think? Raised goose bumps. Hairs on end. Oh, and gag reflex triggered because of how *ridiculous* this is and *God, I hate modern art*. Why did I drag you here?"

The change in tone is so unexpected—and the look of dismay on Kevin's face so out of character—that it takes a minute for me to process what he's said, especially because I'm a few phrases behind to begin with. *(Textural interplay?* I'm thinking. *Why does that sound so sexual?)* Then, once my brain catches up, I start laughing. Like, really laughing. Laughing so hard that I can't remember why I started laughing in the first place, which, of course, only makes me laugh harder. I laugh so hard and for so long that I actually start to tear up, and Kevin looks at me like I've lost my mind.

"Stella?" Kevin says. "You okay there?"

I don't know why he bothers asking. I'm clearly in no state to respond.

"All right," Kevin says. He puts an arm around my shoulders and guides me out of the room, away from the wall-size gray rectangle, and into the hallway. And I guess I can't blame him. The people around us are starting to look freaked out, and the last thing that I would want to do is interrupt them as they soak in the textural, tactile, synesthetic majesty of the great modernist painting *Grey* by Richard Munroe.

23.

It's 4:00 p.m. on a Monday afternoon. Kevin and I are in his room—the door wide open, because his mom is working in the basement—sprawled across his bed. The sun is already low in the sky, because it's November and New England winter is well upon us, and the light slanting in through his window makes his whole room glow reddish-orange. Kevin's room overlooks one of the main roads in town, and every now and then there's a burst of street noise that drowns out the music he's playing from his phone.

Kevin's room is sparser than mine—colder, somehow. I've got childhood gifts scattered throughout the room and dozens of pictures of Katie and Lin and I pinned up on the walls. Kevin's walls are light gray and bare except for one poster of a New York City street in black-and-white; there's a desk pushed into one corner that's piled high with books but doesn't have any pictures.

Kevin, of course, is reading: lying on his stomach at the

foot of the bed, neck craned over our next philosophy book. His shirt has ridden up his back ever-so-slightly, leaving a thin sliver of skin exposed between the top of his jeans and the hem of his shirt.

I'm supposed to be doing the same philosophy reading (by tomorrow, in fact), but I am instead using the time to stare at Kevin, trying to decipher the mess of feelings I experience every time I look at him, the meaning of the knot that seems to have permanently settled in my stomach since the two of us started dating. Sometimes just *thinking* about the past couple of weeks leaves me flustered and overwhelmed and frustrated with my inability to understand my emotions, at which point I usually detox by scrolling through Facebook on my phone. Fortunately, the antics that Bridgemont students put out there on the internet for everyone to see very rarely elicit complex emotions of any sort.

The first thing that comes up this time I refresh my news feed is a picture of Katie and Bobby at an ice-skating rink with Victoria Lee and Justin. I vaguely remember Katie texting me about going out with the two of them on Friday—and then never responding.

But I guess it's actually not so bad that Kevin and I didn't go, because the four of them look—well, perfect, in a way that the two of us would probably ruin. Katie is beaming toward the camera and Victoria is midlaugh, with Justin's right arm slung loosely around her waist. Everyone's cheeks are slightly red from the cold and the exertion. It would look staged if it weren't so candid.

I nudge Kevin in the side with my foot. "Check out this double date we missed," I say.

Kevin looks up. Glances at the photograph for two seconds. Then looks back down. "Mmm," he says.

"I mean, they all look amazing," I say. And I'm trying to say that in a totally normal, happy-for-my-hot-best-friend-and-her-friends kind of way. But I'd be lying if I said that there wasn't a note of jealousy in my voice.

Kevin doesn't even look up this time. "Mmm," he repeats.

A couple of seconds go by. Then something seems to click in his head.

"Hold on a sec," Kevin says. He slides a bookmark into *Waiting for Godot*, places it on the floor and then slides his body up to mine so that he's propped up on one elbow next to me.

"You really shouldn't worry about things like that," he says, all quiet concentration and intense eye contact. He puts his arm around my waist, which, of course, sends my pulse skyrocketing.

"I—I don't," I say.

"You don't?" Kevin says.

"I mean—I do," I say.

It's always hard for me to think straight when Kevin is so close.

He raises an eyebrow.

"*Sometimes* I do," I clarify. "You know, when I'm on Facebook and I see Katie's pictures and I think, Christ, I could never look like that. Because, I mean, Christ, I could never look like that. But it's not like it bothers me every second of every day, really, it's just that—"

"What I'm trying to say," Kevin says, cutting me off, "is that I think you're very beautiful, Stella."

His arm around my waist. His body next to mine. And he thinks I'm beautiful.

Jesus, Stella. Pull it together. Say something.

"Thank you," I say.

Kevin lifts his arm and traces his fingers along my jaw, up one cheek. "Do you believe me?" he says quietly.

And how could I not, when he says it like that?

"Yes," I say.

Kevin looks at me, his blue eyes looking lighter than usual in the golden, predusk light. Silence falls over the room as his phone moves from one track to the next.

"Okay," Kevin murmurs. Then—as if this interaction was completely routine, nothing out of the ordinary at all—he sits back up. Grabs his philosophy book from across the bed. And goes back to reading.

24.

Later that evening, as Kevin and I are about to leave his house, I meet his mother for the first time. She spots us from the kitchen as we round the corner at the bottom of the stairs and says: "Hey, Kev—come here for a second."

Kev? I mouth at him.

Kevin kicks off the one sneaker that he's already put on, looks apologetically at me and then leads me into the kitchen.

Kevin's mom is tall and willowy, with green eyes and wavy brown hair that is the exact same shade as Kevin's. Any other resemblance is hard to find. Kevin's features are all sharp angles—the thin, high bridge of his nose; the curve of his browbone, so prominent that his eyes almost always seem shadowed. His mom's eyes are round and full of warmth, and when she stands and walks toward me, she moves with the grace of a dancer.

"It's so nice to meet you, Stella," she says, and wraps me in a hug.

I shoot Kevin a panicked look. He rolls his eyes.

"It's nice to meet you, too, Ms. Miller," I say.

"Please. It's Eileen."

She pulls back, her hands still on my shoulders, and looks at me. Her eyes move slowly and carefully, and it kind of feels like I'm being studied, committed to memory. Then again, maybe I am. I have just been cooped up for two hours in her son's bedroom, after all.

"Okay," I say. And then I try for, *"Hi, Eileen,"* but it still feels so strange to call her by her first name that I just end up saying the "Hi" and then trailing off awkwardly.

"We should go, Mom," Kevin says. "Stella's parents are expecting her at home."

"Mmm," his mom says, still looking at me. She floats back to the table and sits down again, crosses her right leg over the other. "You know, Stella, you have the most striking eyes."

"Mom," Kevin groans.

"Er—that's—thanks," I say.

Kevin's mom frowns, like that's the wrong reaction.

"I mean, they're just *brown*," I say.

"It's not so much about the color," she says. "The shape. The *depth*. Very expressive. If you're interested, you should come down to the studio sometime and sit for a portra—"

"You *have* to stop doing this to my friends," Kevin says, sounding exasperated. He takes my hand and pulls me toward the door.

"Just being friendly," his mom says.

"Be a more normal version of friendly," Kevin says.

She smiles fondly at him. "Better to be original than to be normal, Kev," she says. "Like I always say."

"I'll be back in twenty," Kevin says.

"Sure," she says. "I'll be downstairs when you get back."

Kevin *mmm-hmm*s in acknowledgment, and the two of us step outside.

25.

"Better to be original than to be normal," I repeat when we're halfway down the turnpike.

I pause, like I'm considering the sentiment carefully.

"That's real deep, Kev. I see where you get it."

"Oh, shut up," Kevin says. But he's laughing.

26.

It's the first time it's been this bad in a while.

Over time, I've learned that my parents have two types of arguments. The first is your standard squabbling-adults type of thing, in which they argue, sometimes voices get a little raised, my father throws around words like *insouciant* and *pertinacious*, my mother throws around words like "Thomas, would you please stop *talking like that*," and the two of them spend the rest of the day ignoring each other. These fights are also known as "it's your fault that Stella isn't doing x" fights, because ninety percent of them are just my parents blaming each other for whatever Stella-related crisis has come up this week. For example, *It's your fault that Stella is unhappy!* Or, *It's your fault that Stella isn't going to therapy!* Or, *It's your fault that Stella won't stay at the dinner table for longer than ten minutes!*

You get the idea.

The trouble arises when things get personal. That's when my dad starts to say things like, "Well, if you did a better job talking to her after school, we'd know why she wasn't doing her homework," or when my mom responds with, "Well, if *you* were home in time for dinner more often, maybe Stella would understand the importance of family time," and *that's* when the first type of fight transforms into the second: the "what the hell is wrong with you?" fight. For example, *What the hell is wrong with you? Don't you care about our daughter's future?* Or, *What the hell is wrong with you? Does spending time with the two of us mean anything to you at all?*

And *that's* how things end up the way they are right now. At two in the morning on a Thursday night. With my parents downstairs shouting at each other about whose fault it is that I've been missing my appointments with Karen. As if the subject of the argument isn't upstairs in her bedroom trying to sleep or anything.

I wish I could say that stuff like this didn't affect me anymore. Because that would be nice—it would be nice to be able to follow up everything I just said with, "And I know this because it's happened countless of times in the past few years, and at this point it doesn't even faze me."

But the truth is, it's hard not to feel upset about it, even the fifth, fiftieth or five hundredth time around. It's hard not to feel upset because there's still a part of me that wants my parents to just work it out and like each other again, as ridiculous as that sounds. And there's a part of me that believes that this is all my fault. If I had known that Karen was going to call my parents this afternoon and tell them that I've been ditching and that it would have triggered this whole disaster, I would have just *gone*. If I had known that eating dinner in ten minutes was going to escalate into an argument about "family values" and "skewed priorities" and all that, I would have just sucked it up and made small talk with my mom.

I don't know what it is that makes me walk across the room, get my cell phone and call Kevin. Part of me is just delirious with exhaustion. I had a big math test yesterday and spent the first three days of the week barely sleeping in an effort to memorize every trigonometric integral known to man. And then there's another part of me that's just…desperate. Desperate for this all to stop. Desperate to think about something, *anything*, other than what's happening downstairs. Desperate to talk to someone. And then, all of a sudden, desperate to hear Kevin's voice.

"Hello?" he says, picking up midway through the fourth ring, right as I'm about to hang up and give up and let him have his sleep. His voice is low, husky. I can hear the yawn at the bottom of his throat.

"I woke you up," I say. All of a sudden I feel terrible.

"I mean, it's the middle of the night, so yeah, I was asleep. But don't worry about it. Are you okay?"

I can hear the sound of Kevin's blankets rustling as he moves around, probably sitting up in bed to check the time, to drink some water. I can picture him so clearly: switching on the light next to his bed, pulling his covers up around his waist, running a hand through his hair. The expression on his face. The way it would feel to be next to him right now.

I can imagine it so clearly that it hurts. And then, all of a sudden, I'm crying.

"Are you okay?" Kevin says. He's starting to sound seriously concerned, which only makes me cry harder.

"I feel stupid," I say. Because I do. This is all so horribly, horribly stupid.

"Talk to me," Kevin says. "What's wrong?"

"I miss you," I say. I crawl back into my bed and pull the covers up around me, thinking about how nice it would be if he were here with me, or if I were there with him, instead of all alone listening to my parents scream at each other.

"Stel…" Kevin says.

"My parents are fighting," I say. I try to take deep, calming breaths, the way Karen and I have practiced thousands of times in therapy. But I can't keep it together long enough to make it through a five-second inhale, so instead I just sound like I'm hyperventilating into a paper bag. "I mean, they fight all the time, but tonight they're *really* fighting and, I don't know, Kevin, I should be used to it, but I'm not, and I should be able to do something about it, but I can't, and I shouldn't have woken you up, but I did. And now I just—I just—want—to be—with you."

Kevin doesn't respond for a couple of seconds. *This is it*, I think. *You went and called him in the middle of the night sobbing and now he probably thinks you're pathetic. Way to go, Stella.*

The thought of that sends me into full breakdown mode, which seems to stir Kevin into action.

"Do you want me to come over?" he says.

"Come over?" I say. "Come over and do what, Kevin? Stand outside in the cold waiting for my parents to stop fighting and freeze to death?"

"I could climb through your window or something," he says.

The suggestion is so absurd that I actually stop crying.

"Climb through my *window*? Have you gone insane?"

"I hear they do that in the movies sometimes," Kevin says drily.

"Yeah, which, in my opinion, is reason enough to rule it out immediately as a valid course of action."

"All right," Kevin says gently. "Consider it ruled out."

"I'm sorry," I say. "I didn't mean to snap at you."

A few moments of silence. My father is storming around downstairs, and I can't hear my mom anymore, which means that she's probably in tears.

"I'm sorry this is happening," Kevin finally says. His voice is quiet, almost a whisper. And with the phone pressed up against my ear, with the way every breath he takes comes through the line, he sounds so, so close.

"Me, too," I say.

"And I really wish I could be with you right now, too," he says.

I start crying again, and this time, I *really* have no idea why. I mean, that wasn't sad, right? I shouldn't feel sad about that. It was really sweet, actually. And yet here I am. Weeping.

"I'm—being—*pathetic*," I say. "God, you must think—"

"Stella," Kevin says. "If someone else called you pathetic, I'd punch them in the face. Well, I wouldn't punch them in the face, because I can't throw a punch to save my life, but I'd be pissed. You're not pathetic, and no one gets to call you pathetic, and you're no exception. All right?"

I hear the sound of the garage door opening downstairs, and then my dad's car starting, which is—well, somewhat shocking, actually. I don't know if that's ever happened before. *He's actually going to spend the night somewhere else?* I think. *Is that how bad tonight's fight was?*

"You still there?" Kevin asks.

"I think my dad just left the house," I say.

"Fuck," Kevin says. "That doesn't sound good."

"It's not good. In fact, I'm pretty sure it's really, really bad. But I'm just—I'm just so tired. Do I even care? I mean, of course I care. But I just—I just want to sleep."

"Let's go to sleep," Kevin says. Low, soothing. "But here— I'll stay on the line with you. Promise I won't hang up. Okay?"

Kevin has the kind of voice you can wrap around your body like a blanket, the kind of voice you could make a home out of.

"Okay," I say.

28.

It goes something like this:

We're in his room. The lamp next to his bed is on, because the sun sets way before 5:30 p.m. these days, and the light throws elongated, blurry shadows of his desk along the floor.

We're lying on our sides facing each other. His arm around my waist. My hand along the side of his shoulder.

Both of our shirts are on the floor.

"Kevin," I murmur, pulling away.

"Mmm," he says, pulling me back in.

I sit up—ignoring the noise of disapproval he makes from the back of his throat—because I really do want to say something to him, something about how I've never felt so vulnerable before in my life, how it's not just the fact that we're half-naked, or lying in bed together, how it's more than that, it's everything about this, being together, being so close, being a part of this moment right now with nothing other than his skin pressed against my skin and his hand in my hair. And I want him to know that even though it's true, I've never felt so vulnerable before in my life, I've also never trusted anyone like this. I've never trusted anyone the way I trust him right now.

But I never get around to saying all of those things. I never even get around to starting. Because when I sit up—between Kevin's disappointed noise and the moment his eyes fly open, irises bright and pupils dilated in the glare of the light—that's when I see them, running along the inside of his upper arm. Slightly raised. So pale the skin is almost pink.

Scars.

"Oh," I say.

Kevin sighs. It's pretty obvious what I'm looking at.

"I didn't know," I say.

"I never told you," Kevin says.

"I can't believe this is the first time I'm noticing," I say. "I mean we've done this—what, how many times?"

"You weren't looking," Kevin says. "A fact that I was perfectly content with."

He sits up, too, and grabs his shirt from off the floor. I guess I've ruined the mood.

"I don't know what to say."

"You don't need to say anything, Stella."

"But I—I want to say something. I want to say the *right* thing."

Kevin sighs, pulls his shirt over his head and onto his body. I get one more glimpse of the scars as he threads his arms through his sleeves, and then they disappear from view.

"You never…?" Kevin asks.

I shake my head.

"Well, that's good," he says. And then, with a bitterness I haven't heard in his voice since he told me about his mom that one afternoon: "Don't."

"Kevin…"

"I'm going to be honest with you, Stella," Kevin says. "Is that okay? Can I be honest with you for a sec here?"

I nod. The truth is, I'm afraid of what Kevin's about to say. What if he tells me that he still cuts sometimes, but makes me promise not to tell his mother? Would I be obligated to tell someone even though it would probably make Kevin hate me forever? Just thinking about that possibility makes my stomach lurch with helplessness.

"There was a period of time when I really hated myself, Stel. It sounds so stupid to say out loud, and I wish that I had a reason for you, some way to explain why I felt the way that I did. But I don't have a reason. I don't even have an excuse. I just really, really fucking hated myself, and I just—one day, I just did it. And I liked it, so I kept doing it, and then I couldn't stop, and honestly, I didn't even want to stop. Okay? I know that sounds bad. I know that *is* bad. But it's the truth."

"Okay," I say. And then, because I really, really don't know what else to say, I reach out and take Kevin's hand. He closes his eyes, but doesn't pull away.

"And I know I should have told you sooner, but I didn't want that to be what you thought of every time you looked at me. I wanted a chance to—I don't know, I guess I wanted a chance to be more than *that*."

Kevin waves his hands in the air. Then he flops down onto the bed and pulls the blanket over his face.

"Thank you for sharing that with me," I say. And is it

wrong that after all of that, after everything he just said, what I want more than anything in the world is just to kiss him? If I could just kiss him right now, then maybe, maybe that would be enough to convey everything that I'm thinking, everything that I can't find a way to put into words.

"You sound like my therapist," Kevin says, voice muffled. And then we snicker, because we both know it's true.

"Did you talk to him about it?" I ask.

"Sometimes," Kevin says.

"Did he help?"

"Sometimes," Kevin repeats.

"And your mom…?"

"She doesn't know," Kevin says flatly, and that's that.

I lie back down, get under the covers so that I'm next to him. Pull the blankets back down so that I can see his face again. Ignore his look of surprise as I drop a kiss on his collarbone.

"I don't know that I've felt that exact way," I say slowly. I'm choosing my words carefully. Part of me doesn't even want to say *anything*, because, well, kissing would be so much easier. But this is the time, and this is the right thing to do, and if I don't say something now, when will I?

"I don't know that I've ever felt that—that pure self-hatred, you know, just, like, sitting there hating myself. I think I just feel very hopeless sometimes. Like there's no point in getting out of bed, there's no point in going to class, there's no point in texting Lin, there's no point in eating, there's no point in— well, anything. And then, at that point, it's like there's this voice in my head that takes over, that starts screaming at me, *Stella, what the fuck are you doing, Stella, why the fuck aren't you at school, Stella, how the fuck are you going to pass history, Stella, you're ruining your parents' marriage,* and just on and on and on."

Kevin nods. He turns onto his side and starts tracing figure-eights on the side of my shoulder with his pointer finger.

This is one of those times when it feels like my chest might explode.

"I guess I should have told you more about this when we were talking on Katie's balcony on Halloween," I say. "I mean, we were already on the subject. But I didn't. Because…"

Our eyes meet, and the intensity makes me feel like I'm about to cry.

"But you were afraid," Kevin says.

I swallow. "Because I was afraid."

"I get that, Stella," he says.

A lot of people have said those words to me before. Karen, of course, because she's my therapist and she gets paid a hefty sum every week to try and make me feel understood. My mom, probably because Karen has told her that empathy is the foundation of any good relationship or something like that. Lin and Katie, because they really don't know what else to say.

But the thing is, I believe Kevin when he says it. I really do.

29.

That is the moment when I know that I have fallen in love.

31.

It is five degrees below freezing outside. The storm has left most of Connecticut without electricity and heat, there are trees uprooted in backyards and trash cans strewn across highways and we have not had school in two days. From where Kevin and I stand in the middle of his bedroom, we can hear the windows rattling throughout the house, the roof groaning under the weight of constant, ceaseless snowfall. There are two lit candles on his desk. It is the only light we have.

But I am not thinking about the storm.

"I wanted to do this at the right time," Kevin whispers. He hooks his index fingers through my belt loops and pulls me in, all the way in, so that I'm pressed up against him.

I pull his shirt off. Trace my fingers up the outside of his arm, then down the inside. Where the skin is smooth, new. So pale it almost glows in the candlelight.

"Stel," he says, and takes my hand in his. "Stella, Stella,

Stella. I have never felt this way about anyone before. You know that, right?"

I don't know what to say.

So I kiss him.

"Do you want this?" he breathes. And then: "Do you want *me*?"

The heat has not worked in over fourteen hours.

I have never felt warmer.

"Of course I do," I say.

And I mean it.

It really does seem very beautiful, at the time.

60. APRIL

We're close to the end.

We're in my room. I'm sitting at the foot of my bed, listening to Kevin shout at me, and I'm crying.

Kevin isn't crying. He's just angry. He's been angry for the better part of the last month.

There was a time when I'd be embarrassed to set the scene like that. When I'd try to say something less dramatic and emotional, something like, "We're having another one of our disagreements," or, "I don't know what's come over the two of us this time." But we've been fighting so much lately that, honestly, I'm numb to it. Yeah, Kevin and I are fighting again, and I'm a mess, just like I always am, and now it's 4:00 p.m. on a Tuesday and I'm sitting on my bed, being yelled at by my boyfriend and sobbing like this hasn't become a weekly routine. What of it?

"I feel like you think this isn't a big deal," Kevin says. "Like

I should just be able to pick myself up and get over it. Well, guess what, Stella? It's not that easy. And maybe if you tried a little harder to understand instead of spending all your time frolicking around with—"

"I'm not saying it's not a big deal!" I say, ignoring the second half of his comment. Snide remarks about me and Jeremy have become so common now that I barely register them.

"So what the *fuck*…" Kevin shouts. He lets the word hang in the air, runs his hand through his hair. There was a time when I found that habit so endearing.

"…are you saying?" Kevin finishes.

There was also a time when I always knew the right thing to say to Kevin. When I could always make him feel better. When I could always make him feel *good*.

"I'm just saying that it happened. That it happened and there's nothing you can do about it now, so what's the point of—"

"Oh, sorry," Kevin says. "I didn't realize that all of my feelings had to have a *point*. You'll have to teach me your ways, since you're so rational and put-together these days."

"That's not what I fucking meant!" I shout.

Something I've learned in the last months is that you can only feel crushed by sadness for so long before the pressure turns it into anger.

"That's exactly what you meant!" Kevin says.

"Kevin," I say. "Kevin, there are other ways to get out of Connecticut. There are other schools. There are plenty of people who—"

"Oh, shut *up*, Stella. I don't know why I came over here. Honestly, it's not like you ever have anything new to say."

"So *leave*," I say. "If I'm not helpful, if I don't understand how you feel, if I can't tell you anything you don't already know, get out of my house!"

And that's when Kevin picks up the math textbook on my desk and throws it at the window.

Which promptly shatters.

My first thought, because the brain works in mysterious ways, is that I really need that textbook in order to finish my homework for tomorrow.

"What the fuck?" I say.

Kevin doesn't respond.

I stand up. There's glass everywhere—all over the floor, scattered along the edge of the bed and probably some that's fallen out into my backyard along with the textbook. The neighbors have probably heard. My mother has *definitely* heard.

"What the fuck?" I repeat.

I'm angry now. I'm angry that Kevin is taking his feelings out on me, and I'm angry that I can't figure out the right thing to say to make him feel better, and I'm angry that he just threw my math textbook out my bedroom window, for God's sake. And I'm angry that now there's proof—proof of how fucked up this situation is, proof of how fucked up this *relationship* is. It's hard to wish away a shattered window.

"What am I supposed to tell my parents about this?" I say.

"Oh, who gives a shit?" Kevin says. "Tell them your boyfriend is a fucking psycho, for all I care."

"It wouldn't be a lie," I say.

Kevin scoffs. "I always liked that about you, you know that?" he says. Voice like acid. "Witty. You were always so witty."

I don't know what to say to that. So instead, I stare out the space where my window used to be. You can hear the birds clearly now, and the street noise is oddly loud.

I wonder if the neighbors can hear us yelling.

"It's too bad you're also such a bitch," Kevin says. And then he leaves.

32.

By the time we're a few days away from winter break, freedom is so close that everyone at Bridgemont just sort of collectively gives up on the semester. The ratio of homework assignments completed to homework assignments given plummets with astonishing velocity toward zero. My parents stop nagging me about my grades in order to nag each other about arrangements for Christmas dinner. And—the truest sign that it's almost vacation—teachers start filling class time with "educational" movies like *Dr. Strangelove* and *The Day After Tomorrow* because they can't be bothered to put together actual lesson plans.

Kevin, Yago and I have spent the better part of the last week binge-watching Netflix episodes while binge-eating Smartfood at Kevin's house instead of doing anything remotely resembling studying, but we're forced to make alternate arrangements on Thursday afternoon when Kevin informs us that his mother is in the process of repainting her basement art studio.

"The entire house smells like paint fumes," Kevin says as we all pile into his car after school. "Stel, can we go to yours instead?"

"Not unless your idea of a fun afternoon involves getting grilled by my mother over tea," I say.

"Yago?" Kevin says. "Feel like inviting us over?"

"Ugh," Yago says, next to me in the backseat. He unzips his backpack, pulls out rolling paper and a plastic bag filled with weed and starts rolling a joint. "I hate my house."

"Yago lives in Crystal Ridge," Kevin says, by way of explanation.

"You live in Crystal Ridge?" I say, dumbfounded.

"My parents live in Crystal Ridge," Yago says. "And I live with my parents, so I suppose that the answer to that question is yeah, I do live in Crystal Ridge."

Yago finishes rolling the joint, pulls out a lighter and takes a long, long drag, as if living in the nicest neighborhood in the Hartford area is a great burden to him. He exhales, and the entire car is flooded with the smell of weed.

"Fine," he finally says. "Let's go to Crystal Ridge."

"Thanks, Yago," Kevin says. He turns the key to start the engine, and the motor revs—but doesn't start.

"Hmm," Kevin says, and frowns. "That's not what's supposed to happen."

"Your car is a piece of shit," Yago says, now blowing smoke rings.

"I like this car," Kevin says. "It's got personality."

He turns the key again—*rev, rev,* nothing.

"It sure does," I say. "The personality of a crotchety old man."

Yago snickers. Kevin turns the key a third time and the engine finally roars to life.

"See? The car is perfectly fine," Kevin says. He shifts into Reverse and backs out of his parking space, ignoring the ominous thumping noises now emanating from the back.

By the time we get to Yago's house, the thumping—perhaps offended by Kevin's outright dismissal—has increased both in volume and in frequency. The car *thump-thump-thump*s as we get on the ramp for the highway, it *thump-thump-thump*s even louder when we take Exit 10 for Crystal Ridge and it *thump-thump-thump*s most insistently of all as Kevin shifts from third gear to first and we make our way down the neighborhood's winding, tree-lined streets.

"Kevin," I start to say, "I understand that it is *very important* to you to drive a stick shift, because, I don't know, that's what Sartre would drive or something, but it's actually very important to *me* to not die before I turn eighteen, because then I'll never make it out of Wethersfield. So could you please just—"

But my plea for Kevin to please, *please* get a new car already never makes it out of my mouth, because now we've pulled into Yago's driveway—practically the length of a street—and his house comes into view. And Yago's house is...not really a house at all. It's a freaking mansion.

"*This* is where you live?" I say.

Yago sighs and kills the joint.

The inside of Yago's house is pretty much exactly what you'd expect based on the outside of Yago's house, a fact that seems to fill Yago with an unhappiness so profound that even

Nietzsche might be impressed. "I thought you said your parents were just 'boring computer nerds,'" I say as Yago leads us into the foyer, past a gleaming kitchen twice the size of my bedroom, and up a flight of stairs. "Did they invent the computer? Is that what you meant?"

Yago takes us down a hallway on the second floor, past another staircase and then through a set of double doors that leads to another wing of the house with *yet more stairs.*

"How many sets of stairs does your house have, Yago?" I say. "And do they move around, like in Hogwarts?"

Yago doesn't respond.

"It's fine," I say. "Don't respond. Probably for the better, anyway. God forbid you get distracted and lead us down the wrong hallway and we get lost. It might be years before someone manages to find their way to us."

Finally—after what seems like half an hour of walking—Yago swings open the door to his bedroom. You can tell that he's tried to make it different from the rest of the house—the walls are covered in posters of rock bands and graphic novels instead of the oil paintings adorning the walls elsewhere, and there's a conspicuous lack of furniture other than his bed and desk—but nothing can really override the fact that his room is the size of a studio apartment and has a massive walk-in closet.

"All this time," I say. "All this time we've been hanging out at Kevin's when you have a closet that could eat his *entire room?*"

"I hate being here," Yago says. "My parents are never around, so it's always empty, and the house is so old that everything's always making weird noises—it's creepy."

"Who are you, Yago? Does anyone else know you live here?

God forbid Katie ever finds out—she'll make it her mission in life to get you to throw a party."

I walk over to his desk and start scanning his books (noticing, by the way, that his window overlooks two tennis courts. Who has tennis courts in their backyard?). There are a few graphic novels in the corner—including *Watchmen*, by Alan Moore, which I remember from freshman year English—and a stack of comic books. Other than that, most of his desk is covered in textbooks and homework assignments. There's also a pile of letters, the first of which is addressed to:

Barron Carter Evans IV
10 Ashboro Lane
Glastonbury, CT 06033

"Don't—" Yago says, but it's too late.

"Your name..." I start.

"Please don't," Yago pleads.

"...is Barron..."

"*Stella*," Yago whines.

"...Carter..."

"I think it's too late," Kevin says, casting Yago a sympathetic look.

"...Evans..."

"Technically, you already knew the *Evans* part," Kevin provides helpfully.

"The fourth?"

Yago—or should I say, Barron Carter "Yago" Evans IV— sighs deeply. "It's Yago," he says.

If this were any other time, any other situation, I might

take a moment to bask in the fact that for once, *I*, Stella Canavas, am not the person in the conversation who is desperate to melt into the ground from mortification. But this is no time for basking.

"No, it's not," I say. I hold the letter up and point to it with my free hand, as if its existence is news to Yago and Kevin. "It's Barron Carter Evans the fourth."

"Please stop repeating that," Yago says.

"Are you British?" I say. "I feel like it's one of those names that only makes sense if you're British. *Barron Carter Evans the fourth*," I say, now in a British accent.

Kevin snorts, then hastily rearranges his face into a solemn expression after Yago shoots him a nasty look.

"All this time, your real name has been one of those longstanding Bridgemont mysteries, you know, like whether or not the hidden classroom in the B wing of the Edgerton building actually exists, or what that horrible statue in front of the Pergis Quad is actually supposed to *be*. And everyone always figured it was something embarrassing like—oh, I don't know, *Apple*, or *West*, or something like that. And it's actually—"

"You don't need to say it again, Stella," Yago says. But I want to. Oh, how I want to.

"Barron-Carter-Evans-the-fourth?"

"My parents are suckers for tradition," Yago says.

"But why *Yago*?" I say. "Why not just go by Jason or Sam or Adam or Steven or anything else in the realm of normal, twenty-first-century men's names?"

Yago sighs again, then flops down into a desk chair. "When I was younger," he says, "it was always *Barron Carter Evans* this, or *Barron Carter Evans* that. *Barron Carter Evans, we are*

going to the country club to see your grandparents, and that's that.
Barron Carter Evans, keep your eyes closed when we say grace and
stop pouting. Everything was always so serious and official.
Even playing video games had to be this ridiculous, proper
affair: *Barron Carter Evans, sit up straight and stop manhandling*
that remote!

"And then one night—I must have been ten or eleven or
something like that—I was at this ridiculous dinner party
being called *Barron Carter Evans* over and over and over again,
listening to a bunch of old people in suits talk about Wall
Street and golf and other crap I didn't care about in the slightest, and I just couldn't take it anymore. I didn't want to be
Barron Carter Evans anymore. So I picked the most ridiculous
sound I could think of—which, to ten-year-old me, ended up
being *Yago*—and told everyone that that was my new name,
and they could either call me that or be ignored."

"Wow," I say. I look over at Kevin, who is scrolling through
something on his phone. He's heard this story before, I guess.

Yago shrugs.

"So then, to really drive the point home, you became a…
stoner?"

"I'm not a stoner," Yago says.

Kevin looks up from his phone. "That's news to me," he
says.

I decide to save my response—that anyone who has as
much advice to dispense about the distinction between *in-*
dica and *sativa* as Yago has definitely qualifies as a stoner—for
another day.

I turn back to the pile of letters. There's one in the stack
that's thicker than the other ones—printed on cream-colored

paper, and unexpectedly heavy in my hand as I pick it up. It's the kind of letter that screams OFFICIAL BUSINESS. The kind of letter that you definitely wouldn't expect to find on the desk of Yago Evans, perennially stoned resident weed dealer of Bridgemont Academy.

And it's also from Harvard University Office of Admissions.

"YOU GOT INTO HARVARD?" I screech.

"We couldn't have hung out at your place?" Yago says, turning to Kevin.

"Sorry, dude," Kevin says. But there's a bit too much of a smirk underneath the apologetic look he shoots Yago for it to be believable.

Yago turns to me. "Yes. I got into Harvard."

There's a few seconds during which the absurdity of this entire situation—the house, the name, the letter—is truly too much for me, and all I can do is turn from Yago to Kevin back to Yago, wide-eyed and slack-jawed.

"Well," I finally say, "congratulations."

"Thanks," Yago says. He manages to muster up a weak grin.

"Seriously," I say. "I know I don't sound very excited for you, because I'm still in shock over the fact that the Yago Evans we've all known, loved and turned to in our darkest, soberest times is actually a trust fund baby named Barron Carter Evans the fourth who lives in a mansion the size of a modest hotel and is going to Harvard next fall. But that's awesome, Yago, really."

"It's not that big of a deal," Yago says. "Everyone from my family going back, like, six generations has gone to Harvard.

There hasn't ever been a Barron Carter Evans that *hasn't* gone to Harvard. They couldn't not let me in."

"Oh, shut up," Kevin says. He rolls his eyes and looks at me. "No one realizes that Yago is actually really smart because of the whole—well, being named Yago and selling weed thing. But he's taken every AP Bridgemont offers. If we had class rankings, he'd definitely be valedictorian. And he's the only reason I passed honors chemistry."

"Yago taught you about covalent and ionic bonds?" I say.

"Yago let me copy his homework. I still don't know jack shit about covalent and ionic bonds."

Now that the shock has started to wear off, what Kevin is saying actually makes sense. Lin did mention that he was in AP Lit with her, and there was that one time that I talked to him in study hall while he was doing homework for AP Physics...

The realization hits me like a ton of bricks.

"Oh, fuck," I say.

Kevin and Yago both look startled by my sudden change in demeanor.

"Oh, *fuck*," I repeat. I grab my coat off Yago's bed and start putting it on.

"What's going on?" Kevin says.

"When did you get this letter?" I ask Yago. Before he can answer, I pick the envelope up off Yago's desk and look at it myself.

"Huh?" Yago says. "Stella, what's going on?"

December 08, 2016, it says. Eleven days ago.

"Oh, *shit*," I say. "Kevin, we have to go. We have to go right now."

I grab my backpack and turn to him, feeling the panic rising inside my chest.

"See, this is why I don't want people finding out," Yago says. "Everyone's going to get all freaked out and start acting weird around me. That's the problem with having a name like Barron Carter with a numeral at the end. No one feels like they can hang out with you like you're a normal human being."

"Right," Kevin says. "Which is why you decided to go by Yago and sell drugs. Nothing remotely conspicuous there."

"This isn't about your name!" I say, pulling Kevin out of Yago's room and down the hallway. I grab his jacket on the way out and dump it into his hands.

"Um, okay," Yago says, trailing behind us.

I speed-walk furiously until we reach a fork in the hallway, where I spin right, then turn back to the left. Was this the point where we turned right and went through the double doors? Or was this the point where we turned left and passed the room with all the bookshelves? I look helplessly at Yago, who arches an eyebrow at me.

"I'm sorry," I say. "I didn't mean to be rude. I just—I really have to go. I'll explain in a second, but could you just— I mean, these hallways are just—what I'm trying to say is, where do we—"

Yago points down the hallway on the right.

I take a deep breath and start walking again. Watch as Kevin puts his jacket on and takes his car keys out of his pocket. He gives me a look: *What is wrong with you?*

"Yago," I say, as we go back through the double doors, down the stairs, past the kitchen and into the foyer. "Congratulations on getting into Harvard. Seriously. That's amazing. And I promise I won't tell anyone about your real name, mostly because I don't think anyone will believe me. But I have to go now, because you found out about Harvard eleven days ago, which means Lin probably found out about Brown eleven days ago, which means that either all of her dreams have come true or she's totally crushed, and I totally forgot. I just completely forgot."

"Oh," Kevin says.

"Oh," Yago repeats.

I pull Kevin out the front door.

33.

It takes twenty minutes for Kevin to drive from Yago's house to Lin's. The car—perhaps out of respect for the gravity of the situation—actually doesn't thump at all on the way there, but I still spend the entire ride terrified that we're going to break down in the middle of the highway, and then who knows when we'd make it to Lin's? (Although, a voice in the back of my head reminds me, it's already been eleven days. What difference is another few hours really going to make?)

"Should I stay?" Kevin asks, shifting into Park in front of Lin's house.

"I don't know," I say. "I mean, if Lin and I end up hanging out for a while, I can just text you and then you can go and I'll have my mom pick me up or something. But if it goes poorly…"

I don't finish the sentence, and I don't have to. "Got it," Kevin says. He switches the engine off and pulls his keys out of the ignition. "I'll just wait here, then, and study for my biology final, I guess. Do you think I can learn all twelve systems of the human body before second period tomorrow?"

"Well, it's only four-thirty," I say. "If you do one per hour, you might even be able to get a couple hours of sleep."

"Sleep," Kevin repeats. Then, drily: "That would be the nervous system."

I grab my backpack from the backseat and open the car door, but before I can swing my legs out of the car, Kevin grabs my shoulder. "Hey," he says.

I turn to face him. "Kevin, I really need to go," I say. The panic has been swelling and swelling inside me and I'm starting to feel like I might throw up from a combination of anxiety and terror and guilt. Mostly guilt.

"I know," Kevin says softly. He hesitates for a second, then leans in and kisses me. Like, *really* kisses me. As if I'm not the worst friend in the world for totally forgetting about Lin's Brown application and the worst girlfriend in the world for making Kevin drive me across town the afternoon before his biology final.

"I just wanted to say good luck," he murmurs.

When he pulls back, he's smiling.

"So—good luck," he says.

"Thanks," I say. And I realize as I step out of the car that despite everything that's happening, despite everything that's about to happen, I'm smiling, too.

I count four seconds between when I ring the doorbell—fingers crossed behind my back, just in case the universe is feeling benevolent today—and when Lin's mom opens the door. Her entire face lights up when she sees me, which, of course, makes me feel like a complete and utter piece of shit. "Stella!" she says. "So good to see you!"

"Hi, Dr. Chen," I say. "Is Lin home?"

"Of course Lin is home," Dr. Chen says. "Studying hard for finals, you know how she is. Come in, come in. Do you want to stay for dinner?"

"Uh," I say.

Lin's mom ushers me through the door and hands me a pair of slippers.

"You girls let me know, okay? I'm making dumplings. Lin is upstairs in her room."

"Thanks, Dr. Chen," I say. I take my shoes off and put on the slippers, and then I rush up the stairs and down the hallway to Lin's room. The door is closed, but I can hear soft instrumental music playing in the room. Lin's study music.

I knock twice.

"Yeah?" Lin says.

I push the door open.

"Mom, I can't really talk right now," Lin says, spinning around in her chair. "I'm worki—oh. Hi."

"Hi," I say.

I wait for her to ask me what I'm doing there or to tell me to leave, but the silence stretches on and Lin doesn't do either of those things. She just looks at me, expression slightly pinched but otherwise inscrutable.

"I texted you," I say. "Fifteen minutes ago. To let you know I was coming. I didn't mean to interrupt."

Lin gestures across the room, where her phone is plugged into a charger.

"Oh," I say.

Silence fills the room.

"Lin. I am so sorry," I say. "And I wish—I wish I had something else to say, you know? I wish I had a reason or—or anything that could remotely justify what I did—or didn't do, I guess—and I wish there was something, anything else I could say other than I'm sorry, but I just—"

"I didn't get in," Lin says abruptly.

"Oh," I say.

"I didn't even get deferred. I just got flat-out rejected. Which is good in some ways, I guess. It's better to know."

"Oh," I say again. And then: "I'm sorry."

Lin shrugs. She spins her desk chair back around and turns her music up. "You didn't have to come here, you know," she says, her back to me. Her voice is calm, almost alarmingly casual. "You could've just texted and asked."

"What?" I say. "I *wanted* to come, Lin. I didn't want to just send you a text. I wanted to apologize here, in person. I wanted to see you."

Lin snorts. "Yeah? Could've fooled me there."

The comment stings, but what stings more is how matter-of-fact she sounds. Like: *Yeah, Stella, you fucked up, but I don't even care enough to be angry about it.*

"Lin," I say, "I deserved that, and I *know* I deserved that. And if you're mad at me, I totally get it. You should be mad at me! I royally screwed up. I've been the worst friend in the world. But you have to know that it's not because I didn't *care*, right? You're still—you're still one of my two best friends, and you always have been, and you always will be—well, until you finally decide that you can't stand to be best friends with someone who hasn't read *East of Eden*, anyway. I fucked up because I'm an idiot, not because I didn't care. Because I did. And I still do."

In the car ride over here, I pictured a thousand versions of this conversation, each more depressing and disastrous than the last. Every gut-wrenching variation involved some combination of Lin yelling at me, Lin bursting into angry tears, Lin throwing stuff around her room, Lin throwing stuff *at* me, all while I apologized, over and over again. But now that I'm actually here, now that Lin and I are face-to-face for the first time in weeks, now that Lin's told me the news I should have known about a week and a half ago, I'm the one falling apart. It's my voice shaking. I'm on the verge of tears, and Lin just turns her desk chair back around and looks at me evenly, coolly.

"People don't just *forget* about the people they really care about," Lin says.

"I didn't forget about *you!*" I say.

Lin snorts—the most emotion I've gotten out of her so far. "Stella, I've been talking about getting into Brown for the last two years. And it's the *only* thing I've talked about for the last, like, four months, not that you've been around for two of those. I slaved over those essays. I spent hours tweaking individual words on my application just in case the difference between saying 'driven' and 'motivated' was enough to make or break my chances—lot of good that turned out to be. The point is, you knew how much this meant to me. *Everyone* knew how much this meant to me. Even *Bobby* bought me this stupid box of chocolates after Katie told him I didn't get in, because *even Bobby fucking Leveux* knew how devastated

I would be. If you hadn't forgotten about me, you wouldn't have forgotten about Brown."

"Lin," I say. I'm starting to sound desperate, I'm starting to sound pathetic, I don't care. I thought I was prepared for this—for the conversation to go badly, for Lin to be angry with me—but now that it's happening, I feel like someone has grabbed on to the inside of my chest and started twisting. It hurts, it really, actually, physically hurts.

"Lin," I say again, choked up. "You have to know that I didn't mean to forget."

"Yeah," Lin says. "But you didn't *try* very hard to remember, either, did you?"

There's not much I can say to that.

"And you know what, Stella?" Lin says. She hits the space bar on her laptop and cuts the music off. I start to wish that she would yell, I really do. If Lin were yelling, I wouldn't have to listen to myself desperately trying to choke back tears and failing.

"It's not just the fact that you forgot the thing that I've worked the hardest for and cared the most about in my entire pathetic life," she says. "It's about the fact that you just—you just got yourself a boyfriend and peaced the fuck out of our lives! Who does that, Stella? We make fun of Katie for being boy crazy, but she's always texted us back when we needed her, she's always showed up when we needed her, she remembered December 10 even though she doesn't give two shits about Brown, because she knew it was a big deal to me—the *biggest* deal to me—and that made it a big deal for her, too. At the end of the day, I know that Katie will be there for me, regardless of what wayward Bridgemont athlete she's managed to stumble into this time. Meanwhile, you find some pseudo-intellectual hipster who thinks that he's way too cool for the rest of us just because he drives a stick shift and disappear off the face of the planet."

I don't know what to say. I don't know if there's anything I *can* say. I don't want to be crying, but I'm crying. I don't want to be angry at myself, but I'm angry at myself. I don't want to be angry at Lin, but for some reason I'm angry at her, too.

"You shouldn't take your feelings out on Kevin," I finally say. Because this is my fault, not his, and Lin should know that.

Lin stares at me. "All that," she finally says, "and what you get out of that whole thing is that I shouldn't take my anger out on Kevin?"

"I said that I'm sorry," I say. I have to say the next sentence in two breaths because I can't make it through the first time I try. "I really—I really am."

"I think you should leave," Lin says flatly.

And what am I supposed to say to that? "No"? "I'm sorry," again, ad nauseum, until she physically kicks me out? I can't just stand here and cry; I can't think of anything else to say; I don't know how to fix this situation and the person who I would ask for advice is ten feet away from me, watching me fall apart with an icy dispassion.

"I know," I say. I'm stuttering. Voice barely above a whisper. "But the problem is, I don't want to leave."

It's a problem without a solution. I am asking her to help me. Please, Lin. Please.

Lin shrugs. She looks out her window at the car parked on the curb outside her house. "Would hate to keep Kevin waiting," she says, and turns back to her computer.

34.

So I leave.

35.

"*Stel*," Kevin says, the moment I've gotten in the car.

"I'm fine," I say. But I'm not. I'm crying, I can barely breathe, I'm a mess. I'm even more of a mess than I was three minutes ago in Lin's room, mostly because Dr. Chen called out, "Too busy for dumplings tonight?" from the kitchen as I made my way down the stairs, and I couldn't even bring myself to respond.

"Stella…" he says quietly.

"Drive," I say. "Drive, just drive, let's go somewhere."

"Do you want me to take you home?" Kevin says.

"*God*, no," I choke out.

"Okay," Kevin says. "I won't take you home."

He starts rubbing circles on my back, the motion rhythmic, soothing. And for some reason, all of a sudden, out of *nowhere*, I am completely and utterly consumed by the desire to push Kevin into a wall and kiss him. Furiously. Stupidly.

"Let's go to your place," I say.

"The paint," Kevin says.

"Who gives a shit? I don't need those brain cells, anyway."

Kevin drums his fingers on the wheel, unsure, but then takes another look at me and seems to decide that I'm in no state to be argued with. "Sure, Stel," he says, starting the engine. "We can go to my place."

Kevin is right. The second we walk into his house, it feels like I'm being suffocated with the smell of paint. But honestly, I don't mind. The strength of it—the sheer toxicity—is welcome. Relieving, almost. It's hard to think about how I've thrown away my best friend of two and a half years when I can barely breathe.

I drop my backpack and my coat onto the floor as he closes his bedroom door, then walk up to him and press my lips into his. Forceful. Desperate.

"Stel…?" he says.

I don't have to open my eyes to hear the surprise in his voice.

"Shh," I say.

I back up toward the bed and pull his shirt off. I don't know what the fuck is wrong with me. I just need—I need to touch him. I need him to touch *me*.

"Don't want to think anymore," I say, pulling him onto the bed and under the covers. I take my shirt off, too, and fling it across the room. His eyes are wide, flickering between my face and my chest like he can't decide where to look, like he can't decide where he *should* be looking. "Just touch me, Kevin, c'mon," I say.

"Stella," Kevin says. He pulls back slightly, but I can still feel the heat radiating off his body, a few centimeters away.

He's so close that the smell of his shampoo is starting to over-power the smell of the paint. It's intoxicating, being so close to him. It always has been.

"This feels wrong," he says. But his voice is low and catches as he says the words and his eyes are bright, bright blue and I never thought it was possible to want someone like this, to be with someone who could make me feel so unlike myself.

"It's not wrong," I say. I reach out and place a hand over his chest, feel his heartbeat pulsing through the gaps between my fingers.

He closes his eyes. I count nine beats before he opens them again.

"I don't want to take—I mean, you're upset. We shouldn't."

He has one hand resting against the small of my back, the other along the side of my face. He pulls it away and his fingers are wet. Am I still crying? I can't even tell. I want to drown in him.

"Please," I whisper. "You're the only thing that gets me out of my head."

I hold my breath.

He bites his lip.

I can barely smell the paint anymore.

He runs his hand down my cheek again. This time, it comes away dry.

I thread my fingers through his. Breath still caught some-where inside my lungs.

Then he leans in and kisses me hard.

And I breathe.

57.

The problem, you see, is that he's locked the door.

"Kevin," I say. My voice is shaking. I've been outside the bathroom door for half an hour now, begging him to open it, alternating between kneeling when I'm too exhausted to stand and standing when I'm too desperate to stay kneeling. As if throwing my entire body weight against the door will make it open somehow. As if I can press myself into the wall and find myself on the other side through sheer force of will.

"Kevin," I repeat, after the door remains a) locked, b) solid, and c) between the two of us. "If you don't open the door, I'm going to call your mother."

"My mom doesn't give a shit," Kevin says. His voice is sharp, bitter.

"Kevin, *please*," I say. I have nothing else. I don't have the energy to think of something better and I don't have the pride to keep from begging. I don't even remember what this fight started over. Was it Columbia? Was it Jeremy? Was it the fact that my parents have forbidden him from coming into the house?

"Please open the door," I say. "Please don't—"

My voice cracks.

"Please don't do this to me," I finish. So quietly I wonder if it's even possible for Kevin to have heard the words.

"Don't do this to you?" Kevin says.

He's heard the words.

"Don't do this to *you*?" he repeats, and I can hear the anger rising in his voice.

"That's not what I meant, Kevin," I say. "You know that's not what I meant. Please don't be upset—"

"I'm not upset," Kevin says. His voice goes totally flat, which is even worse. The last time he talked like this, it took two weeks for him to even *look* at me again. "I'm not upset, because I don't care. It's fine, I've accepted it. I'm not good enough for you and I'm not good enough for my mom and you know what? That's fucking *fine*. I guess I was good enough for Columbia, not that that did any fucking good in the end."

"You *are* good enough for me," I say. "Kevin. You are the *only one* who has ever been good enough for me. You are—you are *better* than me. I don't know what the fuck I would do without you. You know that."

"But Jeremy—"

"I DON'T GIVE A SHIT ABOUT JEREMY, KEVIN," I shout.

There's no response.

"I *know* what you think," I say. "I know. And I'm sorry that you think that, but I've told you a thousand times that

I don't care about him, I really don't, and I know you don't believe me, and you know what, Kevin, I don't even *care* that you don't believe me. I'll tell you a thousand more times, I really will, I just—I don't know—"

I can't finish the sentence.

"Stel…" Kevin says softly.

See, this is the thing. This is how it always goes. He gets angry, or I get angry. The other one of us gets desperate, starts crying, gets on their knees, begs. And then guilt drives out the anger. Kevin suddenly remembers that he loves me. I think of the first time I stayed the night at his house, way back in the fall, when the trees still had leaves and every sentence that came out of Kevin's mouth seemed like a revelation. Kevin remembers what it feels like to hold me, and I remember that I've never felt safer than when I'm in his arms. We have done this a thousand times. I know that the tenderness is as temporary as the flash of anger that preceded it, but I can't help but let myself soak in it, cling on to it like a drowning man to a rope. Everything will be okay if Kevin talks to me like that.

And then I realize that now Kevin is crying, too.

"I'm really sorry," he says.

"*I'm* really sorry," I say. "About Columbia. About me."

I can hear his scoff through the door. "Stella, you haven't done anything. And you know that. And I know that. I just—sometimes I just lose my mind. I don't know, it feels like Columbia was the only thing I was looking forward to for so long, and it could have happened, it really could have, if it weren't for the fact that—"

"Shut up and open the door, Kevin," I say. "I want to kiss you."

A beat of silence.

And then, very quietly: "I'm afraid to."

"You're afraid to open the door?"

"Stella…"

"Kevin, come on. It's not like—"

"Stel."

Something about the tone of his voice stops me short.

"Sometimes I get… Sometimes I feel very out of control, Stel," Kevin says. It's the tone of voice he uses when he's considering every word very carefully before he says it. "And sometimes, when that happens, I do really stupid things."

"You remember who you're talking to, right?" I say.

"I don't… I don't want you to be mad at me."

"I'm not going to be mad at you. I'm just tired of talking to you through this stupid door—oh."

Kevin swings the door open midsentence, and it takes me a moment to register that anything is wrong. I mean, it's just Kevin. His brown hair is slightly messier than usual, but still normal, and his eyes are red and puffy, but it's not like we haven't been there before, and his T-shirt is wrinkled, and his—

"Oh my God," I say.

"Sometimes, I just—I hate myself," Kevin says. He is explaining himself to me. He can see the shock on my face and he wants to make me feel better. He is acting like the bloody razor sitting on the sink and the cuts running up and down the inside of his left arm are things that are actually quite reasonable, if you really think about it—

"…And I just need to—I need to put all of that anger somewhere, you know, I need to just—I need to just get rid of it somehow. I need to make it stop. I'm not trying to kill my-self," Kevin adds hastily, as if that makes everything better.

"Why," I say, "why does it sound like you are trying to convince me that this is no big deal?"

I feel strangely, perhaps even *alarmingly*, calm. I think that my brain has officially exceeded some scientific threshold of panic and I've lost the ability to experience that particular emotion for the next twenty-four hours.

"I'm not saying that it's not a big deal," Kevin says. "I'm just saying that it's a thing that happens sometimes, and I don't want you to be worried about it."

"I'm worried about it," I say flatly.

Kevin bites his lip.

"I thought—I thought you said you stopped," I say.

"I had stopped," Kevin says.

"This could *kill* you," I say.

"No, it couldn't. I don't cut that deep, I promise."

"You really think that *'I don't cut that deep, I promise,'* makes me feel *any* better? Are you insane?"

I guess I was wrong about that panic threshold.

"Look, just please don't tell anyone about this," Kevin says.

"Kevin, I—I have to. I *have* to. You get that, don't you?"

There are droplets of blood along the cuts, shockingly red against the pale skin of his inner arm. A few of them slide down the inside of his arm and leave faded streaks behind them.

"You don't have to," Kevin says. He cups my chin and lifts my head back up so that I'm looking away from his arms, away from the razor, away from the blood. At his eyes. Blue and red-rimmed. His eyelashes are wet.

"If this were me," I say, "you would tell my parents. You would tell Katie. You would tell *someone*. I know you would, Kevin, and *you* know you would, too."

"I wouldn't," Kevin says fiercely. "Not if you didn't want me to."

"How can you say that?" I say. I make it halfway through the sentence and start crying again. Because I need to tell someone. Because I know I can't. Because there is exactly one person in this stupid, fucked-up world who needs me, who *really* needs me right now, and I can't do jack shit to help him. Because half the time, *I'm* the reason why he's upset in the first place.

"I wouldn't tell anyone," Kevin insists. He blinks, and when he opens his eyes again, there are tears trailing down his cheeks. "Not if you didn't want me to."

"How can you say that?" I repeat. Hysterical, this time. I bury my face in my hands because I need to get it together, I don't want Kevin to see me like this, stop crying, Stella, *Jesus*, but then Kevin pulls my hands away and wraps his arms around me, pulls me in until I'm crying into his shirt, until all I can smell is the scent of his body, until it's dark all around and my eyes are squeezed shut and he's everywhere. There's going to be blood on my shirt, but I don't care.

"I wouldn't tell anyone if you didn't want me to because I'd love you, Stella," Kevin says again. His voice is raspy. I can feel the vibrations in his chest when he speaks.

"Even if you couldn't love yourself," he finishes.

58.

So I don't tell anyone.

37.

It wasn't always that bad, of course. The first time Kevin and I fight, the week after winter break, the experience is so new and unexpected that a part of me is excited by the novelty of it all. It starts over something so insignificant, and then escalates so quickly, that it's not until the immediate aftermath—not until after Kevin has walked out of my room, leaving a trail of swears behind him and slamming the door as he goes—when I start to react to what has just happened. Of course, then all of the feelings hit me at once: by the time I hear the front door slam a few seconds later, my stomach hurts and my chest is so tight that it's hard to breathe and I can feel the tears starting to well up behind my eyes.

It's like every nerve in my body is suddenly flooded by panic. All I can think is, *What the fuck have you done, Stella?* And, *Why did you do that, Stella?* And, *You've really gone and ruined things this time, haven't you?* I replay Kevin walking out of the room over and over and over again, picture the look of disgust that he throws me on his way out, think about the possibility that he's never going to talk to me again and feel like I might throw up. And I know that it all sounds so ridiculous and dramatic, and that I should be smart enough to understand that feelings like that aren't rational. But in the moment, I don't care about what's rational. In the moment, the only things that I know are that Kevin is gone, and that I *need* him. I really do.

So I call him. I take long, deep breaths, I feel the tears starting to run down my face, I tell myself that it's going to be fine, he's going to pick up, one ring, two rings—

"What?" Kevin's voice snaps, and I've never been so happy to hear someone address me so rudely.

"Come back," I say.

Kevin hangs up.

My stomach twists. The tears start coming down harder, and I can't get through a breath without gasping.

That look of disgust. It kills me to think about it.

I unlock my phone. Redial his number.

He picks up on the third ring this time. "Look, Stella," he says. "I don't really want to talk to you right now, okay? Just leave me alone."

"I can't," I say.

I actually don't think I could.

Kevin hangs up again.

In the next half hour, I call Kevin ten more times. Each time, the call goes to voice mail, and each time, I hate myself a little bit more. In that half hour, and for the rest of the day, and through the rest of the week, I can think of nothing other than Kevin. I can think of nothing other than how good things were, the color of his eyes, the way he talked about Camus, what it felt like to be close to him, how I might never feel that way again.

By the time Kevin shows up at my locker three days later with open arms and an apologetic look on his face and a letter so sweet that reading it actually makes me cry, I've barely eaten anything at dinner for the past few days, and the only reason I've eaten lunch is because Katie threatens to tell the school guidance counselor if I don't.

Of course, by the time Kevin shows up at my locker three days later with open arms and an apologetic look on his face, none of that matters. Because we're okay again.

All that, over a fight that went like this.

36.

"You should stay over Friday night," Kevin says.

"I can't," I say. "I've 'slept over at Katie's' three times in the last four weekends. They're going to get suspicious."

"Aren't you and Katie best friends?"

"Well, yes. But I never used to sleep over at her house because—well, I don't know. It just wasn't something we did. And it's weird if I start doing it every weekend all of a sudden."

"Okay, sure," Kevin says, going back to his philosophy reading.

"Don't do that," I say.

"Don't do what?" Kevin says.

"Don't—like—don't get upset. Don't be passive aggressive. It's not my fault my parents aren't like your mom."

"I'm not upset," Kevin says. In a tone of voice that screams: *I am very upset.*

"You're clearly upset."

"I'm just trying to do my reading, Stella."

"Kevin, please."

Kevin snaps his book shut and glares at me. "Look. I just wanted to spend time with you. I only ever want to spend time with you, which is why I always ask you if you want to come over on Friday nights. Because we barely see each other at school, and you're always busy with homework after we get out of school, and I just think it's a nice thing, okay? I like being with you. But if you don't want to spend time with me, then that's fucking *fine*. I'm tired of being the one who's always asking."

Then he goes back to reading.

"I feel like you're being unfair," I say quietly.

This time, Kevin snaps his book shut and throws it onto the floor. "What part of that is unfair, Stella?" he says. "Tell me, because I'd really like to know. Is it the part where I want to spend time with you? Or the part where I said that I like being with you? Or the part where I said that if you don't feel the same way, then I'm fine with it? What the *fuck* about any of that could *possibly be unfair?*"

This is the first time that Kevin has yelled around me, and there's something oddly captivating about it: the way his voice gets faster, lower, the way his eyes flash, the way he throws his arms around and starts to speak with his entire body. There is something sick about this, I know, but I can't help but think that the way Kevin looks right now is like a darker, fun-house mirror version of the way he looks when he talks about de Beauvoir, or daydreams about going to Columbia, or reads his notes from Dr. Mulland's lectures out loud. It's the way he talks about things that he's passionate about.

I am not the type of person who is careless with my words, I think, and I remember that intensity, the way everything Kevin says manages to *burn* somehow.

"Or just don't respond," Kevin says. "That's fine, too."

He puts his book into his backpack and grabs his coat from off my bed.

"Are you leaving?" I say.

"You're tired of being bothered and I'm tired of bothering you," he says.

"I'm not bothered!" I say. "Kevin, you're being ridiculous."

Which is, of course, the worst possible thing that I could say right now. But he is. He *is* being ridiculous, and there's a naive part of me that hopes that if I just tell him that—well, he'll listen. Because I'm right.

"Great," Kevin says. "What a fucking supportive girlfriend I have."

"Being supportive of someone doesn't mean supporting someone when they're being *unreasonable*," I say. "It means that—"

But I never finish my thought. Because that's when Kevin says, "Oh, fuck off, Stella," and walks out of the room.

But that's how it always was, with Kevin. We were so compatible, right up until one of us was in tears, until we were shouting at each other, until both of us were swearing up and down that the entire relationship was a mistake and we never should've gotten together in the first place. We were perfectly stable, until someone made one, stupid comment that landed the wrong way, and that one comment led to one more stupid comment that also landed the wrong way, and on and on until both of us were furious but neither of us could remember the comment that started the fight in the first place.

Everything was always so good, is what I'm saying, until it suddenly wasn't.

39.

This time, I suppose that it really is all my fault.

"I feel like you don't take me seriously as an intellectual," Kevin says.

"We're teenagers, Kevin. We can't even legally drink alcohol. You can't be a serious intellectual until you can purchase alcohol. I'm pretty sure that's Jean-Paul Sartre, from *Being and Nothingness*."

"You literally just made that up, Stella," Kevin says.

"Everything in *Being and Nothingness* is made up, Kevin! Just because it was made up by a French guy with a hyphenated first name doesn't make it less made up! In fact, every single book we've read in this class is *equally made up* as what I just said! And everything you say about those books is made up, too! We're all just making shit up!"

I watch as Kevin's expression morphs from one of shock to one that I can't actually read, which is never a good sign. An expression I can't read means that Kevin is thinking, which means that Kevin is *stewing*, which means it's only a matter of time until he gets quiet and mad, or loud and mad, or just leaves.

I should say something, I know, and try to fix this situation before it gets out of hand. I should say, *Kevin, I'm sorry I zoned out two minutes into your fifteen-minute lecture on Beckett and the epistemology of existence, or whatever it is* Waiting for Godot *is actually about. In my defense, I have yet to actually* read Waiting for Godot, *which made your thoughts—which I'm sure were profound and insightful as always—a bit difficult to follow.*

But I can't bring myself to say the words, due in large part to the unfortunate fact that I am not, in fact, really that sorry. Mostly I'm just tired. I'm tired of talking about the meaning of life and the futility of existence and how everything in Bridgemont is cheap and shallow and how much Kevin can't wait to get out of here in a few months. Kevin has been so angsty lately—over whether or not he's going to get into Columbia, over the two of us not spending enough time together, over the fact that he decided to do the reading for next week's class ahead of time and, guess what, Godot never fucking showed up. I miss the days when the two of us actually *laughed* about things, things like dumb modern artwork and the state of his car and Yago's name.

"I thought you appreciated these sorts of things," Kevin says quietly.

He starts putting books into his backpack. Guilt and exhaustion battle it out in my mind: Should I say something? Should I let him go?

"If you didn't want to talk about it, you could've just said something, Stel," Kevin says.

He puts his coat on and heads toward the door.

Exhaustion wins. I let him go.

46.

"How are things going with Kevin?" Katie asks me one day at lockers. Katie still sits with Lin during lunch—which is fine, because I'm usually in the library doing homework—but she makes a point to text me every few days. She still sits next to me in history class and scrawls snarky comments in the margins of my notes. We have brunch sometimes.

Katie is a better friend than I deserve.

"Stella?" Katie says, when I don't respond. "Are things okay?"

I think of the yelling. The scene in my room a few weeks ago. The scene in the diner a few days ago. How far behind on my homework I am. How I really should be talking about this in therapy every week, but the last thing I want to bring up to Karen is how my relationship is going up in flames and that this entire thing was a terrible idea and that she was right all along.

There's concern in Katie's eyes—genuine concern—which somehow makes it all worse.

Maybe Lin told her about what happened at Joe's. Maybe Becca Windham told her what happened at Joe's. Or maybe her fucking *parents* told her, I don't know. They probably talked about it at book club: *Oh, that poor Stella really needs to learn to love herself. I knew that Kevin boy was trouble—didn't we all?*

I imagine the Bridgemont moms sitting in the living room of some boring, nondescript house that looks exactly like the house of every other Bridgemont mom at the table. The concern dripping from their voices. The exaggerated sympathy etched across their faces. Their pity.

"Oh, they're fine," I say.

40.

My dad comes home for the first time since winter break the day after Kevin and I fight about *Being and Nothingness*. That night, my mom bakes lasagna and the three of us have dinner as a family. The conversation goes like this:

"How's school going, Stella?"

"Fine."

"Getting good grades?"

"They're fine."

"Do you need help with any of your homework?"

"I'm all right, but thanks, Dad."

He's still at home the next day, and the first floor of the house becomes so awkward that I claim period cramps and spend the entire evening in bed, waiting for the inevitable storm.

The third night after my dad shows up again, I'm trying to do an entire twenty-question problem set on Riemann sums the night before it's due. At nine-thirty, I finish problem #10. At ten, the storm breaks.

"Stella doesn't have time to add an SAT course to the list of things on her plate right now, Tom," my mom says.

"The SAT is one of the most important components of the college application, and I've barely heard Stella mention it. Isn't she registered to take the exam in March? She'll make time."

I put my pencil down and drop my forehead against my desk. I know how this ends, and it's not with me finishing my problem set before fourth period tomorrow morning.

"Okay," my mom says. "If you want to register her for an SAT class, be my guest. But knowing Stella, she's not going to go, and then the only thing that will have changed come March is that we'll have wasted a couple thousand dollars."

"Do you really have so little faith in our daughter that you think she'll skip the classes?" my father says.

"Do *you* really have so little faith in our daughter that you think she needs the classes in the first place?" my mom fires back.

"I thought you were a proponent of proactive parenting," my dad says. "Isn't that what you always say to me?"

"I guess I just got tired of proactively parenting alone," my mom says.

I put my head between my hands and make a last-ditch effort to focus on question #11—*please define the integral of ln x dx between 0 and 2e as a Riemann sum*—but I can't do it. I'm just so worn down by it all. The arguments. The fighting. There's this stress that seems to permeate every square inch of the house.

And then I think about Kevin. I think about how I don't feel that dread when he's with me, about how being with

Kevin makes me feel like I'm in a universe far, far away from my parents, who can never agree on the best way to fix their daughter, and from Lin, who was right when she said that I'd been a terrible friend, and from my own thoughts. And I think about the other day, when we fought over *nothing* and I just let him walk away. I didn't even try to get him to stay.

I can't take it anymore. I change out of my pajamas. Get my backpack. And walk downstairs, straight into the kitchen, where my mom is sitting at the dinner table with her head in her hands and my dad is waving a pen around in the air.

"I'm going to Katie's," I announce. "I can't sleep."

For a second, the two of them just look at me. There is a part of me that can't help but feel satisfied at their shocked expressions. *That's right*, I think. *I haven't been sleeping. I am NEVER ACTUALLY SLEEPING.*

"We're about to go to bed," my mom says, looking guilty.

"I'm going to Katie's," I repeat.

"Stella," my dad says. "We're very sorry that we've kept you up, and we promise that it won't happen again."

(Bullshit, I think. It always happens again.)

"It's past ten," he continues, "and your mother is right that we should all go to sleep. Perhaps it would be better if—"

"I'm *GOING TO KATIE'S*," I say.

Silence around the dinner table.

It's funny. This is the first time we've all been together around the dinner table in months, and *this* is the occasion.

I'm just about to say, "So it's settled, then," and get my bike when my mom speaks.

"Okay," she says.

"*What?*" my dad says.

"What?" I repeat.

"I get it," she says. "You need some air. You need to get away. I understand that."

"You do?" I say.

Even my dad looks stunned into silence.

My mom smiles a little bit, but it's not really a smile, and then she gives a little laugh, but it's not really a laugh. "I do. Do you need a ride to Katie's?"

I picture my mom driving me to Katie's only to find that everyone in the Brook household is, in fact, asleep.

"Gonna bike," I say.

My mom follows me into the garage, and I'm almost positive that she's going to insist on driving me.

"I'm sorry, Stella," she says instead. Her voice echoes around the garage, oddly loud.

I don't know how to respond to that, so I just say: "It's okay."

My mom just stands there, her arms hanging loosely by her sides, that sad little smile still on her face. I'm taller than her with sneakers on, but only barely.

"Your father and I—we just want the best for you."

"You don't have to make excuses for Dad, you know," I say. "He's being a jerk."

My mom laughs. The corners of her eyes wrinkle, but it's... nice. I guess I haven't heard much of the sound lately.

"He just wants the best for you, too, Stella. Otherwise, why would he care so much about your SAT score? Where you go to college?" She hums a little, thoughtful. "I think he's terrified that you'll end up like me. All alone in an empty house. Not enough ambition. Surrounded by teapots."

She smiles a little wider, crooked.

"You're not all alone," I say.

"That's right," she says. "I'm not. But sometimes, with you at school and Thomas—away…"

In this moment, my mom sound so weary and so tired that there's a part of me that wants to stay. To go back inside and boil some water for tea and sit down at the table and put my arm around my mom and say, *Hey, I know this isn't easy for you, either.*

It would be the right thing to do, I know, and in the coming months, I will spend many nights wondering how the rest of the year would have played out if I had just stayed this one night. If I had found it within myself to be a better daughter. If I had taken the grace my mother is extending to me right now and handed some of it back to her, instead of keeping it all for myself. If I had the presence of mind to think that some things are more important than the boy with blue eyes whose voice is enough to take me far, far away.

But perhaps I am already halfway gone.

"I should go," I say, and my mom nods.

"See you tomorrow," she says.

And I leave.

41.

"What if I hadn't answered your call?" Kevin says, shutting his bedroom door behind us.

"I didn't think about it," I say. "I would have sat outside until morning."

"That's ridiculous," Kevin says. He climbs back into his bed.

"I would have rung the doorbell. I would have rung the doorbell and told your mom that you left your calculus textbook at my house and you needed it to do your homework for tomorrow. I needed," I say, "to see you."

Kevin doesn't respond. His blinds are open, and the moonlight streams through and hits his torso in horizontal bars. Light, dark. Light, dark.

And I want to be close to him.

"Can I come join you?" I say.

"Do you want to join me?" Kevin says. An edge to his voice.

I swallow.

"Yes," I say.

Instead, Kevin throws his covers off, gets out of bed and walks toward me. His steps are unsteady, punch-drunk, like he can't tell if he's walking into the arms of an apparition.

He stops just short of me. Takes me in.

"I'm sorry," I say.

Kevin reaches out with one hand and runs it through my hair, then down the side of my neck, then over the curve of my shoulder and along my collarbone. A trail of goose bumps rises behind his fingertips.

"You're actually here," he whispers.

"Yeah," I say. "I really missed you."

He steps in. Leans into me.

"Stel," he breathes.

And then things are okay again.

38.

Dear Stella,

I don't know how to write this letter.

Letters, you see, are supposed to be crafted. They're supposed to have narrative arcs and messages and themes. Letters are supposed to have beginnings that reveal middles that flow into ends that—if it's a really good letter, the kind that's truly satisfying to read—somehow brings you back to the beginning again.

I don't have any of that. I have an apology. I have a surplus of feelings. Mostly, I just have fear.

The truth is, Stel, that I have never been a particularly brave person, and that you make me weaker than anyone or anything I've ever encountered. When I'm with you, I feel like a six-year-old running around in a park, chasing bubbles, and he's finally caught one. He is holding it in the palm of his hand. It is sparkling under the sun, and in that moment, he is absolutely certain that he is the luckiest little boy alive in the entire universe. The idea that this bubble is a third, maybe half, of a second away from popping doesn't even occur to him—because he's six, and six-year-olds don't think like that.

The problem, I suppose, is that I'm not six, and I do think like that, and I am painfully aware that that bubble is fragile. It's unstable. In a few moments, the wind will pick up, and the bubble will pop, and there will nothing left on this child's hand to suggest that he once held a miracle atop his palm other than, perhaps, the slightest trace of liquid.

When I stormed out of your room the other day, it wasn't really about you staying over my house on Friday night. Which is not to say that I didn't actually want you to stay over, because I did. Of course I did. If I could control time, we would exist in the hours between midnight and daybreak on the nights you stay over, when the entire universe feels so incredibly small, and nothing Beckett or de Beauvoir has ever written could change that.

But that wasn't what I was thinking about as I left. I was thinking about the future. About how in a few months, I'm going to be leaving Wethersfield; how one year after that, you're going to be leaving Wethersfield; how the relationship that we've created between the two of us, like all relationships, is a function of so many different variables that—through some confluence of coincidences—all lined up at the same time to give us what we have now. But these variables are always changing, and I cannot, no matter how hard I try, imagine a future in which the bubble does not pop.

I know that it must seem that I am being awfully callous. Please believe me when I say that I have tried to think otherwise, and my inability to do so—to treat the best relationship I've ever been in like every other normal human would instead of like a ticking bomb waiting to detonate—kills me, it really does.

I guess what I want to say is that I am not asking you to forgive me, *or even to understand. I just think that you deserve to know. When I left the other day, it wasn't because of you, or Katie, or whether or not you could stay over that Friday. It was because every time we argue, there is a part of my brain that insists that every word thrown in anger and desperation is futile, anyway, so why even bother; and every time you make me laugh, or I kiss you the way I know you like to be kissed, that same part of my brain says that this is all just going to make the inevitable collapse more painful, so why even bother with that, either? And every time* either *of those things happens, I am struck with the knowledge that I will come back, over and over again, despite it all. Despite myself. Because I cannot stay away.*

As I said, Stel. You make me weak.

There's one more thing that I want to write about. And I can already picture you rolling your eyes as you read this, but that one thing is a quote from Albert Camus.

Bear with me for a second. Let me explain.

In 1942, Camus published an essay called The Myth of Sisyphus. *At the crux of the essay is Sisyphus, a figure from Greek mythology whom you may remember from freshman year World Literature (although no one could fault you for not remembering, because that class was a fucking bore).*

Sisyphus was a mortal king who represented the best and the worst of humanity: he was clever and quick-witted, but he was also deceitful and arrogant. He made chess pieces out of the living and fools out of the gods, and was punished accordingly. Sisyphus was condemned to spend all eternity rolling a boulder up a hill, only to watch it roll back down again.

So what does Camus say about Sisyphus? Surely, you think, the entire essay is just one long depressing treatise about how all of our lives are just as futile as Sisyphus's eternal labor, how our boulders may take many forms these days, but they are just as heavy and our mountains just as lonely. And you'd be right. Camus is using Sisyphus's eternal condemnation as a metaphor for man's perpetual, fruitless search for meaning. But his conclusion isn't what you might expect. He writes:

"I leave Sisyphus at the foot of the mountain. One always finds one's burden again. But Sisyphus teaches the higher fidelity that negates the gods and raises rocks. He, too, concludes that all is well. This universe henceforth without a master seems to him neither sterile nor futile. Each atom of that stone, each mineral flake of that night-filled mountain, in itself, forms a world. The struggle itself toward the heights is enough to fill a man's heart. One must imagine Sisyphus happy."

I read this passage for the first time a couple of years ago, and I must admit that it was all a bit wasted on me. I pictured Camus at his writing desk, certain in the knowledge that there was no meaning to be found in this world or the next, striving desperately for some note of optimism. Perhaps the idea that Sisyphus could smile in the face of his eternal damnation was the best Camus could come up with at the time. How ironic, I thought. Albert Camus, struggling to relieve the weight of his own boulders.

I thought about this essay for the first time in years last week, a couple of days after we argued. It was two in the morning. I was lying in bed, unable to fall asleep, thinking about how I'd been such an idiot, how perhaps none of it mattered in the end, anyway. And then the thought came to me, unbidden, out of nowhere: one must imagine Sisyphus happy.

Half-delirious from frustration and sleep deprivation, I got my phone from across the room. I Googled the quote. I reread the essay.

And you know what, Stel? It made sense this time. Camus's words, which I had discarded with an eye roll back in freshman year, were sharply, almost painfully resonant. This idea that we must all reconcile ourselves to the absurdity of existence, but that we can and must all be happy in spite of that knowledge, took hold of me. That the victory comes not in denying the reality that lays ahead, but in accepting it with defiant goodwill. That we must.

imagine.

Sisyphus.

happy.

I want to share that thought with you, Stel, and I want to tell you that I do. I do imagine Sisyphus happy. That despite knowing what will come, my eyes are still cast toward the heights and my heart is full of love for you.

Yours,

Kevin.

42.

If you had told me that one month into the second semester of junior year, I'd be standing in front of Jeremy Cox's house at 8:00 p.m. on a Saturday night with a baby in my arms and a backpack full of diapers, I'd have laughed. "Doorstep of a varsity athlete? Evidence of sexual activity? Good joke, but I think you're looking for Katie."

But I guess these are the kinds of things that happen when you subject yourself to four years of Principal Holmquist's renowned Bridgemont Curriculum—or, at least, what happens when your parents willingly subject you to four years of the Bridgemont Curriculum without really ever asking you for your opinion on the matter. I have a year and a half of high school left. By the time I graduate, I won't have learned anything about filing taxes, finding a doctor or balancing a checkbook (do people still use checkbooks?). But worry not, because I *will* have completed a two-month unit in health class in which I raise a fake baby with a partner whose name I drew out of a hat. Because that's how it works in the real world.

Jeremy answers the door wearing a generic Under Armour T-shirt and sweatpants, which is an outfit that would scream I'VE GIVEN UP ON LIFE AND AM MAILING IT IN on any normal human being. But this is Jeremy Cox we're talking about, and he's six-one, with biceps that actually look like they might be carved out of marble, and as he turns around I realize that his generic Under Armour T-shirt has his last name emblazoned across the back of it. So I guess what I'm saying is that it works on Jeremy, a fact which goes from a source of great surprise to a source of great resentment in my head in about thirty seconds. No one should look good in sweatpants.

"Hey, Stella," Jeremy says. He takes the baby rocker out of my hands the second I've stepped into the foyer—who says chivalry is dead?—and looks at the baby inside of it with a vaguely bemused expression on his face. "And hey to you, too, I guess."

I can hear his parents' voices drifting up the stairs from another room in the house as we make our way up to the second floor. Which is weird. It's weird that I'm at Jeremy's house and it's weirder that I'm accidentally listening to his parents talk about whose turn it is to go to the grocery store tomorrow and it's weirdest of all that the two of us—Jeremy Cox, Bridgemont hero whose talents include catching a rubber ball and shotgunning beers at house parties, and me, Bridgemont liability whose talents include ditching therapy and dissolving into hysterics for arbitrary reasons—are now supposed to raise a fake child together.

"Hi," I say, instead of any of that.

"Thanks for coming over to work on the project," he says. He leads me into his room and puts the baby down on his bed. Then he falls onto the bed with an easy, controlled grace and sprawls out on his stomach.

"No problem," I say. Then, when he doesn't respond: "Nice room. Um, lots of trophies."

There are trophies *everywhere*. On his dresser. On his desk. On shelves nailed to the wall. Jeremy has more trophies than I have accomplishments to my name, which is equal parts completely unsurprising and vaguely disheartening.

"Oh," Jeremy says. He smiles, and he almost looks embarrassed. "It's really not that impressive. Half of these are from middle school, you know, when everyone gets a trophy just for showing up to practice. But my mom gets mad at me when I try to take them down, so..."

He shrugs, then adds: "Sorry it's such a mess in here."

"A mess?" I say blankly.

Jeremy points to his floor.

"That's not a mess," I say. "That's literally just four socks. If we were in my room and I said, 'Sorry it's such a mess in here,' and then pointed at the floor, you wouldn't even be able to *see* the floor. It's practically sterile in here."

Jeremy laughs. "Do me a favor," he says. "Say that a bit louder when you're leaving later tonight. Like, loudly enough that my parents can hear you."

Now Jeremy's got this grin on his face, right, that makes him look like he's just been caught doing something against the rules but he knows he's going to be able to get out of it, and that's when it hits me that Jeremy Cox is really, really good-looking. Like, it takes me a couple of seconds to process what he's said, because for a moment I'm just staring at his face and wondering how it could be possible for someone to be that hot, and—even more bafflingly—how it could be possible that I've never noticed this until now. I guess I was always so busy desperately avoiding any and all conversations about topics ending in the suffix "-ball," and resenting the existence of people like Jeremy for making it freaking *impossible* to avoid said conversations, that I just never really looked.

And I'm not saying that all of a sudden I'm, like, totally overcome by lust for Jeremy Cox, because—hundreds of trophies and good bone structure aside—he's still a guy who spends a solid twenty-five percent of his waking hours playing a silly game and slapping people's butts in encouragement. But I guess, three and a half years late, I am finally starting to understand why Katie spent an entire two months in our freshman year doodling Jeremy's name in her chemistry notebook instead of memorizing the many real-world applications of the ideal gas law.

Fortunately for me, I don't have too much time to revel in my newfound appreciation for Jeremy's dark brown eyes and jawline, because our baby chooses this moment to sputter three times and then start crying in earnest.

"Oh," Jeremy says.

"Oh," I repeat.

"It's crying," Jeremy says.

"She, I think," I say.

"She's crying," Jeremy amends.

"Maybe we should name her," I say.

"Will that make her stop crying?"

The crying gets louder. I must admit that as creepy as this

baby is—with its uncanny valley rubber face and huge, un-blinking black eyes—the crying is remarkably, ear-splittingly realistic.

"How about Ashley? Alex? Amy? Aria? Should I move on to B names?"

"Uh," Jeremy says. He is staring at our now-wailing baby with the expression of man who will never have guilt-free sex again.

"Bridget? Bethany? Betsy? Betty? Beatrice?"

"Those don't even sound like real names," Jeremy says. "The last time I met a Beatrice was when I had to volunteer at that nursing home in Hartford to get my ten mandatory community service hours."

"Candace. Camilla. Christina. Caroline. Catherine with a C."

"Rest in peace, Beatrice," Jeremy adds sadly.

"Demi. Diane. Diana. Debby. Danielle. Dasha."

"Suddenly I'm feeling a lot of pressure," Jeremy says. "This is the name that our hypothetical child will be stuck with for the rest of her life. Do we really want to give her a name like *Debby*?"

"Erin. Emily. E…bby? Damn, there really aren't a lot of E names out there, are there?"

"I like Emily," Jeremy says.

"Great," I say.

"Emily," Jeremy says, in a very reasonable, adult tone of voice, as if trying to coach a particularly stubborn five-year-old into throwing a spiral. "Please stop crying."

I stare at him blankly for a second. "You didn't pay attention during class, did you?"

"Uh," Jeremy says.

I walk over the baby—Emily, I tell myself—and tap the wristband we were all given in health class to her chest. The wristband beeps twice, signifying that Emily now knows that I'm here. Emily keeps crying, presumably because even an infant is smart enough to know that I am ill-equipped for motherhood.

"You do it," I say. "Maybe she'll be happier to know both her parents are here."

It takes Jeremy two minutes to fish his wristband out of his backpack. With every second, it seems like the crying grows louder. By the time he's finally found his wristband and tapped it to Emily's chest—without even bothering to put it on; that's how I know that the sound is driving him nuts, too—I'm starting to wonder why anyone would willingly subject him- or herself to a baby.

"It's not working," Jeremy says.

"Because we suck," I say. "I wouldn't stop crying if we were my parents, either."

Jeremy looks helplessly at me.

"Okay," I say. "The next thing Mrs. Croux said to try was rocking her. So… I guess…let's do that."

I try to move the rocker back and forth in a soothing rhythm, one that says, *I'm here, don't worry*, as opposed to what's actually going through my head, which is more like, *Please, for God's sake, stop fucking crying*. But I guess I'm doing a poor job of keeping my agitation from filtering into my rocking technique, because Jeremy pulls my hand off the rocker and says, "Here, let me try."

He rocks Emily once, twice, three times, and then—all at once, almost miraculously—she stops crying.

There is a brief moment of deafening, ringing silence.

Then—with the same frozen, wide-eyed expression on her face—Emily giggles.

"How disturbing," I say.

Jeremy sighs, relieved, and flops back down onto the bed with the baby clutched in one hand. "Thank God," he says.

I sit down next to him, and he folds his legs at the knees so that I have more room. "Thank *God*," I agree, scooting backward until my back is pressed up against the wall. "But what if it hadn't worked? How long are we supposed to rock this baby for before we give up and just throw it out the window?"

"Her," Jeremy corrects.

"How long are you supposed to rock this baby before we give up and just throw her out the window?" I say.

"Stella, I don't think you should throw our child out of the window."

And then, as if she's been listening this entire time, Emily starts crying again.

43.

It is ten at night, and Jeremy is standing in my kitchen.

Jeremy's not the only one. My parents, who now spend the majority of their days (a) furiously avoiding each other, and (b) furiously denying to me that they are avoiding each other, are standing next to each other with matching expressions of steely resolve—united by a common cause for the first time in months.

That common cause is lying in a baby rocker on the table in front of us. And she is *wailing*.

"Was I like this?" I say to my mom. It's Jeremy's turn to rock Emily at the moment, and we're all staring at him with the grim expressions of those who know that he will fail, and that after he fails, it'll be our turn. "Because if so, I am so, so, so sorry. I swear I didn't know better."

"No," my mom says. "With you, the trouble started after you learned to talk."

And then it happens. My dad laughs. It's more of a snort,

really, but still. An expression of emotion. Of *mirth*, even. My mom looks up at him, smiling, and the moment that passes between them is so unexpected that I don't know which to react to first: my mom's sarcasm, or—or *that*.

I don't want to make it seem like my parents have this magical, marriage-fixing moment while standing in the kitchen at two in the morning on a random Thursday night while their daughter and their daughter's health class partner try to wrangle a fake baby into submission, because it's not like that. They don't look at each other like they're young again (which would be weird), or like they're suddenly back in love (which would be gross).

All it is, is this: for this brief moment, my parents seem... content. Content to be in each other's company. Content to be standing next to each other in the house that they bought together, bonding over a joke about their daughter (who is about to get a C in this health class, I swear to God). Not overjoyed, mind you, and I doubt either one of them will look back on this moment as one of the highlights of the year. Just...content.

And I think that contentedness is a fragile thing.

"Sick burn," Jeremy says, which, of course, instantly ruins the moment.

"Was that a joke?" I say, turning to my mom. "Did you just make a joke?" Now that Jeremy's chimed in, I've remembered that the *real* shock of the night is not that my parents can still stand each other sometimes, but that my mother— my mother!—has a sense of humor.

"Well, you have to get it from someone, Stella," my mom says. "And we both know it isn't your father."

"Jesus," I say. We've been up for almost an hour now, and I'm starting to feel delirious. It occurs to me that maybe this is all actually a dream, and that if I can just wake myself up, I'll be in my bed alone, and my mom won't be making out-of-character jokes about me and my sparkling personality, and my dad won't be snickering at the aforementioned jokes, and Jeremy will be back home, saying things like "sick burn" to his friends via text instead of to my mother via real life, and, most importantly of all, I won't have to listen to this *godforsaken shrieking anymore.*

But the weirdest thing of all is that if this entire situation *were* a dream, I don't think I'd want to wake up. I think I'd take this particular brand of delirium any night, screaming baby and all.

47.

Halfway through our lunch period.

"Sorry you couldn't go off-campus with the rest of the team," I say.

"It's all right," Jeremy says. "I'm sure we'll go again before the semester ends."

A pause. Emily wails on.

"You're sure," I say. "You're sure we can't just throw her out the window?"

Jeremy grits his teeth. It takes him a few seconds to remember the correct answer to the question.

"Yes," he says sadly. "I'm sure."

59.

By the time the end of March rolls around and the weather begins its slow, arduous climb from New England winter temperatures (below freezing) to New England spring temperatures (ever-so-slightly above freezing), the sound of Emily's crying has become a persistent, omnipresent, *extremely* unwelcome soundtrack to my life. It accompanies me to school in the morning on most days, switches on and off in the background as I'm doing my homework and, of course, occasionally keeps me up until hours of the night that should be illegal.

I even begin to hallucinate the sound of Emily crying as I walk through the halls on the days when she's with Jeremy, which is seriously concerning until I realize that no, it's actually just someone else's baby crying three feet in front of me as their owner—*parent*, I have to remind myself—stops at his or her locker.

The only person in the universe who finds this health project more irritating than I do is Kevin, who starts looking at

Emily less like she is a cumbersome-but-mostly-harmless academic exercise and more like the spirit of Satan himself resides inside her creepy, plastic, battery-controlled body.

More than anything, I think Emily annoys Kevin because it makes him think of Jeremy, and all the time I spend with Jeremy, and all the time I spend not complaining about Jeremy, which, to Kevin, would be the optimal outcome of this health project: fresh hatred between his girlfriend and the alarmingly sculpted Bridgemont football star. But the truth is that Jeremy is a good partner and, honestly, a pretty nice guy, as much as it pains me to admit that about someone so obsessed with a stupid game centered around men hitting each other as hard as possible, brain damage be damned. Jeremy is the type of person who takes it upon himself to create a three-month "date calendar" at the beginning of the project to make sure that the two of us get to have Emily-less time with Jennie and Kevin, and then presents that "date calendar" to me with the expression of someone who has just laid out a ten-year plan to world peace. I don't want to be type of girl who shit talks someone just to make her boyfriend feel better. So I don't.

So spring drags on, and Kevin and I fight in diners about Jeremy, and Kevin and I fight in my room about philosophy (but also sort of about Jeremy), and Kevin and I fight in his room about whether or not we spend enough time with each other (definitely about Jeremy). Every time we have a new argument, it feels like the very first time he walked out of my house—that sick tightness in my stomach, regret so powerful it's practically indistinguishable from self-loathing. And every time we make up, it's Halloween weekend and I'm up on that balcony again—heart racing and breath held, taking one step forward after another, just waiting for the ground to fall out from underneath me.

One of these times, *I always think to myself,* one of these times, we're not going to make up. *One of these times, he's going to leave and he's not going to come back. There will be no letter. There will be no 4:00 a.m. phone call. One of these days, I'm going to wake up in the morning and whatever sick force of nature keeps us coming back to each other isn't going to be there anymore.*

The magnetism, the pull, the desperation to be with him whenever I'm not and to be closer whenever I am—one day, all of that will be gone.

Isn't that what they always say about young love? It's temporary. The feelings will fade as quickly as they came. The flame always, always burns out in the end.

But that's not how this story ends. It doesn't end with that slow dissipation of energy—where both parties wake up one morning and realize that, for better or for worse, they've both moved on. It's not a gradual burnout; it's a runaway forest fire. A case of arson where the two of us are the criminals, and the victims, and accessories to each other all the while.

It's ironic: the end of this story isn't a particularly happy one, but to get there, we have to go back to a happy note. A happy day. The happiest day of Kevin's life, probably—and, as a result, one of the happiest days of mine. The day that Kevin gets into Columbia.

49.

The day that Kevin gets into Columbia is a quintessential New England spring day, which means that it's about forty-five degrees outside, it is pouring rain and there's still snow on the ground. By the time I arrive at Kevin's house, my bike is mud-splattered and I'm soaking wet.

"So, what's the big emergency?" I say. I'm actually supposed to be at Jeremy's in forty-five minutes to work on a paper about our parenting styles, but I know better than to tell Kevin that, especially since it's only been two weeks since the debacle at the diner.

"Are you and Mulland eloping? Did he finally propose? Also, can I get a towel?"

Kevin throws me a towel and calmly ignores the rest of my questions.

"Stella," he says slowly. "It is very, very important that we savor this moment."

"Why?" I say. "There's nothing special about this moment. It's going to be just as shitty out tomorrow. And probably for the rest of the month. Plus, we have to go to school tomorrow."

"Savor this moment!" Kevin says, laughing.

"Okay, fine," I say. I close my eyes and take a depth breath—a rough approximation of what I imagine it means to "savor a moment" when you're not even sure what the "moment" is that you're supposed to be savoring. "Savoring…savoring…"

I open one eye and peek at Kevin, who is gazing at me with a very solemn expression on his face.

"…savored. Okay, hit me."

"Okay," Kevin says, clearly unable to contain his excitement much longer. He walks over to his desk, picks up an envelope and throws it to me.

"A letter?" I say blankly. "From—*oh, my God*. Is this it? Is this *it*? And you're happy, which must mean…"

I slide the letter out of the side of the envelope, which is already slit open. The page falls open in my hand.

"'Dear Kevin Miller,'" I read out loud, "'we are thrilled to welcome you to the Columbia University Class of 2020. We received an unprecedented number of applications' and blah, blah, blah, holy shit, you're going to Columbia!"

Kevin kisses me. I chuck the letter back toward the general vicinity of his desk.

"I should call Yago," Kevin murmurs. "He'll want to know."

And I should text Jeremy, I think, and tell him that I'll be late. But both those things seem like they can wait.

"Call Yago afterward," I say. Kevin pulls me close and I

can feel his lips curving into a smile against mine and there's this energy between the two of us that makes it feel like we're back at the beginning again, falling into each other for the very first time.

I slide my hands under his shirt.

"Afterward?" Kevin says, but I can hear in the tone of his voice that he's already convinced.

"Yeah," I say. I pull his shirt off and chuck that toward the general vicinity of his desk, too. "I think we should savor the moment."

50.

On Tuesday, it is still raining.

"She won't let me go," Kevin says. He is staring straight at his bedroom wall and saying the words with the flat, shell-shocked tone of someone who has just been hit with really bad news that they have not yet managed to process.

"What do you mean, she won't let you go?" I say. "She *has* to let you go. It's Columbia."

"It is Columbia," Kevin says. "And it is also, as my mother informed me yesterday, 'A bit expensive, don't you think?'"

He closes his eyes. I can see him clenching and unclench-ing his jaw.

"Well, how is expensive is it?" I say.

"Sixty-five thousand dollars a year."

I think about that for a moment.

"I don't know even know what that *means*," I say.

"Neither do I," Kevin admits. "But I just—"

He cuts off. Takes a deep breath. Massages his temples.

It occurs to me that after all this time, and after all these fights, I still don't know how to make Kevin feel *better*. When he's happy, or when I'm happy, when things between the two of us are good, it's so easy for us to be with each other, and it's so easy for me to make him laugh. But I don't know how to get us to that place when things *aren't* good, and I can't help but feel like this is a failure on my part, like I am a lifeguard watching someone drown and realizing only now that they have forgotten how to swim.

"It's because she—she thinks there are more important things than going to an Ivy League school," Kevin says, through gritted teeth. "Like 'personal character' and 'perseverance.' She thinks going to Columbia is going to kill my 'creative spirit.' She's heard that it's cutthroat and she's 'worried about me.' Fucking artists, Stella, I swear to God."

I don't point out that personal character and perseverance probably *are* more important than whether or not you go to an Ivy League school; firstly, because it doesn't seem like the time for that, and secondly, because I was friends with Lin for long enough to know how that conversation ends.

"I have never asked her for anything," Kevin says. His voice is low. "I paid for my car myself. I never ask them for gas money. I never tear my mom away from her precious paintings to have dinner or even to talk. I haven't asked them for anything in, like, ten fucking years, and now *all I fucking want is to go to Columbia.*"

"I'm sorry, Kevin," I say.

"I know that it's a lot of money. And I know that she doesn't believe in schools like that. But *I do*," Kevin says. "Doesn't that count for anything?"

This helplessness. I almost wish he were mad at me. At least then there would be something I could do about it.

"Whatever," Kevin says. "I'll talk to her again tomorrow."

51.

On Wednesday, Kevin talks to his mom again, and she says the same thing. Columbia is so expensive, and there are so many other good schools in the area, and didn't he get a scholarship to UConn? They have a philosophy program there, don't they?

"Well," I say. "*Did* you get a scholarship to UConn?"

"I'm not going to go to fucking UConn," Kevin says.

I try to ignore his flinch when I put my hand on his arm. "Okay," I say. "You're not going to UConn."

52.

On Thursday morning, Kevin finds an article titled "Why an Ivy League Education Is Worth It" and texts it to his mom. She points out that there are probably a million articles on the Internet about Why an Ivy League Education *Isn't* Worth It, and maybe he should look into some of those.

Kevin and I are at lockers together when he sees the text, and he Googles it while I'm trying to cradle Emily in one hand and unlock my locker with the other.

"Ivy League Schools Are Overrated," the first headline announces. "Send Your Kids Elsewhere."

Then Emily starts crying, and I accidentally knock one of my books out of my locker, and the bell rings. Kevin storms off to his statistics class, and even if he hadn't, there isn't much that I can say.

53.

By the end of the weekend, Kevin's belief that he can convince his mom to pay for Columbia is running out, and the determination of the past few days transforms into a permanent undercurrent of fury. He alternates between angry and apologetic with alarming speed and intensity, and I, of course, am useless in the face of it all.

One night, I dream that I am standing on a beach. That I am looking out at the waves. That I am hearing someone begging, crying, *screaming* for help. That I am ready to dive into the water, but all of a sudden my hands and arms are made of sand and they are crumbling, crumbling, crumbling into the ocean.

The tide comes in. The screaming stops.

54.

At 9:00 p.m. on Tuesday night, when Kevin hasn't texted me in six hours despite the fact that I have sent him ten messages asking if he's okay, I bike to his house. I call him. When he doesn't answer, I leave my bike in the middle of his driveway and ring the doorbell.

It's his mom that answers. She's wearing a T-shirt that's smudged with paint and a pair of faded jeans. Her hair is pulled into a ballerina bun. And she looks completely relaxed, which is weird, because I know for a fact that Kevin has been seething over Columbia for the past week.

"Hi, Stella," she says, her voice almost musical. "Are you looking for Kevin?"

"Yeah," I say. It suddenly occurs to me that it's late at night, and that I probably should have called his house or something before showing up, and that I haven't really even spoken to Kevin's mother since the one time I had dinner with the two of them months ago. "Sorry to bother you so late at night," I add hastily.

"Oh, no worries at all," she says. Kevin's mom says every word like she has all the time and patience in the world. It makes me wonder where on Earth Kevin got all of his intensity, the fire behind his eyes, the way he says every word like he is desperate for someone to listen to him. I can't remember ever hearing Kevin speak the way his mother is speaking right now.

She steps back, ushering me in, and I step inside and close the door.

"He's upstairs as usual," she says. "Don't think he even came down for dinner tonight."

She frowns a bit, then gives a helpless little shrug, as if to say: *Kids these days.*

"Well, let me know if you two need anything," she says.

"Will do, Mrs. Miller," I say. "Thanks."

I hear her footsteps padding back down to the basement as I make my way up the stairs.

When I get to Kevin's door, I knock twice. And it's sad, how unsurprised I am when he doesn't answer.

"Kevin," I say. "I'm coming in, all right?"

Then I push open the door.

I don't know what exactly I'm expecting, but what I see when the door opens feels distinctly anticlimactic. There he is: sprawled diagonally across the bed, one hand holding open a book, the other curled into his hair. I feel like I've been transported into an alternate universe: one where everything hasn't gone to shit.

"Hi," I say.

Kevin looks up from his book.

"I don't really want to talk right now," he says shortly.

And we're back to reality.

"Yeah, I got that. You know, from the fact that you didn't answer any of my one hundred text messages. But I was worried, Kevin."

"You don't need to worry about me," Kevin says.

"I know I don't need to," I say. "But I *do.*"

Kevin looks at me, and it's almost a glare, almost like he wants to argue with me for caring about him. But then he sighs, shrugs and goes back to reading.

"Kevin," I say. "Does your mom even know that something is wrong? Did you say anything to her?"

"I said that I wanted to go to Columbia," he says. "We've been talking about this all week, Stella. I gave her a fucking printout. She knows."

"Yeah, but…"

I think of his mom, standing in the doorway, puzzled that he wasn't at dinner. The calmness of her voice. How ordinary everything seemed.

"But does she *really* know?" I say. "Because your mom answered the door when I rang, and she seemed—"

I don't finish the rest of my sentence, because Kevin has lifted his arm and thrown his book across the room. It lands on the floor next to his desk with a dull thud, and I'm so shocked that it takes me a second to realize that my heart is racing and my palms are starting to sweat.

That wasn't fear, I tell myself. *You are not afraid of him, you were just caught off guard. It's just Kevin, it's still Kevin, Stella, get yourself under control.*

"Yes," Kevin is saying. "She seemed fine. Because she is fine. Because that's how she always is. Fine. Everything is always *fine* with her, okay? She's fine with it when you stay over and she's fine with it when I get high with Yago and she's fine with it when their son has to go to a fucking state school instead of Columbia because of money. SHE'S SO ZEN THAT I COULD PROBABLY DIE AND SHE'D JUST DO A PORTRAIT OF ME IN MEMORIAM OR SOMETHING—HAVEN'T WE TALKED ABOUT THIS?"

This is the point at which I should just cut my losses and give up. I should say, *Okay. Okay, Kevin, I'm sorry*, and I should get into the bed and kiss him and hope that tomorrow will be better. But what can I say? I'm just as stubborn as he is, and today is the day it blows up in my face.

"But maybe if you just *showed* HER, you know, how much this actually means to you, and how upset you actually are, maybe then—"

"STELLA," Kevin says. "STOP TALKING."

I stop talking.

Kevin closes his eyes. Takes three deep breaths.

"I feel like you don't understand," Kevin says. "And I'm tired, Stella. Of trying to make you understand."

My feet are at the edge of the water. There is shouting that sounds far, far away. But I cannot find my hands.

"I'm worried about you," I whisper.

Kevin stares at me.

"That's very sweet," he says.

I walk across the floor and pick up the book he was reading. Penguin Modern Classics, the cover says. Albert Camus. *The Outsider.*

I walk over to the bed, book in hand, and sit down next to him.

"Do you want me to stay?" I say, and when I look him in the eye, it hurts in a way that screams, *How can something that feels like this not be worth saving?*

Please, I think.

Kevin drops his gaze.

I put the book on the bed between us and leave.

55.

What kind of person, I think to myself, *lets this happen to some-one she loves?*

56.

On Thursday, Kevin is cutting in the bathroom.
  On Friday, we fight over Jeremy for the fiftieth time.
  And Saturday, I decide, fuck it. I'm going to get drunk.

61.

In hindsight, taking six shots of tequila over the span of one hour probably does not qualify as one of my better decision-making moments.

I don't even have a very good explanation for why I do it. I'm just tired, I guess. I'm tired of feeling sad. I'm tired of feeling angry at myself. I'm tired of feeling frustrated and helpless and desperate. I'm tired of feeling, *period*, and so when Jeremy texts me on Saturday night to tell me that he's throwing a party to celebrate the end of our Childhood and Home Ec unit—or, as I prefer to call it, the Health Unit from Hell—I approach getting fucked up with the manic determination of someone who may never see another drop of alcohol ever again. I know it won't make me happy, and I know it won't fix things with Kevin. But it'll do *something*. It'll get me out of my head. It'll make me forget, or maybe it'll just make me stop caring. Whatever it'll do, I'll take it.

"Listen," I say to Katie as we walk from her house to Jeremy's that night. It's one of the first remotely warm days that we've had this year—not *true* warm, mind you, we're still barely in the fifties—but the snow has melted and it's starting to feel like it might not be winter in Connecticut forever. "Do me a favor?"

"What's up, Stella?"

"Could you just…"

I trail off, trying to think of the best way to word a request that, if I'm honest with myself, is pretty unreasonable. *Just ask her*, I think to myself. *Just spit it out.*

"CouldyounottellKevinaboutthisparty?" I say.

I remember this moment perfectly, because Katie is in the middle of using selfie mode on her phone as a mirror. She's making all of those ridiculous faces that people make when they're checking themselves out, like raising her eyebrows to make sure her eye shadow is even, and opening her mouth to check the corners of her lips for lipstick, and then all of a sudden, her face just…freezes. Midpout. A split second where her face might as well be made of marble. And then she lowers her phone and slips it into her pocket.

"Stella," she says uncertainly.

"Katie?"

"Are you sure that everything is okay?"

If there is a moment for me to say something to someone, it is now. Katie is looking at me with the expression of someone who cares—who really, *really* cares—and I trust her more than I trust anyone else in the world. There's a part of me that's dying to say something. To tell her what I can't tell Karen, and I can't tell my parents, and I certainly can't tell Kevin.

But then I think, *We're on our way to a party, for God's sake. Wasn't the point of tonight to think about something else for once?*

"Everything is okay," I say. I start walking again and keep my gaze pointed firmly in front of me until I hear Katie's footsteps coming up behind me.

"Are you *sure*?" Katie says. "Stella, I'm not trying to interrogate you or make you talk about something that you don't want to talk about."

She pauses for a second.

"Actually, that's kind of exactly what I'm trying to do. Because even though you clearly don't want to talk about this, I really think we should."

She stops again, and this time grabs on to my arm so I can't keep walking.

"I'm serious, Stella. You never respond to my texts. And every time I see you at school, you look like you're on the verge of an emotional meltdown. And now you're keeping secrets from Kevin?"

"It's not like that," I say, tugging on Katie's arm. It's no use. She's planted firmly where she is, so that's where the two of us stay: halfway between Juniper and Oak Street on Bristol Lane, directly under a streetlight so orange that everything feels vaguely surreal.

"Okay," I say. "It's kind of like that. But I'll tell you about it later, okay?" I add, when Katie makes a satisfied noise, "*Not now.* Seriously, I want to have fun tonight. And this isn't the way to do it."

"But—"

"Please?" I say. And I must look pretty damn pathetic, because Katie sighs. Gives into my pulling. And starts moving again.

"Promise you'll hang out with me after school on Monday and tell me what the hell is going on," Katie says.

"I promise," I say.

"Okay," she says.

When I look back on this moment, I can't help but think that maybe if I had told Katie, things would have ended differently. Maybe we wouldn't have gone to Jeremy's at all. Maybe we would've gone back to her house and changed out of the ridiculous outfits that we're wearing and spent the rest of the night talking. Like we used to do.

And maybe, after a couple of hours of talking, I would've mustered up the courage to tell Katie that it often feels like the only good thing in my life is falling apart. That even though I can remember a time when I had other good things—when the two of us texted every day, when Lin and I weren't complete strangers to each other—it's been so long that I don't know how to get to back to that place. That I don't know how to be that person again.

And maybe I would've told her that underneath all of my anger and sadness and frustration is fear. I'm afraid because I was the one who forgot about Lin's Brown application, and I was the one who stopped texting Katie back, and I was the one who got swept up in the moment and threw all of the good things in my life away for a relationship that is going down in flames, and now it feels like it's too late to go back. Maybe I'm just getting what I deserve.

But we don't go back to Katie's house, and I don't tell her any of those things. Instead, I thread my arm through hers, linking them at the elbows like we're fourth graders headed toward the playground at recess. And I walk toward Jeremy's.

By the time we get there, it's 9:45 p.m. and the party is in full swing. I look around and feel a rising sense of panic as I realize that I could add up the number of conversations I have had with every single person at this party other than Katie and fit the total on one hand.

"Oh, God," I say. "I don't know anyone here."

"Huh?" Katie says. She moves us through the crowd and toward the kitchen table, where a stack of red Solo cups a foot high declares that yes, this is going to be *that* kind of high school party. "Sure you do," she says. She takes two cups off the top and starts pouring. "That's Melissa Brochton and her boyfriend, Ben, and there's Ashley, and that's Jennie and Victoria…"

"Those are people that *you* know, Katie!" I say. "I wanted to come to this party so badly that I forgot to think about the *actual party*. Like the fact that it's being hosted by Jeremy Cox… So it's full of Jeremy Cox's friends…none of whom I have ever talked to in my life!"

Katie puts one cup down in front of me. "Stella," she says.

"Please, Katie. Take me home before I embarrass myself further than I already have simply by breathing in the general vicinity of the Bridgemont aristocracy."

I take a breath and look at the drink that Katie's made, which is a very interesting shade of orange.

"But first," I say, "what's in this drink?"

"Drink it and find out," she says with a wink. And then she grabs my arm and pulls me into the crowd.

62. A BRIEF INTERLUDE

Now, I wish I could tell you that I spend the rest of the night meeting new people, and having interesting conversations with those people, and playing beer pong on the living room table that Jeremy has covered entirely in Saran Wrap. You know, *having fun*, like normal people do when they go to parties like this.

But I can't say any of that. And the reason I can't say any of that is not, in fact, because it didn't happen—not necessarily, anyway. The reason why I can't say any of that is because I down the drink that Katie pours me (a sex on the beach, she tells me the next day, her voice rueful) in about ten minutes, and then another one, because it's the best thing I've ever tasted, and then Jeremy and I do a shot of God-knows-what to commemorate the successful disposal of our child, and then I'm doing a shot with one of Jeremy's friends from the football team for reasons that I never really understand, and then…well, I don't know what happens then.

Maybe I *do* spend the rest of the night meeting new people, and having interesting conversations with them, and playing beer pong on the living room table. I wouldn't know, because I don't remember anything that happens between the hours of 10:30 p.m. and 1:30 a.m.

In fact, the next thing that I'm really aware of after my buddy-buddy moment with Carter the Offensive Lineman is linoleum. Specifically, how oddly, intensely cold linoleum feels when your skin is pressed up against it.

And the reason I'm thinking about the thermodynamic properties of linoleum is because I'm on my knees in Jeremy's bathroom, trying not to throw up.

63.

"What is *happening*?" I'm moaning. The entire bathroom is spinning around me and I feel like I have the flu, a stomach virus and really terrible vertigo all at once. "Am I dead?"

I become vaguely aware of the fact that all of my words are spilling out of my mouth at once no matter how slowly I try to say them, so that "Am I dead?" sounds more like, "Ehm-eye-dehhh?"

"You're not dead," Jeremy Cox says behind me, and it hits me, *really hits me*, that I'm ON MY KNEES IN JEREMY COX'S BATHROOM AFTER GETTING DRUNK AT HIS PARTY, TRYING NOT TO THROW UP.

If Kevin was here to see this, he'd laugh. Then he'd probably never talk to me again.

"Where is Katie?" I manage to say. "I need Katie. Have you ever looked at Katie's hair? Katie has amazing hair. Remember when it was purple?"

Then I make retching noises that I'm too ashamed to describe further.

"Katie had to leave an hour ago," Jeremy says patiently. I get the feeling that he's told me this multiple times already.

"Why?" I say. In my current state, the idea that Katie would leave me—well, *in my current state*—is deeply devastating. Like, I don't know that I have ever needed Katie more than I do in this moment, right now, right here, and the fact that she is at her house three miles away instead seems like it should go down as one of the great tragedies of the twenty-first century, up there with the baffling popularity of the Kardashians and the number of Michael Bay films that Hollywood has put out.

"She told her parents that she would be home at one," Jeremy says. "She wanted to stay, but then she'd have to give her parents a good reason, and she didn't want to tell them that you got super-fucked-up, because then her parents would tell everyone else's parents at—"

"I fucking hate the book club!" I say, and it's not until I hear my own voice echoing back at me off the bathroom walls that I realize that I've shouted.

Then I throw up into the toilet.

"How'd you know it was the book club?" Jeremy says, as if he hasn't just watched me *vomit in his bathroom*.

The nausea has subsided, but everything is still spinning, and when I try to turn around and look at Jeremy, I fall over.

"There's water next to you," Jeremy says as I claw my way back up to my knees.

"Did you pour me this?" I say, staring at the glass of water next to me. I don't know why I sound so angry. I think it's because I've spent the last three years thinking that Jeremy was this huge asshole football player type, and I was so pissed when this health project forced me to interact with him, and now *I'm the one* throwing up in his bathroom, and *he's the one* pouring me water.

"Yeah," Jeremy says. "You should drink it."

I take a couple of sips of water.

It is very, very bright in this bathroom.

I'm starting to feel nauseous again.

Everything is terrible.

Then, out of nowhere, a brilliant idea strikes me. Probably the most brilliant idea that I've ever had; certainly more brilliant than that shot with Carter the Offensive Lineman.

The idea goes like this: maybe if I just close my eyes and lie down on the bathroom floor, all of this will go away, and I'll wake up in Katie's room, and Katie will be saying, "Wow, we sure had a wild night. You really met a lot of new people, and had a lot of interesting conversations, and you didn't even embarrass yourself when you tried to play beer pong on the Saran-Wrapped living room table," and I'll remember everything she's referring to with photographic clarity, and I *won't be lying on the floor of Jeremy Cox's bathroom at two in the morning.*

I collapse onto the floor with a truly inspiring lack of co-ordination. "Why are you lying down?" Jeremy asks.

"Ughhhhhhh," I say. "I want to die."

"Yeah, getting too drunk always sucks," Jeremy says, in a tone so agreeable that I can't help but resent him more. "Do you want some Advil?"

"I don't want to die because my head hurts," I say. "I want to die because this is mortifying, and my head hurts so much that I can't even properly appreciate how mortifying it is."

"Stella, it happens to everyone!" Jeremy says. "Okay, don't tell Jennie that I told you this, but after we beat Lexington last season, I got so drunk that I threw up *while we were*— well, never mind."

He pauses.

"The point is, this is totally normal, and you shouldn't feel bad!"

He pauses again.

"Okay, it is a *little* weird that you sound so pissed off and miserable. But it's cool. You're cool, Stella."

"I don't want to be *cool*," I say. "I want to be somewhere that's not your bathroom floor, doing something other than watching the ceiling fan spin around and around and around and around and around even though *it's not even on*."

"Well, Kevin will be here in a few minutes," Jeremy says. "And then you can go lie on his bathroom floor instead."

And all of a sudden I feel totally, totally sober.

"Kevin is going to be here?" I say, sitting up to look at Jeremy in disbelief. My stomach and head both lurch in protest, but it's amazing how distracting sheer panic can be.

"Yeah, in like fifteen minutes. I texted him," Jeremy says. A part of my brain that should have been wiped out by natural selection generations ago chooses this moment to think, *Oh, my God, has Jeremy Cox always been this hot?*

Then, of course, I remember that *Jeremy has just texted Kevin oh my God what the FUCK*, and all thoughts related to Jeremy's fortunate genetics are eradicated from my mental landscape.

"Why would you do that?" I ask, trying (and failing) to keep from shouting.

"I mean, I figured you'd rather be with your boyfriend than with me, so…"

"Oh, God," I moan. I lie back down on the floor and try to become one with the linoleum. "Oh, *God*."

"Is that…bad?" Jeremy says. I can see the gears in his head turning, and I want to throw something at them.

"Yes," I say. "Yes, it's very bad."

"Why?" Jeremy says.

If you had asked me a month ago if I ever in a million years would tell Jeremy Cox about my relationship problems— Jeremy Cox! A man who gave himself motivational pep talks worthy of *Friday Night Lights* every time he had to change the fake diaper of our fake child—I would have first said no, and then suggested a trip to the emergency room for a CAT scan. But what does it matter now? I have less than half an hour to live.

"Our relationship is in pieces," I say tonelessly.

"Oh," Jeremy says.

And then he adds: "I'm sorry to hear that. Why is your relationship in pieces?"

I look from the toilet to the ceiling to Jeremy. Jeremy, with whom I have raised a child. Jeremy, who has poured me water in my greatest time of need. Jeremy, who has the bone structure of a Roman bust.

"Well," I say. "Because of you, really."

"Me?" Jeremy says blankly. The idea that he could be responsible for destroying a relationship—for destroying *anything*, other than the defense of a particularly ill-fated rival football team—is clearly unfathomable to him.

"Yes, you," I say gravely. It's actually starting to freak me

307

out, how calm I feel. It's like I still haven't processed the fact that all of this is *real*—that I actually came to this party, that I drank so much I blacked out, that Kevin is on his way *right now* to pick up his girlfriend from a party she didn't even tell him she was going to. Right now, the entire world is the size of a nine-by-six-foot bathroom with impressively cold linoleum floors, and the fifteen minutes between me and my impending death feel like an entire universe.

"I'm afraid I don't understand," Jeremy says.

"I guess that's not really fair," I say. "I guess it was really the *project* that ruined the relationship. Although, things wouldn't have been nearly so bad if I had gotten paired with Brady Thompson."

"Brady Thompson the mathlete?" Jeremy says.

"What other Brady Thompsons are there at Bridgemont? Look, the point is, Kevin totally hated all of the time we were spending together even though we literally had no fucking choice, and Kevin totally hated that I *didn't* totally hate all of the time we were spending together even though we had no fucking choice, and then he found out he couldn't go to Columbia and everything just really went to shit. I can't believe I'm telling you all this. Do you think I'm still drunk?"

"You drank half a bottle of Fireball," Jeremy says. "You're definitely still drunk."

Then he pauses and starts to look thoughtful. I brace myself for a football metaphor.

"I get why Kevin would feel that way," Jeremy says instead. I blink.

"You do?"

"Yeah!" he says. "I mean, you're a pretty girl, and I think

Kevin is just one of those people who never really liked me, although I'm not sure why…"

He trails off, frowning a bit, and even in my current state, I manage to feel a twinge of guilt.

"And we have been spending a *lot* of time together. Jennie wasn't a huge fan of the project, either. Remember when I had to cancel that date night so we could finish all those stupid journal entries? Plus," he adds, "she felt weird having sex with Emily around."

"So what happened?" I say. Fights with Kevin from the past few months flash through my head—the confrontation at the diner, the argument in my room—only I picture Jeremy and Jennie there instead, superimposed onto the scene in place of Kevin and me. Jeremy, throwing a textbook across the room, his face furious and contorted. Jennie, in full cheerleading uniform, standing in Joe's Kitchen and bursting into tears.

"Well, we talked about it," Jeremy says.

I wait for him to tell me about the screaming, the crying, the fighting, the storming away, the almost-breaking-up, the getting-back-together.

"I was like, 'Nothing is going on between me and Stella, and Emily won't be around forever. Soon her batteries will die.'"

I stare at him. "That's it?"

"Uh," Jeremy says. He thinks back to the conversation. I can tell that this is a very strenuous exercise for him. "Well, then she was like, 'Yeah, I've been feeling sad about you going to Michigan in the fall and it would be nice if you were around to talk about it with me,' and I was like, 'I'll try harder,' and she was like, 'Okay.'"

"That's *it*?" I repeat.

"What do you want me to say?" Jeremy says. "I would never cheat on my girlfriend. Jennie knows that."

"See, this is the difference between people like you and Jennie and people like me and Kevin," I say. "You're the kind of guy who just, like, *says things*, you know?"

"I do say things," Jeremy says uncertainly.

"When you're like, 'Stella, you're a pretty girl'—shut up, by the way—you actually just mean...'Stella, you're a pretty girl.' There's no deeper significance there, you know? You're not, like, tortured by longing or full of internal turmoil or— or *anything*. It's just a thing that you thought that you said out loud."

"I feel like you're insulting me," Jeremy says. "But I don't actually think that anything you're saying is bad."

"Kevin would never just be like, *Oh, you're a pretty girl*. He'd be like..."

I muster up the most dramatic face I can possibly make and imitate the cadence of speech Kevin gets into when he thinks that what he's talking about is very serious, which is always. *"You...are a pretty...girl."*

"Uh-huh," Jeremy says.

"And what he would mean by *Stella, you are a pretty girl* would actually be that he thinks I'm very beautiful, and our relationship is beautiful, but also that all beauty is ephemeral and temporary, and whenever he looks at me, he's struck by the deeply moving and deeply painful duality of existence vis-à-vis beauty. Or something like that."

"Uh-huh," Jeremy says.

"And Jennie is the type of girl who hears, 'Stella is pretty,' and thinks, 'Okay, sure,' and then moves on."

"Because she trusts me," Jeremy says.

"I'm the type of girl who hears, 'Stella is pretty,' and should probably go straight to therapy to figure out why the fuck a compliment is giving me major anxiety. Because I'm insane! If Kevin and Jennie were paired together on this baby project, I'd probably be just as much of a control freak as he's been."

"Don't you trust him?"

"Of course I trust *him*," I say. "*I'm* the problem."

"I don't get the way you think," Jeremy says.

"There was a time when I would have found that fact reassuring," I say. "But now it's just disheartening."

"I feel like what you got out of my story is that I'm not the 'type of guy' who is capable of deep thoughts, and that Jennie isn't the 'type of girl' who gets possessive. Which is…a bit insulting, actually."

"That's not—"

"I'm not an idiot, Stella. Sometimes the things I say can have a deeper meaning. But sometimes I just want to chill, and I like being with Jennie and my friends because things with them are easy and I don't have to try to be deep all the time."

"What I—"

"And Jennie can be jealous, too. Like in sophomore year, when they made Alexis Prader cheer captain instead of her. But the point is, she doesn't feel that way when she's around me."

"But—"

"Also, you're not a 'type of girl.' You're just, like…a girl."

I roll my eyes so hard that I feel another wave of nausea.

"Great. Thank you. I'm not a type of girl—I'm just a girl. Some truly groundbreaking thinking going on over here."

"I'm just saying," Jeremy says, "that—"

But I never find out what other feel-good clichés Jeremy has to throw at me. Because then my phone rings, and it's Kevin calling to say that he's here.

64.

The clock on the dashboard reads 1:47 a.m. when I get in the car.

"Fun party?" Kevin says.

And even though I'm expecting it, even though I've been preparing for this for the last fifteen minutes, even though I know there is no other way this car ride could possibly go, the coldness of his voice still burns.

"Kevin," I say. "I'm so sorry. For everything."

Kevin shifts the car out of Park and into first, then second, then third gear, until we're going fifty miles per hour on a tiny street where the speed limit is probably twenty-five. I'd be lying if I said it didn't make me nervous, but it's the middle of the night, and there's no one around, and criticizing Kevin's driving seems like the worst thing I could do right now. So I keep the thought to myself.

"Please say something," I say.

"I have nothing to say," Kevin says.

"I *know* you have something to say, Kevin. You always have something to say, and that's what—"

The words catch in my throat.

"That's what I love about you," I finish.

The speedometer hits forty-five.

Kevin snorts. It is an ugly sound.

"I know you might not believe me right now," I say. "And I understand why you don't. I understand why you're angry. I should have told you that I was going to this party. But I just—I knew it would make you upset, and we've been fighting so much, and I just didn't know what to do."

Kevin pulls up to my house and hits the brakes so hard that the two of us lurch forward. It takes me a second to register that we're here: I still haven't gotten used to seeing the driveway without my dad's car in it.

"Good night," Kevin says flatly. He's staring straight ahead through the dashboard. The engine is still running.

"Kevin, *please*," I say. "Please just—"

In the moment immediately after I say those two words, I think of all the things that I want right now. All of the things I wish I could ask for. That I wish Kevin could give me.

Please just don't be mad.

Please just think of how things used to be. Don't you remember? How could either of us forget?

Please just believe that we can get back there. Believe me when I say that I will try if you will try.

"Please just look at me," I say.

Kevin turns his head and makes forceful, pointed eye contact.

And he then repeats himself: "We're here."

"Kevin, I couldn't take it anymore!" I say. "I was miserable. Okay? I was absolutely fucking miserable, and I just needed to get out of my head and do something other than sit in my room and wait for a text that I *knew* wasn't coming and *I just didn't know what I was supposed to do anymore*!"

"You don't know what you were supposed to do?" Kevin says. For the first time since picking me up, genuine emotion slips into his voice. But anger isn't exactly the emotion that I'm going for right now.

"You didn't know what you were supposed to do?" Kevin repeats. He looks at me like he has never felt more disgusted with another human being in his life, and that's when I start to cry.

"You were supposed to be here for me!" Kevin shouts. "Not run off to some party and get trashed with the Bridgemont football team!"

"I *tried*!" I say. "I *tried* to be there for you! I came over after school. I listened to you when you needed to vent. I tried to talk about other things—*anything*—when you didn't want to talk about Columbia, but you didn't really want to talk about anything else, either. I came to your house *in the middle of the night* when you wouldn't text me back—"

"And then you left," Kevin says.

"You told me to leave!"

"I did not tell you to leave, Stella. You chose to leave. You have always chosen to leave."

"And I didn't tell *anyone* that you were cutting again because you asked me not to. *Do you know how fucked up that is, Kevin?*"

"Please, enlighten me," he says. "Tell me how fucked up I am. Tell me this is all my fault, go ahead."

"That's not what I'm saying!"

Kevin leans forward and props his elbows up on the wheel, then puts his head in his hands so I can't see his face.

"I would never say that," I say quietly.

And now—

After all that yelling. All that fury.

The car is silent.

And I realize that Kevin is crying.

"Kevin…" I say.

It is now 2:01 a.m. The hum of the engine is loud enough that Kevin's crying is barely audible. But I can hear it.

As we sit in his car for the next five minutes, side by side and silent, it does not occur to me that ten minutes ago, while I was crying, sobbing, *begging* for forgiveness, Kevin could not muster up a single bit of sympathy. I don't feel resentful or angry. I don't even feel scared or sad, which is weird, because it seems like this time is *the* time that things are really fucked for good.

What I feel instead is this tenderness. Like I wish I could reach out and touch him, if only I could do it gently enough.

"This isn't going to work, Stel," Kevin finally says. His voice is weary and muffled by his hands.

"I don't believe that," I say. "And I don't believe you believe that, either."

Kevin sounds exhausted, but I am ready to fight. I am ready to fight for us. I am ready to fight for us even if that means that we have to fight with each other, even if it means that we have to yell until it's five in the morning before we are raw enough to feel that tenderness again.

The problem is, you see, that Kevin is walking away from the ring.

"If you believed that we could work things out, Stel," Kevin says, "I think you would have told me that you were going to Jeremy's."

Kevin takes his head out of his hands and looks at me. His eyes are red, but dry.

"It's not your fault," he adds. "I suppose that I've never been a particularly easy person to work things out with."

Kevin takes a sharp breath—as if to say more—and then seems to change his mind. "Maybe let's talk about this another time," he says instead. He sounds calm, peaceful—like he's come to terms with things—which doesn't make me feel better at all. People don't bother coming to terms with good news.

"I already said I was sorry for not telling you," I whisper.

"I know," Kevin says gently.

Then he reaches over my lap and unlatches the passenger seat door.

A moment of silence.

Then: "For the record," I say, "I am not choosing to leave right now."

"I know," Kevin says.

"You are the one choosing to leave this time, Kevin," I say. I can feel the anger rising inside me. "So don't fucking pin this one on me next week."

"I know," Kevin says again. He drops his head. He might be crying again. I might be crying, too.

I unbuckle my seat belt and step out of the car. *There is something more to say*, I think. Anger begins to give way to disappointment, which in turn collapses into panic. *There must be something more to say—Jesus, Stella, anything. Say* something.

"I love you," I say.

"Have a good night, Stella," Kevin says. "Get some sleep. Drink water before you go to bed, all right?"

"Do you not—"

I choke on the words. Can't finish the sentence.

"You know I do, Stel."

His voice is shaking.

Kevin drives away.

65.

I don't remember how I get back into my house.

I know that it must happen. That I must walk down the driveway and up to my front door. That I must dig through my purse and find my keys. That I must slot my keys into the doorknob, wait for it to click and then step into the foyer.

At some point, I must make my way into the living room and onto the couch. I must have the presence of mind to get a box of tissues. Not a trash can, though—I'm surrounded by dirty tissues by the time my mind clears, however many hours later.

I don't know how long it is. All I know is that at some point the lights turn on, and my mom is standing there, bleary-eyed and confused, still wearing her pajamas. I imagine the sight she's seeing: her daughter, sobbing into the couch, makeup smeared down her cheeks, wearing a black crop top and jeans that probably have vomit on them.

I don't even have the presence of mind to be embarrassed.

"Stella?" she says. "*Oh.* Oh, hon."

I don't respond. I couldn't even respond if I wanted to.

I hear my mom walking through the kitchen. The tap runs, and then stops. The sound of the stove clicking on. Then she's next to me, rubbing my back through the fabric of Katie's too-small shirt in steady, gentle circles, and it feels so nice that it makes me cry harder. I don't deserve this. I don't deserve *any* of this—this kindness, this patience—and I don't understand how—I don't understand why—

"Why—" I say, and try to finish with "—are you *doing this*," but I'm crying so hard that the words come out sounding like gibberish, and my mom just says, "Shh," really softly and keeps rubbing my back, those same small circles, that same even pressure. Eventually, the water boils, and she gets up to get it.

"Drink this," she says when she gets back. She hands me a teacup with a cartoon pug on it. "Whenever you're ready," she adds.

Some unknowable amount of time passes. Four tissues. Four tissues' worth of time, and I manage to move to the cup to my mouth and take a sip.

It's green tea. Light and herbal. The heat of it spreads through my body, somehow both similar to and nothing like the Fireball from earlier tonight.

"It's good," I say, surprised.

"That's why I keep it around," my mom says.

I drink the rest of the tea, hiccupping a few times. When I wipe my face, the back of my hand comes back black and red and beige, some ungodly combination of mascara and blush and eyeliner and foundation and lipstick.

"Kevin just broke up with me," I say. I shut my eyes, but it's no use—a fresh wave of tears seep out from between my lashes. How can I be crying right now? How can there possibly be more inside me when I feel so goddamn empty, so hollow, like the inside of my chest has been carved out?

"I'm so sorry to hear that, Stella," my mom says quietly. Not in the way that adults say *I'm sorry to hear that* when they're just trying to get you to shut up. Like she means it.

"You are?" I say.

"Of course I am," she says. "I know how much he means to you."

"I just thought you'd be happy," I say. I squeeze my eyes together tighter, but it's no use. "Jesse Rogers's mom called you. You thought he was bad for me. Everyone thought he was bad for me. My grades have been so bad this semester."

"Of course I'm not happy, Stella," she says. "I'd do anything to keep you from feeling like this. I'd go back in time and keep you from ever meeting Kevin in the first place. But no—that's not the right answer, either."

"I just don't understand," I say. "I don't understand how the person who always answered the phone when I called him crying at two in the morning could be the same person who threw a book out my window because of a stupid health project. I don't understand how the person who laughed with me about stupid gray paintings at art museums could be the same person who thought life would be over if he couldn't go to Columbia. I don't understand how someone who could talk about the meaningless nature of existence like it was the most beautiful thing in the world—"

I cut off, choked up.

"I don't understand how someone like that could hate himself so much," I say.

Then there are the versions of Kevin that I doubt I'll ever tell my mother about: the Kevin who turned me into the kind of girl who ditched school to ruminate over park graffiti; the Kevin who read *Waiting for Godot* in the fading sunlight and put it down long enough to tell me he thought I was beautiful; the Kevin who held my hand while a snowstorm howled outside and said, *Do you want me?* like he didn't already know the answer, like the answer could possibly be no.

"People are complicated," my mom says. "They can be full of love one moment and full of anger the next. Beautiful and ugly at once, kind and cruel in turns. And the worst part and the best part about loving someone is learning that they're no exception."

She smiles a little, sharp and sad, and I think—*oh*.

"I'm sorry that I've been a terrible daughter," I say, crying with renewed vigor. Scenes from the school year play in my head, and I feel guilt like a tidal wave, like I'm suffocating with it.

"Oh, Stella. You know that's not what I meant. You haven't been a terrible daughter," my mom says, sounding amused.

"I haven't been there for you when you and Dad have been fighting and I—I said those terrible things to you that one time, and that other time I should have just stayed, and—"

"Shh," my mom says, and smooths down my hair. "Honey, it's okay."

"I hate that he's not here," I say. Thinking about my dad makes me feel angry, and feeling angry makes me feel a little bit less sad, and feeling a little bit less sad makes me feel like maybe one day my chest won't feel so hollow and things will start being okay again.

"Please," my mom says. "Don't make this about your dad. He really does just want—"

"The best for me, I know," I say, annoyed. "You said that. It doesn't change that he wasn't here all spring, that he left you all alone—I know that I did it, too, so I guess I should also hate—"

"Stop," my mom says sharply.

I stop.

My mom sips her tea. She looks like she's conflicted over something. She looks like she's *tired*. Outside, the sun is starting to come up over the horizon, fracturing the indigo of the sky with pretty rose-gold streaks. I don't know how long we've been sitting here. Sixty tissues, I'd guess. Sixty tissues' worth of time.

"This probably isn't the best time to tell you this…" my mom starts. "But your father and I—we're separating."

It takes a few seconds for that to get through.

"You're getting divorced?" I say blankly.

"We've been doing a trial separation," my mom says. "It might be temporary."

"You don't sound very confident," I say.

She chuckles. "I'm not. But…people change. Circumstances change. I don't know who your father will be in one year and he doesn't know who I'll be in one year. Perhaps we'll find our way back together."

"Okay," I say. Sixty tissues later, and I'm finally numb.

"We probably should have told you sooner," my mom says

ruefully. "We probably should have told you together. But—ah, well."

I'm tired. I'm so, so very tired.

"I think maybe the three of us should all go see Karen together," my mom says, and now there's really nothing else to do: I laugh.

66.

"Thank you all for taking the time to come in today," Karen says.

I know that I am probably imagining the faint note of smugness in her voice, and that she probably doesn't actually linger on the word *all* just a few beats longer than necessary, but I still can't help but resent her for this. All of this.

"As I'm sure Stella has mentioned to you," Karen continues, "I have been a huge advocate for this family session over the past few months."

I try to sink farther into the couch, but there's nowhere left to go.

"So," Karen says. "Is there something specific that you'd like for us to discuss today?"

On my right, my dad clears his throat—*a-heh-hem*—and then abruptly falls silent, probably because he doesn't want to be here any more than I do and wouldn't know how to talk about his feelings even if someone wrote him cue cards.

"Thomas and I are separating," my mom says diplomatically. "And Stella has had a tumultuous semester. We thought that it might be—*valuable*—for us to come and have a discussion as a family about—about—"

My mom trails off, frowning a little.

"It sounds like there's quite a bit to discuss," Karen says.

"Yes," my mom says. "Quite a bit."

"Why don't we start with you, Stella?" Karen says.

"Yes, *why don't we*," I say, sarcastic. I notice that the quote on the bulletin board today reads:

I Am Safe Here.

—which doesn't seem like a very good representation of the situation at hand, all things considered.

"Well, let's see," I say. "I loved someone, and he loved me, too, but then that crashed and burned. I had two best friends, but that crashed and burned, too. I had an okay grade in calculus, but it turns out that it's rather difficult to focus on derivatives and integrals when life is going up in flames, so that also crashed and burned. Should I keep going?"

"It sounds like it's been a difficult semester," Karen says.

"Oh, does it?" I say.

"Have you found any of the coping mechanisms we've discussed to be helpful in dealing with those events, Stella?" Karen says.

"Arson," I say. "And petty theft."

A moment of silence. Karen crosses her legs, then uncrosses them again.

"Stella…" my mom says. She looks pained, which makes me feel kind of bad. But it's only been a week since Jeremy's party, and I'm just not ready to talk about all of this yet.

It's one thing if my parents want to spend an hour working through their feelings about the impending separation and who gets to keep the china in the dining room dresser, but—I can't. I just can't.

"Look, Mom," I say. "I know I agreed to come do this with you guys, but—I think I need some time. Isn't that normal? Didn't they try to teach us this at camp? Sometimes you just need time."

"Ah, yes…" Karen says. "Camp."

Her voice is a practiced, deceptive casual, and there are alarm bells ringing in my head before she even finishes her thought.

"You know, Camp Ugunduzi," I say. "'Camp Ugunduzi is an experimental four-week wilderness program—'"

"We think it might be beneficial for you to spend another summer at Ugunduzi," Karen says.

"'—for teenagers aged fifteen to seventeen and' wait, what?" I say.

"Your parents and I have been discussing this, and we all believe that you would benefit from another summer at Ugunduzi," Karen repeats.

I look in disbelief from my mother, whose pasted-on look of determination is wobbly at best, to my father, who gives me his best *trust-me-I'm-a-lawyer* grimace.

"Is that a joke?" I say.

"Stella, after you got back from Ugunduzi last summer, it genuinely seemed like you were in a much better place," Karen says. "Think back to the fall. You told me you felt much better, do you remember that?"

"Yeah," I say. "But that was *in spite* of camp, not because of it. Who could feel like a normal person when they're stuck in upstate New York playing mental health charades all day?"

"I reached out to Jessie, your former counselor at Ugunduzi, and she said that she would be willing to keep a spot open for you if we let her know in the next few weeks. Personally, Stella, I think that we're quite lucky."

And that's when I begin to understand that this was not just some impromptu family session, cobbled together at the last minute. This was an ambush.

"What is this?" I say. "Did you—did *any* of you—ever think at some point during the many conversations you've apparently been having all year about what would be best for Stella and what Stella needs and how Stella's feeling that maybe, just maybe, you should have *asked Stella*?"

"Look," my mom says. "We understand that you might be upset or angry right now…"

"I'm not upset with you. I'm not angry. And I'm *not*," I add, "going to talk about any of this at Ugunduzi. Because I'm not going."

"You're going," my mom says.

"I would like to pursue legal emancipation," I say to Karen.

"Don't be so dramatic," my dad says.

"I'd like to bring the conversation back to Ugunduzi," Karen says. "Stella, we all understand that in an ideal world you would spend this summer in Wethersfield."

"In an ideal world," I mutter, "I would spend this summer on Mars. Where there are no people."

"But we've agreed that another summer at Ugunduzi is the best course of action for the world we're dealing with right now, especially given the alarming trend toward impulsive and self-destructive behavior that we've seen over the past few months!"

"What does that even mean?" I moan.

Karen turns to my parents.

"Anne and Thomas, I have a colleague who works with many parents who are considering separation," Karen says. "I'd be happy to put you in touch if that's something you're interested in."

Then she turns to look at me.

"How are you feeling about the separation, Stella?" she says.

"Is it really my turn again?" I groan. "What about Dad? He's barely said anything since we've gotten here!"

I take a moment to revel in my father's obvious discomfort at being in the one place on Earth where an abundance of four-syllable words won't save him—a therapist's office. Then Karen says:

"I'm happy to do another family session next week if you don't feel like everyone has participated—"

And the moment ends.

"All right, *fine*," I say. I close my eyes and try to get in touch with my emotions, to really dig deep into the place where there's usually roiling turmoil or soul-crushing despair, or— like the night after Jeremy's party—this awful, aching emptiness. But the thing is, there's...not really anything there.

"I'm feeling...like I should be feeling...more than what I'm actually feeling right now," I say. "Does that make sense?"

"Sure," Karen says. "It can sometimes take a while for our emotions to catch up to a big life change like this."

"No, that's just it," I say. "I think I have processed it, but I just…don't feel any which way about it. I mean, it's not like you guys—"

I look at my dad, who is in the middle of a particularly vigorous readjustment of his glasses.

"—were super happy, and now there's been some huge tragedy that's forcing you apart. I mean, come on. Do you guys even like each other? I'm pretty sure you don't."

Then I turn to my mom, who has a guilty expression on her face that practically screams, I HATE YOUR FATHER'S GUTS. I start to feel like maybe the reason why my parents sat on either side of me was not so that they could prevent me from getting up and flinging myself out of the window, but instead so that they wouldn't have to sit next to each other.

"You were both miserable," I say. "Mom was crying all the time. I hadn't gotten eight hours of sleep in months. Everyone was miserable. So…this literally just seems like the right thing to do."

I look back at Karen, who is nodding despite the fact that I stopped talking ten seconds ago, and at her clock, which informs me that we only have three minutes left.

"Am I being crazy right now?" I say. "I feel crazy for not feeling crazier about this."

"You're not being crazy," my mom says. "And I'm—*we're*—sorry that our difficulties made your junior year harder than it needed to be."

She looks pointedly at my dad, who clears his throat and says: "Yes. Yes, your mother is right, Stella. We're very sorry for that."

"I think you're being perfectly reasonable," Karen says. "You've observed that your parents are not happy together, and perhaps subconsciously realized that separation would make both of them happier months before they themselves came to that conclusion."

"Exactly," I say.

Karen drums her fingers against her notebook.

"Do you ever feel like you could feel that way about Kevin?" she asks.

"What?"

"Like you weren't happy together, and perhaps separation would make both of you happier in the long run," Karen clarifies.

I feel like I'm being punched in the gut for the second time this afternoon.

"It's different," I say. "We just established that my parents don't even like each other. Kevin and I actually—I mean, we genuinely love each other. I still love him even though it's over, and I know that he still loves me, too, even though…"

I pause. Swallow hard.

"Even though he decided it wasn't worth it to fight anymore."

There's a sharp twist in my chest, so sudden that I lose a breath.

Karen looks at me sympathetically, and for once I wish that she'd just say something. Something about healthy coping mechanisms or how maybe mindfulness can help me or that no feelings are permanent and everything will eventually pass—something corny and therapeutic, because for once in my life, I sure as hell need it.

But we're finally out of time.

67.

By the time I get home, that twinge I felt in Karen's office has detonated into a searing ache, the kind that feels like there's a black hole inside your chest and it's threatening to consume you from the inside out.

It's over.

I mean, it's been "over" with Kevin countless times now, but never has it felt so final. Never has it felt like it is actually too late for one of us to make things right. And never has it felt like even if I *were* given the chance to try and make things right—to fix it one more time, to look into Kevin's eyes and pull him close until both of us feel that gravity, that tenderness again—I don't know that I would.

So I do the only thing I can do. I pull on my old, worn-down Nikes. And I go for a run.

I started this story at the end, on a Tuesday afternoon in April when spring was in full bloom outside my window and I let Kevin walk away for the very last time.

I hope you understand how we got there now. And I hope you understand why I don't want to leave things there—not with that therapy session, not with me crying in bed and certainly not with Kevin storming out of my room after I refused to give things a fiftieth final try.

No, there are two more conversations that I want to tell you about. The first comes soon after that last fight in the spring, and the second comes much later—after April is over, after AP exams wipe out the first half of May, after I've skipped prom and passed almost all of my finals and even gotten a 1950 on the SATs.

I'd like to think that maybe these two conversations are the real end of this story, if only because endings are lot less depressing when you can find some semblance of a beginning in them, too.

69.

Five days after Jeremy's party and two days after my last fight with Kevin, Jennie von Haller walks up to the table where Katie and I are eating lunch and says, "Hey, Stella. Can you talk for a sec?"

At first, I'm so certain that she's here to talk to Katie that I don't even really hear her say my name. But then Katie elbows me in the side and says: "Stella. You all right there?"

"Uh," I say. I look up from my lunch and realize that Jennie is making eye contact with me.

"Sure," I say. "Yeah. What's up?"

"I meant, like, alone," Jennie says.

"I was just going to go to the library to print out my history homework," Katie says, standing up. Which is a *blatant lie*. We don't even have history homework due today. But before I can grab her arm or beg her to stay or pass her a note that says PLEASE DON'T LEAVE ME ALONE WITH THE EXTREMELY POPULAR GIRL WHOSE BOYFRIEND

FATHERED MY CHILD, she leaves, and Jennie slides into the seat across from me.

"What do you want to talk about?" I ask.

I'm starting to get really nervous. The last time Jennie and I talked to each other was at Katie's Halloween party right before Jeremy shotgunned that beer, and even then, it was more Jennie talking toward my general vicinity than Jennie talking to me. Of course, it's quite possible that Jennie and I had any number of conversations at Jeremy's party over the weekend, but those hours are lost to me, so I guess I'll never know.

"Jeremy told me about what happened the other night," Jennie says, her voice low. I figure that this is not the appropriate time to ask why on Earth she is wearing her cheerleading uniform despite the fact that the football season ended five months ago.

"Oh," I say. And then, because I can truly think of nothing else, I add, "I'm sorry."

"Why are you sorry?" Jennie says, frowning.

"Uh," I say. "Well, I threw up. A lot."

"Oh," Jennie says. "Oh! Don't worry about *that*, Stella, oh my gosh. It happens to everyone."

She leans in conspiratorially, which is very confusing, because from what I understand, that's something that you do when you're talking to someone who you're trying to become friends with, and the only possible explanation I can come up with for why Jennie von Haller would want to become friends with me is that she has suddenly realized that graduation is six weeks away and she's still short of the ten-hour community service requirement.

"Don't tell Jeremy I told you this," Jennie is saying, her

voice as alarmingly conspiratorial as her posture, "but one time, after we won this really big game last season, he got so drunk that he threw up while the two of us were—well, you know where I'm going with this."

"Yes," I say. "I know where you're going with this. And I am starting to get the impression that no one else is particularly embarrassed by the things they do when they drink to excess."

"But that's not even what I was talking about," Jennie says. She tucks a few strands of her long, blond hair behind her ear and bites her lip. "He told me about when you were telling him about Kevin."

"Oh," I say.

And I'll admit it. It hurts to hear his name.

I know that that doesn't really make any sense, because it's not like I haven't been thinking about Kevin all day, nonstop, for the past week, in between crying in the bathroom when I can't hold it together in class anymore and going to the nurse with fake period cramps so she lets me spend the next hour lying down. It shouldn't feel worse than it already does just because someone said his name out loud.

"We broke up," I say shortly. "I don't really want to talk about it."

"Oh, gosh," Jennie says. "I'm really sorry."

I shrug.

"Hey, hear me out for a sec, okay?" Jennie says. She looks at me, wide-eyed and sympathetic and earnest, and it's the earnestness that does me in. It's the same quality that Jeremy has: effortless sincerity. Like they're just saying what they're saying because it's true to them, and that's enough to say it without irony or sarcasm or endless internal deliberation.

"Okay," I say.

"When I was a freshman, the year before you got to Bridgemont, I dated this guy. He was a junior at the time, so you may have known him, actually—Corey Andrews?"

"Didn't know him," I say. "But he's got two first names, which is never a good sign."

Jennie laughs. "Wish I'd had you around to tell me that at the time," she says. "Not that it would've changed my mind about him, but at least I could've laughed about it later."

"Oh, okay," I say. "I see where this is going. You're going to tell me that Corey was a terrible guy but you were still madly in love with him, because you were a freshman and all freshmen are idiots. Then it ended disastrously, because that's how these things always end, but eventually you realized that it was actually a good thing that it ended, because now you're with Jeremy, who is perfect and nice and aggressively hot. Is that it?"

"Er," Jennie says. "Well. I wasn't really going to talk about why Corey and I got together, or why I'm grateful that it ended—although I am grateful that it ended, and not just because my current boyfriend is perfect and nice and aggressively hot."

"I didn't mean that in a weird way," I add hastily. "Jeremy and I were just—"

"Just friends, I know," Jennie says.

I choose to take the complete lack of concern on Jennie's face as a testament to her trust in Jeremy rather than my utter lack of sex appeal.

"Where you've got the story wrong is that Corey wasn't a terrible guy," Jennie says. "He was just a regular guy who liked playing baseball with his brothers and went to church on Sundays and really wanted to go to college somewhere warm."

"Okay," I say.

"But the *relationship*," Jennie continues, "was terrible, and it ended terribly. And after it ended terribly, the thing that bothered me the most—more than the fact that I spent six months with him, more than the fact that I no longer had an invite to junior prom—was that he wasn't a terrible guy. He wasn't a terrible guy, and I certainly didn't think I was a terrible girl, so the fact that our time together was such a shitshow—well, it just didn't make any sense."

"Okay," I repeat.

"And I spent months beating myself up over that, trying to figure out *why* things were the way they were. Was it him? Was it me? Was it school? Was it his chemistry lab partner who he started dating two weeks after we broke up?

"I thought about those questions, like, every second of every day. I stopped going to cheer practice—*that's* how upset I was. But no matter how much I thought about it, I couldn't come up with an answer. And eventually I realized that sometimes, things just don't work. You bring out the worst of each other. You fight even though you have no reason to. You break up even though you're still totally convinced that you're perfect together. And you drive yourself nuts trying to explain it all, but there *is no explanation*. Sometimes you just have to let it go. Does that make sense?" Jennie says.

"Yeah," I say.

"Okay, good." She stands up and picks up her notebooks

with the satisfied expression of someone who has completed their community service for the day. "I'm going to tell Katie to give you my number, okay? Text me if you want to talk."

"Okay," I say.

As Jennie walks away—her heels clicking against the bricks on the ground as she goes—I find myself feeling grateful that Jennie came over at lunch, even if the reason why I find myself feeling grateful is not, in fact, Jennie's Disney Channel sentiment that "sometimes you just have to let things go." The part of that conversation that sticks with me and occasionally even makes me smile over the next few days is the part when I backtracked furiously after calling Jeremy aggressively hot.

"Jeremy and I were just—" I started. And even though I had every intention of finishing the sentence with "health class partners," I never got around to saying the words. Because then Jennie cut me off and said, "Just friends, I know."

It's a silly thing to take away from that conversation, and I spend as much time rolling my eyes at myself for being happy about it as I do...well, actually being happy about it. But still. Given the state of my life, I suppose I'll take what I can get.

70.

I'm not expecting to run into Lin on the day that I do, but when it happens, there's this sense of inevitability about it all. Like, of course Lin is at Joe's Kitchen on the Saturday morning before her graduation, reading *The Complete Short Stories of Ernest Hemingway*. And of course I choose that day to stop by and pick up a breakfast sandwich on my way back home after a run.

And of course I'm going to walk up to her and sit down at her table, and of course she's going to look up at me with an expression somewhere between surprise and embarrassment, and of course we're both going to sit there in screaming awkwardness for half a minute while neither of us can figure out what to say.

"Good book?" I ask.

"It's all right," Lin responds slowly. She looks taken aback, and I can't say I blame her for that. It's been a long time.

"I find Hemingway's prose to be irritatingly spare at times," Lin adds, "but the short stories are way better than the novels."

"I'll have to read one sometime," I say. "After I finish *East of Eden*, that is."

Lin laughs. Well, half laughs—something between a sharp exhale and a snort, something that says: *Progress. We're not all the way there, but we're making progress.*

"Katie told me what happened with you and Kevin," Lin says. "And I'm sorry, Stella, I really am. I know you really cared about him."

"It was for the better," I say. "And it was a couple of months ago, so..."

Then I think about what I'm saying. And who I'm talking to.

"But yeah," I admit. "It still fucking sucks."

Lin slides a bookmark between the pages of her book and closes it. She pushes it to the side of the table.

"Katie tells me you're going to Yale," I say. "Congratulations."

"Thanks," Lin says.

We're quiet for a bit, and that's okay, I think. It's not always easy to fall back into the rhythm of an old friendship. But I have faith that the two of us will be able to keep count if only we can find a familiar first note to grab on to.

"Hey," I say. "Listen. I don't know if you want to talk about this right now, but—I'm sorry. About what happened in December, I mean. And I'm sorry that it's taken so long for me to come up to you and say that again. I should've done it ages ago, but I was afraid that it would end the same way it did last time."

"It could still end the same way it did last time," Lin says sharply.

"I know," I say. "And I'm okay with that. You deserve to make the call."

There's a split second during which it seems like Lin may very well tell me to get out of the diner and leave her alone. She's silent, and her shoulders are tense, and there's hurt in her eyes that looks real, and raw, and resentful.

But then her body relaxes. And the walls behind her eyes come down. And I think to myself: *Of course*.

"I've missed you a lot," Lin says.

"I've missed you, too," I say.

"Katie made me go to prom, and it was terrible," Lin continues. "And then she made me go to afterprom, which was somehow even *more* terrible."

"Unsurprising," I say. "But unfortunate."

"I got drunk and accidentally made out with Yago Evans," Lin says, looking far more proud than embarrassed. "You know he got into *Harvard*? But I feel bad about that," she adds. "Because I know that he and—"

"Trust me," I say. "There's nothing to feel bad about."

Lin takes a sip of coffee.

"Are you okay, Stella?" she says. "Like, generally? It's okay if the answer's no, I swear. I just really want to know how you're doing."

"Yeah," I say. "I'm okay."

I pause.

"I'm not, like, super thrilled about how junior year went," I say. "And my parents are making me go back to camp this summer. But… I'm okay, I think."

Lin nods.

"It's just hard," I say.

"Yeah," Lin says softly.

"And everyone's got some kind of lesson that they think I should take away from all this, you know? My therapist thinks it's that love isn't enough to make relationships work, and my parents think it's that I should go back to camp, and Jennie von Haller—"

"Jennie von Haller gave you relationship advice?"

"Yes," I say. "Life has gotten weird."

"Clearly," Lin says. "So what was it?"

"Oh, right. Well, Jennie von Haller thinks it's that sometimes bad things happen for no real reason and you just have to accept them and let them go."

"That's not bad," Lin says, looking impressed.

"Well, sure," I say. "But I don't want a lesson. I don't want a cute, feel-good saying to embroider onto my pillow or copy into my journal a thousand times. I just want none of this to have happened."

"I get that," Lin says.

"Plus, I have my own lesson that I got out of this year, and it has nothing to do with love, or camp, or the universal nature of unexplainable misfortune. The lesson that I got out of all this is about *me*. It's that people like me shouldn't be in relationships because we're just going to fuck everything up."

Lin takes that one in for a second, and then two, and then three. She starts to look very thoughtful, which makes me increasingly worried that what comes next is a going to be a reference to a classic American novel that I haven't read. But then she takes a deep breath and says: "Listen, Stella. Everyone is going to project their own experiences onto yours and tell you what they think the moral of the story should be, because that's what people do. You can't control any of that. You can't control what your therapist tells you, and you can't control what your parents make you do this summer. The only thing that you can control is what *you* tell yourself the moral of the story is."

"Ugh," I say. "No wonder you got into Yale."

"It sounds like the moral you've decided on is that people 'like you' don't deserve to be in happy relationships. And I have to be honest, Stella—I don't even know what that means. People who are kind and witty and smart? People who have had a rough couple of years? People who really need to read *East of Eden*?"

I'm tearing up, even as I laugh. I should probably be embarrassed, but—

It's Lin.

"So I guess what I'm saying is: *Pick a better moral for yourself.* All right?"

"I'll try," I say.

"Okay," Lin says.

The silence is comfortable, this time.

"So you and Yago…" I say, and the look I give her is so aggressively suggestive that the two of us burst into laughter at the exact same time.

And it's one of those moments, you know? That's kind of silly, and kind of stupid, and kind of moving despite it all. That you remember even though there's no way to explain it to anyone who wasn't there.

Two friends rediscovering an old rhythm. A small, simple,

fragile thing. Like a bubble sitting on a six-year-old's palm that may very well be about to burst.

But still. Given the state of my life, I suppose that I'll take this one, too.

★ ★ ★ ★ ★

ACKNOWLEDGMENTS

I wrote this novel over the course of a two-and-a-half-year period that included a number of highly distracting milestones, including:

- Graduating from college (which was sad)

- Publishing my first book (which was terrifying)

- Turning twenty-one (which was long overdue)

- Learning how to drive, ski and play a number of new Taylor Swift songs on the guitar (which precipitated much swearing, many bruises and countless unwelcome renditions of "All Too Well")

- Surviving my first full year of real-world employment (which was, to be honest, a very close call)

That I managed to complete *Imagine Us Happy* while being dragged kicking and screaming into adulthood is far less a testament to my skill and determination (which are sort of like the Loch Ness Monster and Bigfoot in that they have been sighted very rarely and only by shady characters with highly questionable motives), and far more a testament to the support of the following friends, mentors, accomplices, drinking buddies, etc.:

- Christina Teodorescu, who has been reading my shitty first drafts since the days when "beta readers" were just known as "suckers with poor taste in friends"

- Jesse Victoroff and Shinri Kamei, who provided feedback and invaluable pats on the head from their respective SPG hotels

- Molly, Ana, Hannah, Dorothy, Ami and Russell, whose kindness, compassion and faith have been with me in my lowest moments

- Laura Dail, who continues to devote her time, her energy and a steady stream of "don't panic" emails to my writing career despite my deficit of time management skills and social media prowess

- T. S. Ferguson, whose support and guidance shaped Stella and Kevin's story into the novel before you today